"You need to go, [...] [...] be done." His deep [...] face, rasped warmly [...] her forehead. "You. Leave," he said haltingly. "Before . . ."

*Before what?*

She moistened her lips.

He followed the motion of her tongue with his hot-eyed gaze and she thought she heard him . . . groan? It was soft. Perhaps he was in pain from slicing his neck?

Her gaze flicked back to his throat. She lifted the linen from his throat. "Let me see if the bleeding has stopped."

His fingers firmly circled her wrist again, halting her. "I don't care if I'm bleeding out. You need to go . . ." His voice faded and his eyes dropped to her mouth. "Before I do something we will both regret."

*Something like kiss her?*

Her heart lurched into her throat, and she did not know if it was alarm or thrill at the prospect.

She curled her fingers into fists, her nails digging into the tender skin of her palms to stay the impulse to touch him, to haul him against her, to force him to mash his lips against hers. She felt as though she'd been given her first sip of water after being stranded at sea. She desperately wanted to drink her fill. She craved it . . . needed it to live.

## Also by Sophie Jordan

# Sophie Jordan

# The Duke Starts a Scandal

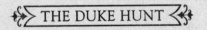

THE DUKE HUNT

AVON

*An Imprint of HarperCollinsPublishers*

THE DUKE STARTS A SCANDAL. Copyright © 2023 by Sharie Kohler. All rights reserved. Printed in the United States of America. No part of this book may be used or reproduced in any manner whatsoever without written permission except in the case of brief quotations embodied in critical articles and reviews. For information, address HarperCollins Publishers, 195 Broadway, New York, NY 10007.

First Avon Books mass market printing: October 2023

Print Edition ISBN: 978-0-06-303575-1
Digital Edition ISBN: 978-0-06-303576-8

*Cover design by Amy Halperin*
*Cover art by Alan Ayers*
*Cover images © iStock/Getty Images; © Depositphotos*

Avon, Avon & logo, and Avon Books & logo are registered trademarks of HarperCollins Publishers in the United States of America and other countries.

HarperCollins is a registered trademark of HarperCollins Publishers in the United States of America and other countries.

FIRST EDITION

23 24 25 26 27  BVGM  10 9 8 7 6 5 4 3 2 1

*For the first little girl in my life,*
*my sweet niece, Shelby:*
*We have been kindred souls since*
*the day you were born.*
*You will forever own a piece of my heart.*

# The Duke Starts a Scandal

# Prologue ❧

$\mathcal{I}$t was her own fault, she supposed.

She should have known better than to be caught out in the countryside after dark amid a storm. She was no green girl. No untested maid. Susanna Lockhart was the Duke of Penning's housekeeper, and she held herself higher than such foolish behavior.

Susanna minded her steps in the falling darkness. She knew these lands well. Every well-trod path, every pasture, every field of wildflowers was known to her like the back of her hand.

Still, in the fast-fading light, one could not be too careful and she had no wish to turn an ankle. The last thing she needed was to be relegated to her bed. How would she serve Penning Hall then?

Her boots plodded along cautiously over the ground, for all that she was eager to reach the warmth and safety of the hall. She was envisioning the cozy fire in the kitchens, a bowl of Cook's heavenly pottage waiting for her, the fragrant steam wafting to her nose as she filled her stomach with the thick, savory broth.

Susanna shook her head in disgust. She should

have returned hours ago. She had spent far too long in the village. At least the basket she held was now empty and lighter for it. It swung easily, looped around her arm. The vicar and Mr. Gupta had been most grateful for the baked goods she brought them today. The Penning cook was renowned in these parts, and Susanna made certain to spread the wealth of her culinary talents to the good people of Shropshire.

The storm had rolled in suddenly, darkening the skies prematurely. She should have had another hour of light. The rain started with a few fat drops, landing on her nose, cheek, hair. Then the skies opened in a heavy deluge. She was soaked immediately. Her steps grew labored, the wet, spongy ground sucking at her boots.

The familiar path curved and she stopped, breathing heavily, looking down the hill to the grand residence of the Duke of Penning spread out in sprawling splendor below. Lights twinkled in the many windows, beckoning her. Home. It should not have been to a woman of such humble birth, but it was more home to her than the one she left behind so many years ago. *Almost there.* Dry clothes, a warm fire and a hearty meal were only a short walk away.

She heard the horse and rider before she saw them.

The pounding of hooves rang like thunder, rivaling the loud rumblings in the sky. The staccato thuds increased, growing closer. She turned, whirled around just as beast and man rounded the path, straight for her.

Her scream was lost in the air, swallowed up by rain and the clap of thunder and the horse's panicked neigh. She flung up an arm in front of her as though that would stop the violent impact. As though that would shield her—save her from imminent collision.

As terror seized her, so, too, did a sense of mortification. Regret coupled with a sense of shame that she should die this way and not in her bed at a ripe old age. Indeed not. *Trampled to death.* That would be her ignominious end.

The horse reared. Hooves clawed the air overhead in a wild frenzy and she fell back, landing hard on the wet ground in her attempt to scramble out of the way. She bit the inside of her cheek and the coppery taste of blood filled her mouth.

She turned her face and jammed her eyes tightly shut, recoiling, shrinking inside herself as she waited for the sensation of steel hooves to come down, to cut into her flesh and bones and smash her apart, leaving her broken in the mud.

They never came. There was no pain. No breaking of her body.

Instead a litany of stinging curses burned her ears and the earth shook as the horse came down near her head, shuddering the ground, spraying her with fresh mud. Near her head, though. Not *on* her head. There was that blessing.

A body landed not far with an *oompf*. A long groan followed.

She could not move at first, breathless and stunned, gazing up at the water-soaked night. She pressed a hand over her chest. Her heart felt like it might burst through her rib cage.

"What in bloody hell is wrong with you?" The hard voice tore through the storm raging around them.

She blinked against the falling rain, sitting up slowly and looking around, finding the rider inches away, unmoving on his back.

Her lips parted, moving without making a sound. Her voice was lodged in her throat.

In the gloom, she could see very little of his face, but she could hear the heavy huff of his breaths . . . and, of course, his cruelly biting words: "Are you trying to kill yourself, lass? Or just me?"

She scowled, finding her voice finally. "You're talking, aren't you?"

He grunted.

"Then you are not dead," she added succinctly.

"No thanks to you." With another grunt, he sat

up. "It was no easy trick, but *I* avoided *you*." He hauled himself to his feet, his hand going to his side, rubbing at some invisible ache with a hiss of breath. "Even if that meant flinging myself off my horse."

"So heroic," she tsked, even though she allowed, to herself, at any rate, that it was quite the feat. "You should not have been riding so recklessly," she charged.

"Me? Reckless?" he scoffed with a wide wave of his arm. "What do you call someone strolling about the countryside in the dark in the midst of a storm?"

Disliking how vulnerable she felt sitting at his feet, she lifted herself up, slipping on the slick ground but managing to catch and balance herself.

That was little better. Goodness, he was big. On her feet again, she could see at once that he still towered over her.

His shadowed figure moved, cloak whipping around him as he inspected his horse for injuries—all the while grumbling beneath his breath.

"This is private property. Who are you?" she demanded.

He continued attending to his horse, ignoring her as though she were so very . . . *ignorable*.

"Do you not hear me? This is the Duke of

Penning's estate," she pressed. "I am certain he would not approve of you tearing about at night on his lands like some, some wild—"

He whirled around to face her. Rain fell between them like needles, but he fixed his attention on her, no longer ignoring her. "*I* am the Duke of Penning."

She hesitated only a moment before letting loose a laugh.

"No. You are not." She knew the duke. She was his housekeeper, after all.

"Oh, yes. I am." He pronounced this with such complete confidence that her laughter faded. A small current of apprehension trembled through her. Then her certainty reasserted itself. The newly minted Duke of Penning and his son had been in residence for months now. This man was lying. He was a liar. He was a lying liar.

Doubtlessly he thought she was someone who did not know any better and would not question him on the matter. Her chin went up and she lifted her voice over the increasing pound of rain. "You lie."

"I lie?" He snorted.

"Yes. You're lying . . . a *liar*," she added at the end as though she wanted there to be no confusion about it. "I do not know what game you are playing at, sirrah, but the Duke of Penning is down that hill, cozily ensconced in his drawing room as we speak."

The stranger took his mount's reins in hand and moved then, gingerly. Evidently his tumble had not been the easiest of falls and was not without physical cost to himself. He stopped in front of her and she had to crane her neck to look up at him.

In the falling rain, she was granted a shadowy view of his features. Deep-set eyes. Thick, slashing eyebrows. A patrician nose. A wide mouth that now moved, over-enunciating his words as though to encourage her understanding, as though she were somehow slow to comprehend what he was telling her—or perhaps he wished to simply be heard over the storm. "I play no game. I *am* the Duke of Penning, and I am here to claim what is mine." He nodded in the direction of the manor house, water streaming from the brim of his hat. "That man down there is a pretender. A clever fraud . . . cozily ensconced in *my* drawing room."

She flinched at the echo of her own words hurled back at her, but she forced a mirthless laugh. Nervously. Awkwardly.

Shaking her head, she spit out, "No . . ." She could say nothing more than that. It was all she could manage as doubt took hold of her, creeping in and sinking deep.

He countered with a simple: "Yes."

Lightning lit the sky, illuminating his face, and she gasped. He was handsome. Young. And angry. *Very angry.* She saw that at once. Recognized it.

He continued, "I am the legitimate heir to the dukedom with agents of the estate traveling in a carriage behind me to prove it. That man"—he nodded down the hill to the house—"is an imposter." Water glinted in his lashes as he looked her drenched person up and down like she was something unsavory, and in her present state, she was certain she looked it. "And who are you?"

"I am . . ." *The duke's housekeeper. Your housekeeper?* She gave her head a hard shake. After this bit of awkwardness, she hoped she still was.

The corners of his wide lips pulled down in a frown. "Are you unwell? Did you hit your head, lass?"

She felt as though she had. She felt as though she had suffered a great blow and didn't know what to think or how to respond.

For weeks now she had been serving two very nice men who claimed to be the duke and his son and now this rude, ill-tempered man was telling her she had been duped—that he was the true Penning, that *he* was her employer.

With a grunt of disdain, he moved ahead of her, leading his horse back onto the path and in the direction of the hall. "You coming?" he called over his shoulder.

Another flash of lightning lit the night sky. With little choice, she picked up her basket and followed the lion into his den.

# Chapter One ❦

*Two months later . . .*

*T*he true Duke of Penning was a terrible man.

Susanna had suspected it from the moment she first met him on that stormy night, and time had revealed her to be correct.

She knew something of terrible men. Unfortunately, she had known more than a few in the course of her life. At ten and seven, she had been too inexperienced and naive to recognize such men when faced with them, but now, as a jaded and thoroughly seasoned woman of eight and twenty, she knew one when she met one. And Penning was one such man.

Normally she would steer clear of his ilk, but he was her employer, a fact Susanna was wise enough to never forget, especially considering their fraught initial meeting. She supposed she was fortunate he had kept her on. She had insulted him. Called him a liar. Treated him to scorn. Every time he looked at her she read the memory of that reflected in his gaze . . . felt it like a bothersome pebble caught, trapped in her shoe.

Terrible man or not, she lived in service to him. Such was her lot. She must listen to him, obey him, cater to his every whim without complaint or she would be replaced. That was the way of things. There was no avoiding him. No shirking of her duties. No escape lest she wanted to be set free, wandering like a vagabond, searching for hearth and home, as fragile as a tulip on the hill. Being set free did not mean *freedom*. Not in this sense. She was worldly enough to understand that.

Presently, she stood before him with a smile of deference pasted to her face, nodding circumspectly and reminding herself that she was fortunate enough to have this position, a position of respect and authority in her own right.

She was fortunate to have a roof over her head, a healthy wage, a comfortable bed, and ample food on her plate every day. *And* she was fortunate enough to be in possession of her good name, which, let us recognize, was everything to a woman in this day and age. Especially *to* a woman like Susanna who had very nearly lost it once upon a time.

Serving the Duke of Penning was a small price to pay for all of that. A woman of humble roots and precarious background ought never overestimate the value of those things.

The duke had requested this audience, summoning her through his valet, the young Mr. Carter, whose soft, pitying gaze warned her that this would not be an easy meeting.

Nor was it.

Penning let her know that at once with his announcement. A house party was coming to Penning Hall.

*A house party.*

Her mind raced with all that must be done in preparation. And *much* must be done.

Of course, everything would have to meet the duke's exacting requirements. It would be a significant undertaking.

"On the fifth day there will be an assembly—" He did not lift his dark, bent head from where he sat at his desk, scribbling furiously into a ledger as he spoke, as though he were in great haste . . . or angry.

He always seemed angry, or at the very least *afflicted* . . . burdened. Of course, she often felt the subject of his chronic displeasure. Ever since he arrived at Penning Hall, he surveyed his new domain and all within it with an expression that bordered disdain.

She could not fathom such disdain. What a great inconvenience to inherit a dukedom! All that money and property and instant esteem. Such a hindrance.

She suppressed an eye roll and clasped her hands in front of her. "An assembly, Your Grace?"

He looked up then, and she rather wished he had not. Or rather that she had not spoken and drawn his attention to herself.

Those blue eyes of his were as frosty as an arctic wind breezing over her. She preferred *not* to have him so focused upon her. An impossibility, of course, as she was his housekeeper, and must attend to the man daily. A mere two months had passed since his arrival at Penning Hall and she still struggled with that . . . with those eyes, with that perpetual expression of disdain . . . with *him*.

He was nothing like the previous duke to hold the Penning title. Or dukes, rather. In her eleven years at Penning Hall, there had been a total of three. *Well.* In a manner, there had been three. There had been the two and then the swindler. She would have preferred the swindler over him, though. What she would give to have *any* of them instead of *this duke* and his judgmental stares and acerbic attitude.

He cocked a dark, supercilious eyebrow at her. He may be newly minted to the role, but he had the haughty and arrogant airs down to perfection. It was as though Providence had crafted him this way, knowing he was destined for such a role. Just as he possessed blue eyes and dark hair and good looks, he had this in him, too . . . this streak of severity, this ability to be a perfectly arrogant arse.

"An assembly, yes, Miss Lockhart. That is when a group of people come together for food, drink and dance."

*Arrogant arse.*

He leaned back in his chair.

She flushed. "Yes, Your Grace. I am aware."

"A good thing as you are my housekeeper, Miss Lockhart. For now . . ."

*For now.*

She twisted and squeezed her fingers. There was no mistaking the implication of that.

She was strangling. "Y-yes . . . Your Grace." She did not know what else to say. Nothing else was required. As with most servants. They were to merely nod and obey. Acquiesce dutifully and be invisible until required to speak.

"It is my understanding that my *counterfeit* predecessor hosted a ball for the entire village of Shropshire." He paused and it seemed that his eyes held a smidge of accusation as he leveled it upon her. As though *she* were somehow responsible for the fact that before his arrival, another man, a clever charlatan, a consummate trickster, had passed himself off as the Duke of

Penning. "I should do no less, I imagine," he finished tersely.

"Yes, Your Grace."

He blinked his frosty gaze once more in a way that seemed to say she was dismissed, and then returned his attention to his ledger, as though the sight of her now bored him.

She started to turn away and then he spoke again, asking rather harshly, "Can you offer more than vague platitudes, Miss Lockhart? This is to be an important event and I need your assurances that you can manage it."

*Manage* it? As the Penning housekeeper, that was what she did. All the time. Every day. For years now, *managing things* was her singular talent.

She compressed her lips, annoyance prickling over her. The man clearly did not like her, and she could relate because she felt the same way about him. Not that she dared to reveal that. She was not that foolhardy. Not after their less-than-glorious beginning. She knew she should be grateful that he had not sacked her on the spot after that dreadful start.

She needed this position.

She was determined that he see she was highly competent at her post, and therefore indispensable.

"I shall meet with Cook this very afternoon and construct a menu and present it to you tomorrow—"

"This evening," he corrected, the tip of his quill scratching as he wrote upon parchment, not even glancing to her. "Before I retire tonight we shall review your list. Only the best, mind you. Spare no expense. We have several important guests coming from London."

More important than him? She did not think this arrogant duke believed anyone above him.

She took a careful breath, keeping her smile in place. "Very good, Your Grace. This evening, then." She nodded. "I assure you everything will be faultless."

"I hope so, Miss Lockhart."

The words were mild in themselves, but they rang in her ears with implicit threat.

"How many guests are we expecting?"

He handed her a sheet off his desk. "They are all listed here."

She gave the list a quick glance, noting the names of several ranked personages upon it. He had not been exaggerating. Important people, indeed. It would be a fete boasting only the highest echelons of Society.

She was familiar with several of the names. The young Lady Miranda was constantly in the gossip rags, renowned for her beauty and charm. And the Dowager Countess of Lippton was one of the reigning doyens of the *ton*. She would have to be put in the very best chamber.

He nodded to the list in her hand. "I am certain you can see why I need this to go smoothly."

"Yes. It will, Your Grace," she promised.

He was clearly shopping for a bride. One could not reside beneath this roof without knowing a future Duchess of Penning was on the horizon.

Perhaps he was even after husbands for his younger sisters. The girls were of age, and there were some young gentlemen on the list, too.

Or perhaps the wife he sought would usher his sisters through Good Society for him and find the girls suitable matches. A proper wife well versed in Society would certainly assist him in that endeavor.

"I will hold you to that promise, Miss Lockhart." And just like that he was done with her. He returned his attention to the ledger before him, clearly dismissing her. "I will see you later."

"Good day, Your Grace." She executed a brief curtsy that he did not appreciate at all as his attention remained on his desk.

She sent him a backward glance as she departed the room. Still nary a look from him, and his lack of interest both offended and relieved her. It was a paradox, to be sure, and spoke to her contrary nature.

Closing the double doors behind her, she exhaled a heavy, reproachful breath. The man, however, was not a paradox. He was unequivocally beastly, but she supposed most dukes were. Her problem was that she possessed expectations. Expectations that existed because the previous dukes had been perfectly pleasant and charming gentlemen.

The duke she had worked beneath for most of her tenure at Penning Hall was now Mr. Butler. Such an ordinary and common name for a man who had been brought up with all the pomp and privileges of a nobleman.

Unfortunately it had been discovered he was illegitimate, born before his late father married his mother. He had lost everything: his title and all entailed therein. Following his exodus, the hunt for the next Duke of Penning began.

Agents of the estate thought they had discovered him, but it turned out that man was a charlatan, posing as the Duke of Penning, with his son in tow, no less. The pair of them had quite fooled everyone.

Frauds or no, they had been perfectly pleasant gentlemen and Susanna had been happy to have them here, to serve them. Again, that should have made her suspicious. Perfectly pleasant and affable men were not likely to be dukes. Indeed not.

No, the great lummox sitting in the study behind her was the duke—as he had proclaimed that rain-soaked night after he had very nearly run her down with his horse.

The bloody Duke of Penning. And she was his housekeeper.

She swallowed against the sudden thickness in her throat. At least for the time being.

# Chapter Two ❧

The housekeeper had to go. His housekeeper. *His.* That was the rub of it.

Lucian had known the moment he clapped eyes on her on that rain-soaked hill that there would be trouble, that *she* would be a problem.

He had an instinct for such things. It never failed him. His nape tingled. He *felt* trouble before it struck, and Susanna Lockhart was every bit that. She was defiance and pertinacity through and through. She might be a domestic, but there was nothing submissive or meek about her. Her amber-brown eyes gleamed with rebellion.

Oh, yes. She had to go.

Ever since his father died, he had lived by his wits. Gut sense guided him, informing him when to extricate himself from situations. It was the only way he had survived and provided for his sisters all these years.

He had made mistakes certainly, but he had never ended up dead, in a gutter, or in prison. Three things that had seemed very possible in his former life. Not that anyone would surmise that now of him, installed, as he was, in his new role of duke.

He had managed to feed himself and his sisters and keep a roof over their heads. Good fortune might have befallen him now, lifting him up from his hardscrabble existence, but his sense of survival remained, and it was on screaming alert now.

Everything within him told him that Susanna Lockhart was someone he had to remove from this new life he was carving out for himself and his sisters posthaste.

*Perhaps in my old life . . .*

No, no. He shook his head swiftly. That was neither here nor there. No sense in making suppositions on whether he would have welcomed Miss Lockhart into his life *before*. It was not *before* anymore. What *could have been* in his old life did not matter anymore.

That life was gone.

Only this new life remained.

This new life with Susanna Lockhart as his housekeeper.

*But not for long.*

There was nothing the least bit deferential about her. Oh, she said all the right things. Proper and respectful words only ever passed her lips, but he saw beyond that. He read the glittering resentment in her eyes. He recognized that at once. He knew the truth. He knew the reality between them—the reality that had been there in the rain and mud with thunder cracking around them and his body aching from very nearly breaking his neck.

She saw him for what he was. And she found him lacking in his newfound role as the Duke of Penning. It was as though she could see to the very core of him.

He was a fraud and she knew it.

Oh, he was the legitimate Duke of Penning. His late father was a distant cousin to the last true Duke of Penning to hold the seat and that tenuous connection made him the present Duke of Penning.

The *true* Duke of Penning.

He was a fraud in another sense, though. Perhaps the truest sense.

He did not *deserve* to be the Duke of Penning. He was not a good man. There was nothing noble about him. He was besmirched. Unworthy.

The things he had seen and done . . .

There was not even the regret in him there ought to be. He wished he could look back and hate all those things. That was how he *ought* to feel. That was perhaps the deepest shame of it. However, remorse was elusive. In fact, at times he missed the debauchery. He had reveled in it. He had been good at it.

As a lad of seven and ten, when he first entered that dark world of vice, it had been out of necessity. There had been no choice. Not when fighting for survival. He had no knowledge he would be quite so good at it, though. That he would bask in it.

He had swum among the sharks for so long, he himself had become one.

A good man ought to regret the wickedness and vice. Except alone, in the dark of night, in his bed, in the quiet still of his thoughts . . . he longed for it. Longed for yielding flesh and sweet, unbridled release. The kind not to be found in a proper young lady's bed.

Clearly he was not a good man.

He inhaled sharply and whirled around in his chair, pushing up from his desk. Standing, he gazed down at his view of the impressive gardens: the copious flowers, the lemon trees, the rosebushes, the intricate maze of yew hedges beyond. Several gardeners were at work among the shrubs, toiling to make certain the grounds remained impressive.

This place was his. Incredibly. All of it. He would not fuck it up. If that meant burying himself deep down, repressing the core of himself and trapping all his unholy impulses in a box, then so be it.

No one knew the truth of his past.

No one knew the wickedness hidden deep inside him.

Not even his housekeeper with her too-keen gaze.

Despite her judging stare, she did not *know*. Oh, she might sense something wasn't right with him, but that was only suspicion. She did not know for a fact. Nor would she ever know. His true nature, which felt very close to unraveling whenever in her presence, would remain under wraps.

Miss Lockhart was his housekeeper. A member of his upper staff, but a servant nonetheless. *She* worked for *him*.

He should not feel anything at all about her. He should not find her obstinate chin intriguing. He should not find her scornful gaze challenging, filling him with all manner of improper notions these last couple of months, making her a less-than-ideal housekeeper.

No good would come of such thinking.

Perhaps if they had not started out toe-to-toe, sparring as adversaries, things would be different between them. There would be only civility. Proper thoughts and dignified words.

Instead of this tension that throbbed between them.

He should not care if she thought him undeserving of a dukedom. Her opinion did not matter. He was the bloody duke.

And yet he *did* care.

He cared what his scornful little housekeeper in her colorless dresses thought of him.

It was an untenable situation. He really should have sacked her already and replaced her with a proper housekeeper. One old enough to be his grandmother. Someone whose plump mouth did not incite unholy ideas.

It was confounding. Who ever heard of a woman like *her* running a household as grand as Penning Hall? He snorted. What had the previous *legitimate* Duke of Penning been thinking to have placed someone so young in such an elevated and important position? The old man had clearly been daft. That would explain his attempt to pass off his bastard as his legitimate heir to the world.

Of course none of this would be a problem if Lucian were a different sort of man. A nobleman who didn't care what his housekeeper thought of him. Or a nobleman who wasn't reluctant to act on his impulses.

He knew such men existed. Haughty nobles

who took whatever they wanted, whomever they wanted—including pretty servants. Nothing would stop those men from cornering one of their housemaids, grabbing her from behind and hiking her skirts up for a quick tumble. He was not that man.

Lucian was . . . well, he was not one to take advantage of someone in a position less privileged than his own. He had struggled enough in his own life. He would not knowingly inflict suffering on anyone else.

He lifted his arm and grasped the window frame in a white-knuckled grip, staring down at the grounds and yet seeing nothing.

No perhaps about it. He needed to let her go. He would give her a proper recommendation, of course. Something that would easily land her another position elsewhere. He was not such a cad that he would sack her and cast her out without any prospects. Perhaps he could even see about securing a position for her so that he was not turning her out with nowhere to go. His conscience demanded he make such an effort.

Resolute with this decision, he moved from the window and rang for his valet. He would put the task to Mr. Carter. That good man could handle her dismissal and the hiring of a new housekeeper.

His valet had been indispensable to him since

he arrived at Penning Hall. Carter was young and bright. Ambitious. He had been instrumental in helping Lucian acclimate to his new position.

Lucian knew he was leaning on him more than one might lean on a valet, but he was a little at sea in his sudden role of a nobleman, and Carter had served as valet to the previous duke . . . the previous *two* dukes if one counted the swindler. He well knew the habits of a nobleman and he kept Lucian from looking like a fool on most days.

Lucian would have to increase the man's wages. Perhaps promote him to the role of secretary. He gave a single nod of decisiveness. Indeed.

Especially if he was foisting the unpleasant business of sacking members of the staff on Carter. He gave the valet's bell rope another tug and returned to his desk. Carter would see to the matter. With any luck, he would have a new housekeeper by the week's end—one that did not provoke him and stir uncomfortable things inside of him.

# Chapter Three ❦

"Contemplating murder, Miss Lockhart?"

Susanna lurched off the door with a gasp at the sudden voice. She had been so lost in her cross thoughts that she had not noticed the approach of Miss Ross.

"Miss Ross," she said in what she hoped was an even and composed voice. "Whatever do you mean?"

She glanced over her shoulder to the room where the duke remained. She couldn't see him, but she imagined he was still at that desk, that stupid handsome face of his poring over his list of victims . . . er, bridal prospects.

She wanted to think it would be difficult for him to win an eligible lady to wife. That no woman would want him, but, of course, that would not be the case. It would be the opposite, unfortunately. He would be much desired. Feted. Pursued. Every Society Mama would be pelting him with their marriageable daughters.

Such was the unfairness of life. Beautiful money-eyed people generally got what they wanted. And let's not forget he was a duke, too. A vagary of birth and twist of fate that made him more advantaged than just about everyone else on the planet.

"Come, now." Miss Ross offered a cajoling smile. "I know my brother can be a trial."

*A trial? He is an arse.*

"Oh, no! Not at all, Miss Ross," she stammered, hoping and praying that she had not conveyed that attitude.

The young woman was well out of the school room but still younger than Susanna. Like Susanna, she was unmarried. Although *un*like Susanna, she was not likely to remain so.

Now that Mathilda Ross was the sister of a duke she would have her pick of suitors. With her fair looks and generous dowry, she would likely snag herself a lord by the end of the season. She would have her pick of husbands. Both Ross sisters would likely not be here for very long. They would be running households of their own soon. Young, attractive sisters of dukes did not remain unwed.

Miss Ross stood with the morning light limned behind her. She was a vision in her lovely day dress of periwinkle blue. Unlike her dark-haired brother, she was fair, her thick curls shining like spun gold.

Her dress was a simple confection of muslin. Simple for *her*—this sister of a duke. Susanna had never owned anything so fine in all her life.

She had led a humble existence in a sparsely populated fishing town by the name of Kennaughly on the Isle of Man. Her mother had worked in the kitchens of a gentry family—when she was not working alongside her fisherman husband. The family was English and only in residence half the year. When not working as a kitchen maid, Mama spent the rest of her time on the docks or on the boat or at home sewing and repairing nets.

When Mama overheard the lady of the house complaining that her young daughter was in need of companionship, Susanna's mother had quickly volunteered her for the position.

Susanna had been called up to the big house for a nail-biting interview. She remembered the day well. She had stood before the elegant English lady in awe. Susanna was only eleven, standing in the well-appointed parlor of a house she had only observed from afar, wringing her hands as she was eyed critically by this lady with milk-pale skin and hands that looked as tender and fresh as a newborn babe's.

Whilst Mrs. Davies had not liked Susanna's meager English and too-thin frame, she'd thought Susanna clean and pleasing of face. She'd hired Susanna on the spot.

Soon, Susanna found herself swept up in a strange new world of manners and fine clothes and an abundance of food—tea and scones every day! As many as her heart desired. Her thin frame quickly filled out and her face took on a healthy glow, much to Mrs. Davies's satisfaction.

Her world grew exponentially as she began taking lessons alongside the precocious Ruth, who was hungry for a friend and welcomed Susanna full-heartedly. Mrs. Davies insisted that Susanna be educated alongside her daughter—so that Ruth would not feel so alone in her studies.

For no other reason could Susanna speak like a proper Englishwoman today. It was because of Ruth and her governess that she could speak English at all instead of exclusively Manx, the tongue she had spoken since she formed her first word.

She had learned not only English, but arithmetic, literature, science and a spattering of French and Latin. The governess had a special fondness for the classics, and Susanna had soaked it all in, sharing that love, losing herself in stories of Theseus and Aphrodite and Persephone and Zeus and all the other Greek gods, reveling in the drama, the struggles and foibles of characters who felt so very real in her mind, all the while appreciating the education she would not have received in the normal course of her life.

Growing up in that household, Susanna had seen pretty frocks before. Even Ruth, however, had not worn anything as fine as Miss Ross's dress. Susanna had not seen such elegant gowns since moving to the mainland, to Shropshire. She had observed countless sumptuous gowns in her tenure at Penning Hall; first as a maid and later as a housekeeper. She admired them with secret longing in her heart, knowing she would never wear one herself. Never feel fine silk against her skin.

It was a foolish longing. Shallow for her to want something as silly as a pretty dress she would never have cause or occasion to wear.

Her life was good. Things could have been so much worse. That thing that drove her from Kennaughly could have followed her here.

She quickly glanced down at herself and stifled a wince. She wore a serviceable wool gown of blue and it was more than adequate. It was one of five dresses she owned. In addition to this dark blue one (her favorite), she owned a gray one and three others in varying shades of brown. These were the colors of her life. No patterns or prints. No silk or muslin. All adequate.

"Come. Now that we have settled in at Penning Hall, we needn't be so formal. Call me Mathilda. Or Mattie, as my friends do."

Susanna could not possibly. Unlike her brother, this girl was not natural to the role of haughty and superior aristocrat.

Miss Ross continued, "And you? What is your name, Miss Lockhart?"

She hesitated only a beat. If the duke's sister wished to address her by her Christian name, then that was her right. She was the duke's sister, after all, and Susanna but a servant of the house. She could call her whatever she wished. "Susanna."

Miss Ross's lips spread in a smile. "Susanna. That is lovely. It suits you." Her gaze flicked to the doors of the study and she pulled a pout. "Is my brother being his usual tyrant self?"

"Er . . . I . . ." *Yes.*

"You can agree. I won't betray your confidences to him."

Susanna glanced around her as though sensing a trap. "Your brother is . . . a fair man." She did not know that to be true—he had not been here long enough for her to know—but she certainly was not about to confess her dislike and that she thought him to be terrible.

"Hmm," Mathilda murmured as though she was not convinced. Her eyes, a much lighter (and warmer) shade of blue than her brother's, twinkled in merriment. "He rather is, but I don't expect you to believe that as I've seen the way he's behaved toward you since we arrived."

She straightened, beyond curious at what this

young woman believed herself to have witnessed. "Indeed?"

"He's been a bear. A regular grump, and I don't know why. He is usually so much more courteous. Especially to the ladies. They adore him."

Perhaps that was the problem, then. Susanna was no lady. He was not courteous, and she definitely did not adore him.

Mathilda continued, "I quite understand if you do not like him."

"You do?" She blinked warily.

"Forgive me for defending him, but he really is the dearest of brothers. You simply need to understand him."

Susanna struggled to school her expression into passivity at that astonishing pronouncement. Mathilda Ross really was an innocent. The girl thought it necessary for the housekeeper to *understand* her employer. The lord of the manor. The duke.

Oh, sweet, naive girl.

Intrigued, she could not help but ask, "And what, pray tell, should I understand, Miss Ross?" As far as she could determine, the Duke of Penning came from wealth and privilege. He possessed youth and beauty and other attributes too many and exhaustive to account. Suffice it to say, the man was blessed.

"He is new to this role . . . and I don't know if you know much about us, about where we come from, about who we were before . . ." Her voice faded.

*Before the windfall of a dukedom that landed in his lap?*

No. Susanna knew very little about the Duke of Penning and his sisters—merely that they had been living a modest life in London. A gentleman's life, she had been told. No more than that had been imparted. No more explanation was she owed.

Mathilda shook her head as though ridding herself of some particularly unpleasant thought. "Let us just say that he takes his new position very seriously. He means to do right by the dukedom and right by us. Er, me and Evelyn," she clarified as though Susanna might not understand.

Such a challenge! However could he juggle all the copious power and vast wealth gifted to him? Oh, the plight of the rich and privileged was indeed a weighty burden. She resisted rolling her eyes, and instead said, "I am certain he will."

Mathilda gave her an inquiring look. "*I* am not certain you mean that."

Susanna shook her head in sharp denial. For a sweetly innocent young woman, she was rather discerning. "Of course, I mean it. I wish the duke only success in his new role—"

Mathilda laughed lightly. "Fret not. I'll not tattle to my brother."

She exhaled.

Mathilda continued, "I like you, Susanna." She smiled with this declaration as though she had just reached that decision. Heavens knew why it took her two months. "I think you're quite needed here. You seem like someone who will be good for my brother."

Her cheeks caught fire. That sounded vastly . . . inappropriate. Almost as though she was a romantic prospect, which was the absolute furthest thing from the truth.

"Oh," she mumbled, squaring her shoulders as she attempted to prevent Miss Ross's kind words from going to her head—even if she knew she worked most diligently and that this place functioned like a well-oiled machine because of her. "Er. Thank you . . ."

"Anyone can see that this place is what it is because of you." She gestured around them.

Of course that was what she meant. She meant Susanna was good for Penning Hall. Not the duke . . . well. Not directly the duke.

Miss Ross added, "Soon my brother will realize that, too."

*Ah. So then the duke does not think I am needed.*

Her stomach knotted. That felt like confirmation of her fears.

"Thank you." Hopefully, Miss Ross was correct and Susanna's position was not in peril as she suspected.

A sudden commotion rose up from the bowels of the house. The two women exchanged startled glances before hastening along the corridor and down the stairs, pausing on the landing.

Several other members of the staff were already gathered, surrounding something . . . *someone*.

Susanna pushed her way forward to find Mr. Carter groaning on the floor of the landing at the center of the group.

She dropped down beside him. "Mr. Carter! What happened?"

He released a chagrined gust of breath as he reached for his ankle. "I was rushing on the stairs and lost my footing. I feel quite foolish."

"Nonsense. These things happen."

"I've really gone and done it, haven't I?"

"You will be fine. Don't fret."

Miss Ross materialized beside Susanna, her pretty features creased with worry. "Oh, Mr. Carter! Does it pain you very much?"

The young gentleman flushed, attempting an unaffected, dignified expression, but the pain was still there, in every line and hollow of his face. "'Tis nothing, Miss Ross. Do not concern yourself."

Susanna looked up and snapped at one of the gawking footmen. "Peter, fetch Dr. Merrit."

"Yes, ma'am." With a brisk nod, he hastened away.

It was no surprise that Mr. Bird had not done so yet. In any other household, the butler would have stepped to quick action, but the Penning butler had slowed down considerably in the last few years. He was no longer so quick to perform—or quick to think. Or quick to do anything.

The elderly butler stood on the fringes of the group, blinking his rheumy eyes. She suspected his vision was failing him—along with everything else. Poor man. He was the oldest staff member. He'd been at the hall longer than even her aunt. Those eyes had witnessed a great many things—the reign of several dukes.

No one voiced a complaint at Mr. Bird's less-than-stellar performance, but everyone knew. *Everyone* was aware. Mr. Bird was absentminded and if he moved at all these days it was at a snail's pace. Everyone held their tongues out of consideration for him. No one wanted to see him forced to resign from his post. He had no family. Where would he go? To some dank little hut on the outskirts of Shropshire? Or perhaps he would take a room somewhere. In a boardinghouse among strangers.

Susanna swallowed thickly because she felt the bleakness of his fate keenly . . . because it was a reflection of her own.

By the time she reached the end and was ready to retire, she would have no one, either. No one and nowhere to go.

She would be as alone as Mr. Bird.

Presumably her mother and stepfather would be gone by then—not that they would welcome her back to Kennaughly. Indeed not. As far as they were concerned, she was already dead to them.

Not that she would wish to return there to them if she could. As much as she missed the sea and the taste of salty air on her skin, as much as she missed watching the boats come into dock and listening to the rhythmic lap of water on the shoreline, she had no wish to return there. Not to that place where she had been scorned and de-rided and expelled as though she carried some horrible contagion, where her mother had so horribly failed her.

She had no siblings, and no other family—only Aunt Ferelith, who was actually Susanna's great-aunt and over sixty. She would likely not be around, either, when Susanna was ready to retire.

She was careful with her money, putting away for the inevitable future, one where she would have no one except herself upon whom to rely.

Hopefully she could find a small cottage, some place where she could grow a garden, keep a few pets, a fat tabby cat to curl up on her lap before the fire and an energetic dog to accompany her on invigorating strolls.

As clearly as she visualized this fate for herself, her lonely fate, she acknowledged it was not all that bleak. Oh, to the outside world, it assuredly looked a forlorn existence. And yet aloneness did not frighten her. There were far worse things than finding yourself alone in the world. She felt no despair at the prospect. She enjoyed her company. Her books. Sketching. Country walks. She enjoyed baking. Cook had long ago accepted her occasional presence in the kitchen.

Baking was something she had done in her youth, with her mother, when times had been good. Simple. Peaceful. The rhythmic kneading of bread . . . the kiss of sugar and mixed spices on the air. A time when her stepfather had not loathed the sight of her. Before she had learned that family, the people who were supposed to love her unconditionally, had conditions on that love, after all. That hearts could turn cold and turn on you and break your own heart. That the people who were supposed to care about you the most could hurt you the most and cast you from their lives. A painful lesson, but one that had stayed with her to this day.

Indeed, there were worse things than solitude.

Being with others, stuck with someone whose company was regrettable or repugnant or even just dull, was worse. She would rather be alone. At least she liked herself and did not regret her own company.

Susanna directed her attention back to Mr. Carter. "Let us see you to your room."

She motioned for two of the larger footmen to help him up off the floor. Together, they carried Mr. Carter between them down the steps. She followed, trailing them into the servants' stairs to Mr. Carter's room.

Mr. Bird panted as he struggled to keep pace beside her even though they were not moving quickly. "What will we do with Mr. Carter incapacitated?" he fretted.

"We don't know the extent of his injuries, Mr. Bird. Let us wait and see what the doctor says." She paused with a hopeful breath. "It might not be so very bad."

# Chapter Four ❧

$\mathcal{I}$t was bad.

"At least a week in bed. For now keep your foot elevated," Dr. Merrit pronounced, closing up his bag and stepping back from the bed. "And when you are up and about, keep that ankle tightly wrapped lest you wish to injure yourself all over again and end up bedridden for an even longer spell."

No one spoke for several moments, absorbing that, absorbing how the very essential Mr. Carter would be incapacitated. Without a functioning butler and without Mr. Carter . . .

Susanna sighed. Her burden just became that much heavier.

Dr. Merrit's cheerful smile faded a bit as he took in the grim expressions surrounding him. He gathered up his bag. "Feel free to send for me. Although I don't imagine you will need to." He fixed a stern gaze on Carter. "Not if he does as instructed."

They held silent as the physician departed the room.

Then Mr. Carter erupted, "I cannot remain in

this bed." He sat up, moving as though to rise to his feet. "There is too much to do."

Before Susanna could even protest, Mathilda was reacting. The young woman pressed a hand to his shoulder to stay him. "Mr. Carter!" she tsked. "Did you not hear the good doctor?"

He looked down at her hand on his chest, clearly uncomfortable at the touch. He sent Susanna a look that seemed to say: *She should not be in here.*

Susanna knew he was correct, but the duke's sister did not appear to be a young woman easily managed. That task fell to her brother. There was no one else charged with her. She was too old for a nurse or a governess. She had no mother. Her lady's maid stood behind her, not about to intervene. That was not Miss Barrow's role, and it certainly was not Susanna's—or Carter's.

Susanna sent the valet a small, single-shoulder shrug.

"The duke needs attending," he insisted.

No one replied.

"Who is going to attend to the duke?" he pressed into the silence. "Someone must attend him."

Susanna looked pointedly at the butler. As the highest-ranking male servant, clearly it should fall to him. She winced. Except sometimes he confused his socks for gloves.

Mathilda snorted, thankfully, so that Susanna did not have to. "Lucian will survive a week without you just fine."

Mr. Carter's eyes fairly bulged. The Duke of Penning going a week without the services of a valet did not strike him as survival. Mathilda might as well have suggested that her brother perform surgery on himself with garden shears.

"A week on his own?" Mr. Carter uttered the words as though they were the foulest of epithets. "By himself? Oh, no, no, no."

"He's gone without a valet for years," Mathilda pointed out. "Long before he—"

"Forgive me for disagreeing with you, Miss Ross, but the man is the Duke of Penning now. Past oversights do not signify. He is not just a man any longer. He cannot do without a valet." Carter attempted once more to gain his feet. Mathilda pushed him back down again, sending Susanna a beseeching look.

Susanna dutifully found her voice. "Now you're being foolish, Mr. Carter."

He frowned and leveled an injured look on Susanna. "Miss Lockhart, you understand my obligations better than anyone."

Of course she did.

"I do." Susanna gestured to his foot. "And yet you cannot walk." That was the crux of the matter.

The valet fell back against the pillows with a defeated sigh. He dragged a hand over his face. "Then what shall we do? What do you suggest?" At this question he was, of course, looking to Susanna.

"Someone else shall step forward and act as his valet until you're well enough to attend the duke." Simple. Except it was not so simple as that.

Carter lifted his head from the pillow. "Who? Who on staff is prepared for such a task? No one is trained for the role."

She bit her lip, considering. A valid question. A footman could not merely slip into the role as though he were donning a new shirt. There was a great deal of skill involved. One trained to become a valet over time. Years. It was a much-coveted position among servants. Susanna did not think even one of the grooms could tie a proper cravat. Not with the mastery Carter possessed.

In the past, Mr. Bird would have been the obvious choice. But that was in the past. Sadly, the butler was no longer capable. The man could scarcely attend himself and perform the tasks of a butler. He surely could not step in as valet to the duke.

Still . . . Susanna found herself looking rather helplessly to where Mr. Bird stood near the window, gazing out vacantly rather than attending to what was presently happening with Mr. Carter.

Carter followed her gaze. "Him? You jest."

Mr. Bird did not even react to their remarks, which were so obviously in reference to him. It was not uncommon. At times he would drift away, so lost in himself that he failed to note his surroundings.

She sighed. "I know." Mr. Bird could not be considered.

"Then who?" he challenged.

"Miss Lockhart, of course, is the only viable option."

The outrageous suggestion dropped in the air between them like a stone plopping through water. Susanna blinked and then looked sharply to where Miss Barrow stood.

The woman stared back at Susanna with her dark, intelligent eyes as though she had not just suggested anything extraordinary.

She was always so quiet. And yet very efficient. The duke had arrived with his sisters and two ladies' maids were required. Susanna had not needed to ponder overly long on the matter of which housemaid to promote. Miss Barrow had been the immediate and obvious choice to step into the role of lady's maid to the eldest Miss Ross. Susanna had needed to ponder a bit longer to arrive at an appropriate candidate for the younger Miss Ross, however.

Carter was the first to fill the silence following Miss Barrow's outrageous suggestion. "Miss Lockhart?"

Why did his voice sound so very contemplative and not incredulous?

"Yes. She could do it," Miss Ross asserted as though she knew about such things.

"B-but," Susanna sputtered.

*I am not a valet. I am a woman.*

"But what?" Miss Barrow countered. "You are the housekeeper. As such, it is not beyond the pale."

"Is it not?" Susanna demanded.

"You possess the keys to the house. You are the chatelaine. In days of old, you would see to the comforts of prominent guests and to the lord of the manor, attending to him yourself . . . even at his bath."

Her face caught fire. Suddenly Susanna could only think about that. About bathing the duke, about putting her hands on the duke—the very naked duke. Catering to all his needs, whilst he was at his bath and outside of it.

The wicked prospect turned her face into an inferno. She pressed the back of her hand to one cheek, wondering if it would ever cool . . . if she would ever *not* feel aflame at that prospect.

Miss Barrow looked around at everyone in the room. "Is that not so?"

Mr. Carter's mouth parted as an expression of deep thought came over him.

Mathilda made a humming sound. "Hmm. That is true. I read that in my history lessons."

"But that was centuries ago. This is not a feudal manor," Susanna weakly reminded them.

"Some things have not changed so very much," Miss Barrow mused. "A housekeeper is second only to the lady of the house and the last time I checked there is no Duchess of Penning to hold sway here." She arched a reddish eyebrow in challenge at Susanna.

Carter nodded slowly as he, too, eyed Susanna. "True, it is not ideal, but we find ourselves in a unique situation here. Clearly it should fall on you to attend to His Grace."

*Clearly?*

"I fear it is not clear to me," she protested hotly.

"Well, who more than you is suited to the task?" He nodded. "It is not as though I wait on the man hand and foot. You would not have to do *everything* for him, of course. His Grace is far more independent than he ought to be." He sent a careful glance to the duke's sister, who listened raptly to the discussion. Obviously he did not wish to malign the duke in present company. "No one need know outside of the house. We can be discreet on that matter." He sent everyone in the chamber a meaningful glance as though to affirm that discretion would be the order of the day.

"I cannot act as his valet," Susanna insisted with a determined shake of her head.

"It is not as though I will be bedridden indefinitely," Carter continued. "I should only be indisposed for a week at the most. Your assistance would not be required for very long. You can manage that. It is only temporary."

Susanna fell silent, thinking on that. *Temporary.*

He was correct, of course. She was being missish.

There was no one else more suited than she to step into Mr. Carter's shoes.

Her aunt had trained her well. She knew how the duke should dress and the manner in which he spent his days.

She swallowed thickly. Indeed. There was no one better.

Carter looked at her beseechingly. He knew it. So did she.

Perhaps they should have taken on an underbutler after all, training him to step in when needed; then they would not be in this predicament. An underbutler would have been the ideal choice to act as valet in Carter's absence. Stubborn loyalty had stayed the impulse, and now she was being punished for the oversight.

She sighed, feeling herself relent. "I suppose I *can* manage it for a week." *A mere seven days.* She could endure that. She had weathered worse.

At the first opportunity, she would hire that underbutler. For now, however, it was too late.

Carter expelled a relieved breath. "Very good."

Miss Barrow nodded as though it was the obvious conclusion.

Miss Ross appeared unaffected. It obviously did not occur to her that Susanna attending to her brother could lend itself to awkwardness.

"He bathes before dinner," Carter unnecessarily reminded her. As though she did not know his schedule. She knew everything that went on in this house. Nothing happened under this roof without her knowledge.

"I know," she grumbled.

He nodded approvingly. "Of course you do, which is precisely why you are so suited for this task."

She forced a smile that felt brittle on her face.

"We are so fortunate to have you, Susanna," Miss Ross asserted in that kind way of hers. She was yet untouched by the life of privilege and excess that had befallen her. She was still humble.

Perhaps time would change that. Time and a future married to some blue-blooded toff. Gazing at her wide, guileless eyes, Susanna felt a pinch of regret over that.

The sweet girl turned a militant eye on the valet. "And you, Mr. Carter, will stay put right here until you are fully mended." She wagged a finger at him in the bed. "I will check on you each day to make certain."

Carter flushed, splotches breaking out over his handsome face. "You are much too kind, Miss Ross." Kind. And terrifying. Susanna read that in the young valet's gaze immediately.

The man did not quite know how to cope with the overly friendly sister of the nobleman he served.

Susanna sent a glance to the window, noting the purpling skies. The duke would want that bath soon. She would have to see it readied for him.

But first she would have to call on him and inform him that his valet would be incapacitated for a short time.

She took a shuddering inhale. He would have to rely on her. She wondered which one of them would hate that more.

# Chapter Five ❧

Susanna arrived late to the duke's chamber, clutching an armful of fresh linens to her chest, an apology for her tardiness on her lips.

She needn't have been so late. It was not like her. She was never tardy. Never one to be remiss in her duties. She *could* have arrived at his door sooner—promptly on time. She *could* have been the consummate professional, as was her usual custom.

She could not help herself, though. She needed the time to compose herself—to fortify herself before facing him and explaining that he would temporarily be without Carter. That he would have *her* instead. No one else would have explained that to him. Who would want to? The task of delivering that unwelcome news fell to her.

The duke bathed before dinner. That was his habit. Of course she knew that. She knew every routine in this house, including his. He had not been here a very long time, but in the span of two months she had learned his preferences.

She might not be his valet, but it was her business to know all the duties of the staff. She was the one to assign them, after all. Once upon a time it had been Mr. Bird's purview, but over the last few years it had become her task. Every morning following breakfast she met with the senior staff members and discussed the staff's obligations for the day.

She was late this evening, which meant his bath was late, which meant he would be late to dinner, too. She grimaced. It really was not well done of her. Especially as she had just vowed this very day to do better, to *be* better, to be invaluable.

She knocked once, the sound brisk and efficient, precisely the image she hoped to project. Once inside his chamber she would ring for his water.

This was simply another duty. She told herself that with a firm nod. Like any other she would perform in the course of her day. As Miss Barrow said, it was not beyond the pale.

Even as she repeated this to herself, her hand trembled as she rapped her knuckles for a second time. Firmer.

At the muffled sound of his voice bidding entry, she turned the latch and entered the chamber. She could not recall the last time she had even entered the room. Not since the arrival of this new duke, to be certain. The housemaids cleaned and tidied every day. Mr. Carter handled everything else. Her presence in this space had never been required. Until now.

She entered . . . and found the Duke of Penning stark naked, standing beside a steaming tub, clearly on the verge of climbing into his waiting bath. Apparently the footmen had already delivered his water.

She froze.

He froze.

Heat swamped her, first flooding her face and then every inch of her.

His cheeks went ruddy beneath the tanned hue of his skin, but he did nothing to shield himself. No diving behind furniture. No snatching up a linen. No hands flying to cover that impressive member hanging between his thighs.

He held her stare with all the dignity of a . . . well, a duke. There was not the slightest bit of modesty to him. If anything, he seemed to square his shoulders and stand taller.

Her mouth dried.

She forced herself to hold her ground and not whirl around with a squeak. She was no child. No squeamish maid. She was not even an innocent.

Aside from her brief lapse all those years ago—that shameful romance which expelled her from her tiny island home and landed her in Shropshire—she felt a complete novice.

Discounting that instance, Susanna had seen naked men before. She had helped her aunt attend to the men in the household that fell ill, and after her aunt retired she had continued in that custom. She had even seen the original Duke of Penning (how he would forever be remembered in her mind) a time or two in his twilight years when he fell ill and needed assistance.

And yet this was no sickly, aging man. Indeed not.

She swallowed down a whimper as she struggled to view him with a dispassionate air. He was virile and young and the very definition of strapping. She had known he was well formed but possessed no full concept that *this* was what hid beneath his clothes.

His body was long and lean. Shoulders wide. Chest and stomach flat with interesting ridges and shadowed lines. Hips narrow. A dark line of hair started at his navel and trailed into the hair nestling around his member.

This, she thought rather grimly, was a body bred for labor, a weapon to be used at a plow or on a battlefield—*or on a lover.*

That latter thought was like a smoky whisper

threading through her mind, unbidden, but once it surfaced she could not banish it.

Her gaze continued to linger where it should not. That manhood of his was impossible to miss. Impressive. Daunting.

Floating across a ballroom seemed the least ideal use of that body. A wasted resource, to be certain. Not that she was well experienced in that arena, but he—*it*—was impossible not to look upon, not to take measure, and consequently imagine how it might be used . . . the pleasure it could happily inflict.

Her face turned to flame.

She knew what a cock could do, both theoretically and physically.

Resolve tightened her jaw, resistant to that seductive little voice and the way it caused her to pulse between her legs. That kind of pleasure also destroyed.

She knew about such destruction. Had experienced it firsthand. A weapon indeed.

Once had been enough.

One time, one relationship or foray with that part of a man's anatomy, had very nearly destroyed her. Destroyed her heart. Her pride. Her good name. Her family. Erased her entirely from existence. That misstep had cast her here, far from home. Now she lived with no past of which to speak. At least no past she dared to share.

Gazing upon the Duke of Penning, the throb between her thighs twisted, demanding an end to the aching hollowness.

He was altogether an appalling display of vitality. Truly. The kind of man the young women in the household would salivate over were he a mortal man and not a bloody toff—not that they had not already made fools of themselves waxing on about the new Duke of Penning and how very handsome he was. Susanna had put an abrupt end to that—at least where she might overhear.

It was one thing for them to proclaim about the good looks of a local tradesman or yeoman. Penning, however, was their employer. A nobleman, as far removed from them as the stars in the sky. It was vastly inappropriate for them to ogle him as though he were some stable lad with bulging muscles to be admired.

She blinked at the reminder.

Just as *they* should not gawk at him neither should *she*.

She gave her head a slight shake, determined to maintain an air of propriety.

He finally spoke. "You're not Carter." Perhaps not *finally*, though. It had only been moments since she unceremoniously charged into his sanctuary, since she leered at him and his swelling member—a fact he seemed indifferent to—but time had seemed to freeze amid the shock of finding him thusly.

"I am not," she agreed dumbly, which she supposed was forgivable as his declaration had been equally stupid. She motioned to the door. "You bade me enter."

"I was not expecting *you*."

That much was evident.

Perhaps if she had not dallied, overcome with dread at facing him, at explaining that *she* would be stepping in for Carter, this uncomfortable encounter could have been avoided.

He turned with his usual air of dismissal, giving her a glimpse of two well-rounded, taut cheeks, twin dimples above the swells, directly below the small of his back. As though nothing awkward passed between them. As though she had not burst in upon him naked. As though her entire body did not burn with equal parts mortification and arousal.

She could not recall ever seeing a man's arse before, and it astonished her that such a sight should increase the insistent tug in her belly.

*Experienced* did not mean *experienced*, she acknowledged.

He lifted a foot and stepped into his tub, his long body descending into the water. His dismissal felt usual, but only that. Nothing about any of this was usual. All of this was extraordinary and new. Awkwardly, regrettably new.

But he was out of sight now. Thankfully out of sight. At least there was that.

She released a gust of breath. She had only his chest and shoulder and stern features to endure and that was quite enough.

"I thought you were Carter."

"Obviously."

His eyes narrowed. "As that is so obvious . . . could you explain what *you* are doing here? What are you *still* doing here?" He settled his arms on the edges of the tub. Even those naked limbs were manly. Well formed and sinewy, offering a peek of dark hair beneath his armpits. How was even that enticing? "Because that is not obvious to me."

She moved deeper inside the room, setting the fresh linens down on a nearby side table with hands that treacherously trembled. She would not reveal how very much he had discombobulated her. "Unfortunately, Mr. Carter has met with an accident—"

"What happened?" A line drew between his eyes.

"He took a spill down the stairs, but he will be fine. It was not too far a fall. He turned his ankle. It's quite swollen. We called for the physician. Dr. Merrit said he will need some time off his feet."

He digested that and then nodded. "I suppose

that explains his absence. I rang for him some time ago. It was not like him to keep me waiting."

"No, it is not," she agreed.

She knew Carter well enough to know that he usually anticipated the duke's every need, appearing well before he was even summoned.

Penning grunted.

She took a breath. "I have come to attend to you in his place."

"You?"

"Yes. Me." She adjusted her spine. "I am here to help you however Mr. Carter would have."

He took a moment before answering, his gaze gliding over her in slow, spine-tingling deliberation. "Are you in the habit of attending gentlemen in their baths? Is that within your area of expertise, Miss Lockhart?"

Was it her imagination or did his gaze turn mocking? He thought to scandalize her. That was his intent. Of course, she had no intention of helping him *bathe*—that would be the height of inappropriateness—but his infuriating smirk stopped her from pointing that out to him.

She lifted her chin. "You will not be my first, Your Grace."

That wiped the smirk from his face. *Of course, her first had been an old, infirm man.* "Indeed?" If possible, his eyes darkened. "Interesting."

And why did it feel as though they were no longer discussing *bathing*? She realized with some consternation that the same words would apply to fornication—and that what she said would still be true. He would not be her first. She was no dewy-eyed maid, but a woman with experience when it came to matters of the flesh. Heat returned to her cheeks.

He looked away from her then, slipping lower in the water and resting his head on the back lip of the tub. "You are not needed here, Miss Lockhart. I can bathe myself." He gestured to the table. "If you will just fetch me the washcloth and soap, you may take your leave."

He closed his eyes as though prepared to nap in that tub and forget she was even in the room.

After a moment, she crossed the chamber and claimed the washcloth and soap. Moving to the tub, she stretched out the soap and washcloth in a perfunctory manner. "I will be taking over Mr. Carter's duties until he is on his feet again."

He scowled and opened one of his eyes a crack to peer at her. Clearly he did not like that notion. "Will you now?"

Determined to prove herself useful, she added, "I am quite capable—"

"No," he snapped, glancing down at the soap and washcloth in her hands as though they were poison. "Your self-professed experience aside, I do not require your assistance. I will be fine until my valet can resume his duties. I lived for years without one."

She blinked, feeling like a fool. He clearly did not want her here. Just as well. The sight of him was overwhelming to her senses.

She moistened her lips, doing her best to keep her gaze trained on his face and not look south—of course, this was after she had already subjected his body to a thorough examination moments ago. She could still envision him. She needed to escape to her own chamber, where she could exorcise the imprint of him from her mind.

So why was she lingering here?

"Do you have something else to say, Miss Lockhart?" The question was deep and rumbly and did funny things to her inside.

Fire burned her cheeks and she snapped her gaze north from where it had drifted for a split second to the inky depths of his bathwater. "Er. No. Good evening." She dipped a hasty curtsy.

She was almost to the door when he called out after her. "I still expect to see that menu from you, Miss Lockhart."

*Drat!*

She had promised him the menu. She had not even managed a moment alone with Cook. Of course, he had not forgotten. Nor would he. Nothing mattered more to him than the upcoming assembly and all it signified. *Landing a wife.*

Some proper English rose who would be a perfect wife and usher his sisters and future children through Society. The perfect ornament at his side. A wife who would share his bed and look her fill at his body without shame or guilt or embarrassment.

Hopefully this unknown lady would like Susanna more than Penning did and she did not have to fret over being sacked.

Susanna turned slowly to face him again. "Yes, Your Grace." She nodded deferentially. "I will return posthaste."

"Not posthaste. I will finish bathing and then dine with my sisters. Afterward, I will send for you. Be ready."

"Yes, of course." Nodding, she turned around again and took her leave, her hands shaking at her sides with indignation. She was not one to struggle with taking orders or harbor lofty aspirations. She had been in service much of her life and was accustomed to authority figures commanding her to and fro. And yet for some reason taking orders from *this* man only served to vex her.

It was evident that he did not approve of her acting as his valet. Susanna snorted and kicked herself for permitting Carter and everyone else to persuade her into stepping into the role. He scarcely stomached her as his housekeeper. What made her think he would accept her as someone who interacted with him even more frequently?

Once in the corridor, she hastened to her own bedchamber, needing solitude . . . and her desk upon which to write the required menu.

Her chamber consisted of one bed, a washstand, a wardrobe and a dressing table that also served as a desk.

As the Penning housekeeper, she was fortunate to have a room to herself. She'd occupied it ever since Aunt Ferelith left to live with her longtime friend, Agatha. The only other servant on staff who could boast of such a claim was Mr. Bird.

A handmade quilt Aunt Ferelith crafted covered the bed along with several velvet and damask pillows. Framed watercolors that she and her aunt had painted over the years filled the walls, saving them from complete bareness.

A single shelf lined one of the walls, holding her collection of books. Nearly a dozen, read and reread over the years. A few were gifts from her aunt. Others were books she had saved up to purchase for herself.

This chamber was the only place in the house that felt like her own, like her sanctuary. No one else entered the space. Only Susanna. It was the one place she could go to at the end of each day and strip off her dreadful brown dress. Alone in her shift, she could brush out her hair and curl up on her bed and read or work on a puzzle or write a letter to Aunt Ferelith.

It did not matter what it was she did in here because she did it for herself. She was free to do whatever she wanted in her bedchamber. In her space. Hers alone.

She grimaced slightly because even that was false.

This chamber was *not* her own.

This room belonged to the Duke of Penning just as this house did. She was a servant. There was no place in this entire world that was hers alone.

Her autonomy in this life was based on her employment . . . and on the lies she had crafted about who she was—and who she wasn't.

On the decency of others, on the whims of the blasted blue-blooded arse upstairs who did not seem to want or need her.

Suddenly she felt keenly, achingly alone.

She missed her aunt, and wondered if it would be a terrible thing to abandon all of this and go to her, invade the life she and Agatha had built for themselves. They did not live too far away. She managed to get away and visit them a couple of times a year.

Agatha had been her aunt's longtime friend who owned a millinery shop in Shropshire. The pair had scrimped and saved to buy their own home: a lovely cottage where they could spend out the remainder of their lives, a day's ride from Shropshire near tiny Hamford.

They lived as independent women of adequate means, and Susanna loathed the weak notion of falling upon them, behaving as a leech with no prospects when every penny they possessed had been earmarked and planned for *their* future.

*No.* She inhaled a shuddering breath. She would *not* do it.

She must remain strong and stalwart and continue on her course of proving herself to the duke.

Staving off the bleak feelings, she sank down at her desk and pulled out a sheet of parchment.

Forcing herself to the task at hand, she set quill to paper and started creating a menu that would be fit for a king . . . and hoped it would be good enough for the discerning eye of the Duke of Penning.

# Chapter Six ❧

*A*s soon as Miss Lockhart left him Lucian slid all the way down in the tub, submerging himself under the surface and letting the warm water engulf him.

Fuck all. This was *not* supposed to happen.

He was contemplating sacking the woman . . . not using her as his valet.

A valet was present for all manner of intimacies. Intimacies such as witnessing him in a state of undress. A fact he never thought twice about with Carter, but with her . . .

He breathed out from his nose, bubbles escaping to the surface. Even if it was only for a week and Carter was back on his feet, the situation was untenable. He might have acted aloof and unaffected as her gaze skimmed him, but that had been all pretense.

He had learned how to hide his emotions from an early age. He had used that skill since then. He had not blinked an eye at her sudden appearance—or during her scrutiny of him. Lucian had feigned nonchalance as heat erupted over his skin everywhere her gaze touched.

He stayed beneath the water as long as he could, until his lungs burned and he needed oxygen. When he broke above the surface he was no longer suffering an aching cock. There was that, at least. He'd climbed into the tub as a necessity, to hide his growing erection from her.

He swept his hair back from his eyes, slicking it over the crown of his head with a curse. He simply had been stuck too long in the country and away from the many diversions of Town. Too long away from available and eager women to bed.

There was no other explanation. He was no green lad, unable to control his urges. Finding a woman eyeing him in his altogether should *not* have impacted him.

His previous life had been full of amenable women. He had never considered himself dependent upon the fairer sex, but they had always been there. Always available for him to take his ease. Always a part of his world.

He had been five and ten when his father passed away. Papa's death had caught them all by surprise. Papa had still been a relatively young man when he expired and they had been living a comfortable life. It had been a great shock. He'd dropped dead at breakfast over his eggs. He could still hear his mother's and sisters' shrill screams.

His father had left them nothing. No tidy nest egg. No property. Nothing more than the few notes and coins in his pocket and a mountain of debt. That had been perhaps more of a shock than his sudden death. They were destitute.

Papa had enjoyed steady employment. Only later had they learned of his fondness for the gaming tables—and the reality of their circumstances. They lived from one day to the next, surviving on his father's weekly wage with nothing left over. Nothing saved. No assets amassed.

Everything screeched to a halt. Lucian's education ended. As did the fencing and riding and pianoforte and all other lessons his parents had somehow managed for him and his sisters. All the things a well-bred lad like him enjoyed ceased to be.

They had been forced to move from their comfortable house with its staff of three to a shabby boardinghouse in a less-than-quality neighborhood with other lodgers—questionable people with shifty eyes.

They had shared a room, the four of them, he and his mother and sisters, crowding in, all pretending to ignore the raucous sounds of the boardinghouse that seemed to never stop pulsing around them, day or night.

Mama toiled, something she'd never had to do before. She took in sewing and helped the proprietress of the boardinghouse with the laundry and other domestic tasks. Still it was not enough. Not enough to support herself and three children. Gone were their effortless lives and in place of that was penury, drudgery, and shame.

Money might not be everything. That was what people oft said. And yet there was no dignity in poverty.

Lucian discovered firsthand what it meant to go without. To have nothing. He learned about the nature of desperation, of doing what one must to make ends meet.

He had learned very quickly there was almost nothing too unacceptable or offensive. Not when it came to survival.

That had never been emphasized more than the evening his mother went out dressed in one of her fanciest gowns, rouge on her cheeks and paint on her lips. She'd left with no explanation, ignoring his questions. The hour had been late and she had left looking as he had never seen her appear before, and that only knotted his stomach with foreboding.

He did not sleep that night.

He lay awake, listening for her footsteps outside their room, waiting for her return, scarcely recognizing the shadow of her that eventually did return, coins clinking in her reticule.

That went on for another fortnight: Mama disappearing each night once his sisters fell asleep. Her shrinking, withering shadow returning until one day she could not even rouse herself from bed. She could not clamber to her feet. She could not eat.

She sank into the thin mattress of her bed, a deadweight, her eyes wide and unblinking, gazing ahead unseeingly like a glassy pair of marbles.

He knew. He was a lad of ten and seven then, but he knew. He had lived enough by then, especially in the boardinghouse. He had heard things, seen things a gently bred lad should not have.

She had remained in that bed the following morning and through the next day. And the next. She never roused. It was as though something had broken beyond her spirit. As though her body truly ceased to function.

He often wondered if something specific had happened that last night she went out. Some ugly encounter, an incident uglier than all the others that had come before. Or perhaps it had been the totality of everything piled upon her that made her give up.

He tried to wake her, urging her from her bed. Not only him. Mathilda and Evelyn had crawled all over her in the bed, tugging on her arms, cajoling, pleading with her for attention.

Nothing. She didn't move. Didn't speak. She was done.

Eventually he had no other choice. The landlady wanted her rent and the clawing ache of their stomachs demanded food. He was forced to go out for himself and look for work, leaving his young sisters with their listless mother and hoping Mama might blink and be her old self again, that she might return to the woman she had once been, the mother who nurtured and loved them.

Unfortunately the little work he found did not pay enough to accomplish those things. He could not pay for their room *and* buy food for all of them.

The solution had been offered to him by the lady in the room next door—the same woman who had loaned his mother the kohl and paint for her face. She had lingered in the threshold of her room as he started down the corridor.

"A handsome lad like you could be right popular," she remarked.

He'd paused. "I beg your pardon, ma'am?"

Her eyes twinkled. She was pretty. Older than himself by a solid ten years, but she seemed so much more worldly and sophisticated. Likely because she was.

"And such fine manners and speech," she marveled, assessing him from head to toe. "You've turned into quite the man over the last year."

He was well aware that he had grown nearly half a foot since Boxing Day. There were times when his heels ached and his mother informed him (when she had been speaking, of course) that was the normal course of things. Growing pains, she had called it, advising him to stretch his feet and limbs. Mama had been forced to let out the hems in his trousers, but still they fell too short.

"You could earn enough blunt to see you and your family into far better accommodations than this." Their neighbor had leaned against her doorjamb, indifferent to the fact that she was attired in naught more than a night rail. The sheer fabric did nothing at all to disguise the shape of her.

He'd stared at her for a long moment, unable to look away from her melon-size breasts that threatened to spill from the loose ties of her bodice.

Her hair was an improbable red and her eyes lined heavily with kohl. She was attractive in a sharp, predatory way that made him feel strangely alert.

"How?" he asked.

She smiled slowly. "By being nice to the ladies. Fine, proper ladies with deep purses and a penchant for pretty lads such as yourself."

He'd stared at her uncomprehendingly for a long moment.

She smiled and shook her head ruefully. Pushing off the door, she advanced on him, clearly intent on enlightening him.

Still smiling, she stroked a hand down his chest. He startled when she cupped him through his trousers. "There now, lad," she tsked. "Don't be skittish. Just seeing for myself."

She palmed his crotch, and he reacted. It didn't take much. Even as green as he was, he was surging against her expert fingers.

She laughed. "There's my randy lad." She opened his trousers and dipped her fingers inside, closing her hand around his cock and rubbing him harder until he was panting and spending himself. "That's lovely," she murmured, apparently not embarrassed in the least at the mess he'd just made against her hand. "You like that? How about you do this and help your family at the same time?"

He grappled to steady his breathing and then asked, "H-how?"

"Oh, there are plenty of nice ladies with blunt to spare that would worship a fine lad like you. It will be good. Not at all like what happened with your dear mam, poor thing. You're young and strapping and will have your pick of patrons.

You'll have only the best. You'll not have to endure the wretched companions your mam—"

"Silence. Please." He did not wish to hear what his mother had endured. At least not the grim particulars. Oh, he knew what she had done and that it had destroyed her. Broken her. But he could do without the details. He wanted to know nothing of the men.

He held his neighbor's dark, liquid gaze in the dim corridor of that boardinghouse and felt compelled, enticed.

She nodded her head toward her room and cajoled in a throaty whisper, "Shall I show you what it's all about, love?"

He peered over her shoulder to the inside of her chamber, where the flickering candlelight cast shadows over her waiting bed.

He dropped his attention back to her form. Her tongue glided over her bottom lip as she looked him over. "You could have quite the vetted clientele. Ladies would love you."

He sent a long look to the door of his family's rented room, where the three most important people in his life, in his world, waited for his return. Waited for him. Waited for food, for a brighter future than the one he could provide them.

"Do you know any of these . . . *ladies*?" he asked.

Her chin went up in convincing determination. "I am certain I can find them for you."

And he was certain she could, too. She was an industrious sort. Her plump curves attested to the fact that she never missed a meal. She clearly earned more than enough blunt to support herself.

"You would do that for me?" he asked. "Why?"

She leaned into the doorjamb, her hand drifting to the loose laces at the front of her night rail. She played with the end of one frayed ribbon, tugging until the fabric gaped open wider, exposing the dusky edge of an areola.

His cock stiffened anew at the sight. He'd never seen a lady's bare breast before and he leaned forward eagerly, entranced at the half glimpse.

"I would take a small fee, of course. It could be profitable for both of us." Her attention dropped to his thickening cock. "Oy, you *are* an impressive lad. I am sure we could come to a pleasurable arrangement for both of us. If you're agreeable?"

Like the green lad he was, he could not look away from that breast. He finally released a ragged breath and nodded.

She smiled slowly and extended a hand for him to shake. "Brilliant. My name is Meg." She cocked her head to the side and tugged him closer. "Would you like to come inside? We can talk. We have much to discuss, I think."

# Chapter Seven 🖙

$N$o truer words had been spoken. They had discussed much that night, he and Meg. And words had not been the all of it. There had been a demonstration, too.

Meg had led him into her room, to her bed, and following a very informative and rigorous induction into what would be expected of him with these ladies she would introduce him to, they set forth a plan for him to meet his first paramour—a very kind and generous widow two decades his senior who taught him all about the giving and receiving of pleasure. Beyond what he had already learned with the lusty Meg, of course.

He had a standing appointment with his first client, the seasoned widow, twice a week. She even introduced him to a few of her friends. His enterprise spread from there. He was soon able to relocate his bedridden mother and sisters into a more appropriate home.

It was a decidedly dissolute way to earn a living. There was the rare degrading moment, but thankfully those were few . . . and did not outnumber the pleasant and tolerable. Just the same, it was a past he wanted to stay buried. No one could know the Duke of Penning had peddled his flesh for coin. Such licentious activity would never be understood or forgiven.

And yet he could not regret it.

He had been able to support his family in a suitable manner. His sisters thrived. He hired a governess to finish their schooling and a maid to attend to Mama, who never fully recovered.

His mother spent most of her days in silence, staring out the window and onto the street until the day of her death, several years after they left the boardinghouse behind. He supposed *she* had never left that time behind. The memories of those days when she had slipped from their room to earn enough blunt to support herself and her children haunted her to the end.

He didn't know the details of what she had done, nor had he ever wished to know. Just the same, those undisclosed *things* remained etched in the lines of her face—until the morning he woke to discover she had passed away in her sleep. Only then had her features been at ease and relaxed, the anguish gone.

He did his best to hide his occupation from his sisters, conducting himself as a gentleman and keeping his affairs to himself in the most clandestine manner. Fortunately, the ladies he consorted with never talked. Nor did Meg, whom he kept on as a secretary of sorts, managing his appointments.

Discretion was of the utmost importance to his clients. They certainly did not want knowledge of their activities getting out. They all had that in common.

They used him. Paid him. Repeat. That was the cycle. That was the rhythm of his life in those days.

He didn't hate it, either. He supposed he should. He supposed he should feel a deep abiding shame, but he could not summon the sentiment. Not when his actions brought food to the table and a roof over their heads. Not when his sisters could be safe and enjoy their remaining childhoods.

His clients were more often than not kind. Neglected wives or lonely widows. Not all of his assignations were even carnal in nature.

There was one lady who only wished to be held in his arms as he read her poetry. Another one wanted him to listen as she talked about the son she lost to the blue death, since her husband had forbidden the mention of the lost child within their home. They appreciated him and he appreciated their generosity. It was an amicable exchange.

On occasion a lady called him rude names and

commanded him about as though he had not a brain in his head. He understood the origin of such behavior and he managed to empathize. Those were ladies seeking a semblance of control, however fleeting, over their lives. He took no offense and let them play out their fantasies.

If ever he felt uncomfortable in an encounter—which rarely happened—he left.

There had been one time too disturbing for him to remain. A lady had wanted him to tie her up . . . to use his fists, to squeeze his hands around her throat in the midst of their coupling. He could not do it. No matter how she insisted it would titillate her, he would not. He had walked out and never met with her again.

His life would have continued that way indefinitely. He would have continued meeting with his clients, providing assignations in exchange for money. That would have been his existence if an agent for the Penning estate had not turned up on his doorstep, informing him of his change of fortune.

He knew he had not lived a respectable life, but discretion came easily when one did not live in the public eye. Now he did. This secret past of his would ruin lives—not only his own—if it ever came out, if it ceased to be secret. He could only hope the knowledge of it never surfaced.

He never imagined a respectable future was possible for him—certainly not one of such prestige and wealth. He had not even been aware that his father possessed family ties to a duke.

In a single moment he had become the Duke of Penning. Then and there, he vowed he would never have to fight and scrape for survival again. His sisters would never go without, their futures never fall into question again. And his past must remain buried.

He would triumph in his role as the Duke of Penning. He would thrive and be all that was respectable and right. A nobleman in the truest sense. The world would look at him and know no better duke. No better man fit for the role.

Only every time he looked at Miss Lockhart, he read the disapproval in her eyes, in the defiant set of her chin, in the pursing of her lips. He did not fool her. She was not convinced. He did not impress her—his own bloody housekeeper!

He felt a snob at the very thought, unrecognizable to himself, but why should a senior member of his staff make him feel so wretchedly uncomfortable in his own skin?

Quite clearly, she found him . . . lacking.

Miss Lockhart thought him a fraud, which was the height of irony since the last presumed Duke of Penning had actually been a fraud and she had thought him a delight.

Here he was, the *true* Duke of Penning, and her lip curled in his presence. It was bewildering.

Infuriating.

For some reason, when she looked at him, she *knew* he wasn't good enough.

He felt this truth in the marrow of his bones. One glimpse of her face was enough to tell him that.

That said . . . she stirred him. Roused his darker impulses ever since their first meeting.

It was maddening, but he wanted to revert to his former self and charm her, use his many practiced wiles on her and watch the disapproval fade from her eyes and become something wild, hungry, insatiable. He longed to unleash himself and watch her unravel, watch her come apart in his arms . . .

He knew he could do it. He was confident in his abilities. It was what he knew, after all. What he did, what he had been—what he *had done*. Seduction was his forte.

He shook his head and dragged a hand over his face. He needed a trip to Town, where he could embrace anonymity and lose himself in the warm, pliant body of a willing woman.

A woman who did not look at him with scorn, but instead with hot-eyed appreciation. The kind of woman who would know exactly what to do if she happened upon him naked—and it was *not* to gawk at him as though he were a three-legged troll.

Miss Lockhart had stared at him for so long he was certain the sight of him offended her. No doubt her maidenly sensibilities had been affronted.

He certainly was not going to find a woman inclined to bed play here. *Correction.* He would not permit himself to find *that* woman *here.*

The women here, in this world, in his new glittering life, were forbidden. His own sense of honor demanded that.

He was the Duke of Penning and not about to cavort with any member of his staff *or* a woman in the local village *or* any of the genteel ladies about to descend upon Penning Hall. Luckily, none of his staff or the women in Shropshire had captured his interest.

*Except Miss Lockhart.*

He scowled. She was precisely to his tastes. Evidently. He had not known prickly females were his preference. He'd had little experience with women who did not *want* him, after all. It was simply a fact. He had spent little time with ladies in the last decade who did not wish to take him to bed and explore every inch of him.

And that was why she had to go.

Clearly. Obviously. Undeniably.

He would not be the manner of nobleman to take advantage of those under him.

He finished his bath and emerged, rubbing himself dry briskly, deliberately *not* thinking about her eyes on his skin. *Not* thinking about her hands on him *instead* of her gaze. Because that led to other wayward thoughts. Thoughts of her fingers gliding over his body, taking hold of his cock, lathering it with soap and squeezing him, fondling him, slipping up and down his length until he—

*Blasted woman.*

With a sharp intake of breath, he looked down at himself. His cock stood at attention. He closed his eyes in a pained blink and shook his head.

It was damned annoying. She would be horrified. Her lips would likely disappear into her face in prudish aversion if her hand even so much as brushed against him.

Finished drying off, he donned a dressing robe and moved to pull the rope, but then stopped himself, recalling it would not be Carter to answer his call. It would be Miss Lockhart.

Instead, sighing, he collapsed in a wingback chair before the fireplace and attempted, once more, to steer his thoughts in a direction that would not touch upon his disapproving, pursed-lipped housekeeper.

A more difficult task than one might expect.

## Chapter Eight ❧

After taking dinner with his sisters, Lucian left them to their lively quarrel over the latest fashion plates delivered from London. The girls had more time on their hands out here in the country and that led to the nonsensical bickering.

It really was uncharacteristic of them. Oh, they'd had mild disagreements before, but they had always been allies. Friends, not just sisters. The frequent bickering was a new development. As much as they reveled in their newfound fortune, he suspected they missed the bustle of Town. Evelyn especially was oft inquiring when they would return to London.

As the Duke of Penning, he was in possession of a house in Mayfair, and Evie was salivating to make use of it. Unlike Lucian. Up until now, he had spent most of his life in London, plying his trade . . . and he was happy to be gone from it. Happy for new scenery. He felt at peace in the countryside. Free in a way he had never experienced. He never needed to see London again. He would like to travel abroad and see the places he only read about in books, faraway and marvelous sights that made him forget the past.

Evie and Mattie did not remember London the way he did. Naturally. They did not know of its darkness or debaucheries. He'd done everything to make certain they would never have memories like his own.

Evie especially missed her friends. It did not occur to his youngest sister that she might forge new friendships now. Friends with fathers in possession of old and venerable titles that dated back to the Conqueror. She had no thought to advancing herself or bettering her social connections. As far as she was concerned, Katie, the daughter of a haberdasher; and Caroline, a merchant's daughter, would seamlessly fit into her new life of privilege and wealth. They were not friends she intended to leave behind.

That was her inherent goodness. She and Mattie both were simply that way. *Good*. Kind and not yet spoiled by the harsh realities of the world. They were the complete opposite of him and he would not have them *become* him for anything. He would not have them tainted.

The task fell to him to find good men for them. Not merely lofty noblemen (yes, that, of course), but men who deserved them. Gentlemen in the truest sense. Noble. Honorable. A daunting task, to be certain, for did any men like that truly exist? Men deserving of his little sisters?

He retired alone to his office and rang for Miss Lockhart with a resigned sigh. It could no longer be avoided.

He had not seen her since she had barged into his chambers during his bath, but they still had the menu to discuss.

He supposed he *could* leave her to her own devices regarding the menu and all things relating to his impending house party, but no. He would not permit himself to do that. It was too important. The food had to be fit for royalty. Everything must be considered. He must approve all matters pertaining to this affair. The first event he was to host at Penning Hall must be faultless.

Carter had been especially helpful in building the guest list. He knew everyone who was anyone in the *ton*. Lucian had been quite clear in his goals for his sisters—and himself—and Carter had at once gotten to work on it, investigating and building a list of eligible noblemen and ladies—although eligible noblemen for his sisters took priority. Always, Mattie and Evie came first.

His sisters' futures were tied to the success of this dreaded house party. He owed it to his mother, even his wastrel of a father. He had failed to protect his mother. He would not fail in protecting the girls.

This house party needed to be a triumph.

There were defined goals. Prominent husbands for Mattie and Evie, and a wife of high station for himself. Such spouses would better position them for the very real likelihood of his sordid past coming to light. *Untouchables*. That is whom he sought for the three of them. That is what he would have them become. That was the hope. Given the illustrious names on his guest list, the opportunity was not out of the realm of possibility.

With luck, possibly one, if not both, of his sisters would be betrothed by the end of it. Perhaps even himself.

As much as he had no wish to see Miss Lockhart again so soon—she had an unfortunate way of affecting his equilibrium—they had a menu to discuss.

With a fresh glass of brandy in hand, he seated himself on the comfortable sofa before the fireplace, appreciating its crackling warmth as he waited. Glancing around the room with its fine appointments, he marveled that this was his life now.

His father had been considerably older than his mother. As a young man, he had served as an officer in the British army. Upon returning from abroad, he'd taken a post in the Home Office.

Prior to the age of ten and five, when his father lived, Lucian knew only nice things.

He had a proper tutor who even taught him the pianoforte alongside his Latin and French. He'd had friends. Holidays at the seaside. His father taught him to ride, fence, box and fire a pistol. He took him to Tattersalls and showed him how to judge quality horseflesh. It was a good and easy life with no hint of the storm to come. And yet even that *good* life was very unlike this one.

This one had all the comforts of his youth and more. So much more. His new life was all about excess. It was the height of opulence. Fresh flowers in every room. A bed with the softest, cleanest sheets that could sleep a regiment. Decadent food, steaming baths . . . whatever he desired with a snap of his fingers.

And yet it all came with a price.

Responsibilities. Eyes forever on him. Watching. Assessing. Every step measured. It wasn't the steps *forward* that worried him, though. It was the steps he had already taken. The steps behind him. The ones he could not undo, the footprints etched deeply and irrevocably. *His past*. It could be revealed at any time.

Miss Lockhart did not make him wait very long and he suspected she had been awaiting his summons. At her knock, he bade her enter.

She came into the room with, presumably, the menu in her hands. She'd been good to her word, then. That was something to recommend her, he grudgingly acknowledged.

"Your Grace." She stopped before him and extended the parchment to him with a wary expression. He studied her for a moment. The firelight gilded her loosely upswept hair and it was a thing of beauty. Reds, browns, and golds: it was a splendid combination of all three, reminiscent of a forest caught in the glow of sunset.

He clutched his glass in one hand and gripped the arm of his chair with the other until his knuckles went white—as though he needed to do that to resist the impulse to touch that lovely, soft mass . . . to bury his fingers in the fiery strands and gather them up in his palms.

God help him. He was in dire need of a woman. Perhaps he would take a short trip to London before the house party and avail himself of female companionship. A lass with plump thighs and sweet-smelling burnished hair that spilled over in his hands and reminded him of a forest at sunset.

*Bloody hell.*

With a clearing of his throat, he accepted the list from her, careful that their fingers not touch, and glanced down at her neat penmanship, scanning what she had outlined for the full week of the house party and asking himself if this was good enough to impress his very lauded and high-ranking guests. Nowhere in his mind did he yet consider himself an esteemed member of the peerage, even though he knew, by rights, he was. It would take time for him to consider himself one of them. Perhaps that day would never come. Perhaps he would spend all the days of his life pretending, faking that he belonged among them.

"Vichyssoise?" he questioned.

She nodded. "Cook's version is delicious—"

"You don't think it a little too . . . pedestrian?" He fluttered the paper. "I mean . . . potatoes and leeks." It was something he had eaten so often in the boardinghouse. Except they only called it potato and leek soup then and not vichyssoise.

She flinched, and he marveled at that. He thought she was made of sterner stuff. So far she had stood up to him with aggravating and somewhat surprising mettle.

"Would you prefer something else?"

"What about a consommé?"

Her lip curled and he knew she found his suggestion lacking when compared to vichyssoise.

"If that is your preference."

After studying for a few more moments, he returned the parchment to her.

She added, "Does the rest of the menu meet your approval?"

It was more than adequate. Oysters. Lobster in cream and butter pottage. Venison and quail pastries. His mouth was watering although he had already eaten dinner. He grunted. "It's adequate."

Her lips pressed together and he knew she did not care for that response from him. It was all he could summon. He could not very well praise her if he intended to send her on her way.

"Thank you, Your Grace." Her amber-brown eyes sparked and he felt his cock stir beneath his robe. Standing before him in the glow of firelight, she was altogether too much for his senses.

He glanced away. "How long have you worked here, Miss Lockhart?"

He heard her swift inhale. "Eleven years." Defiance rang in her voice.

"Eleven? You must have been a child when you started here."

"Seventeen."

"And did you grow up here? In Shropshire?"

"My aunt lived here. I came to be with her. She secured me a position as a housemaid. That is how I began."

*I came to be with her.* She was not the most forthcoming. "You have yet to answer my question. Where did you grow up?"

She hesitated only slightly. "London."

"Indeed? You don't sound like a Londoner. I do detect something in your voice." A hint of an accent he had never noted before. Welsh perhaps? Irish?

Her expression hardened. "London," she repeated.

She was lying. Instantly he knew. He was certain.

He did not know *why* she sought to hide her past from him, but she did. He angled his head in bemusement. Apparently they had that in common.

As her elusiveness in this did not signify, he let it stand. "Perhaps you have an interest to return there?" At her blank stare, he clarified, "To London?"

Wariness crept back into her face. "I do not. I like it here."

"You're still a young woman. London has many more diversions and opportunities."

She stiffened at the word *opportunities* and he knew she had a sense of what he was about. "I am content here," she insisted.

He considered her for a long moment and then dove into the matter. "I think it might be time for you to move on and think of a future elsewhere."

Her face paled. "You are sacking me?"

"I am not," he stated. Rather, *not yet*. He would not be so callous as to do that. And yet if she found another arrangement and left of her own accord, that could only be a good thing. "But I am not certain we . . . suit, Miss Lockhart." He winced as soon as he said the words. It felt as though he were speaking romantically and he was decidedly *not*.

"Please." She took a halting step closer and then stopped directly before him where he sat. "This is my home . . . I will do whatever you want, *whatever* you like. I can learn to . . . suit you."

"I would not have you go against your nature."

She lowered her head and gave it a little shake, a puff of breath escaping her that reached his ears. When she looked up again, she settled brightly determined eyes on him. "It is a servant's role, is it not? To make oneself amenable? That is our function. Our nature. And . . . this is the only home I have."

Suddenly he felt a cad. The impulse to sweep her up in his arms overwhelmed him. And that was a terrible impulse given this was a respectable woman, his employee, a woman he ought not feel anything for other than the most appropriate and brusque of emotions. Embracing her was *not* the proper impulse. Given that he was not a man to deny himself, it was most certainly inconvenient.

He knew just how a comforting embrace could turn into something else. How *any* embrace could turn into something else. It was the *something else* that he knew very well. The *something else* that he must avoid.

He cleared his throat. "You are young. Clever. Presentable." *Damn fetching*, but he did not say that. That was irrelevant and it revealed far too much of his attraction for her. To say nothing of being highly improper. And *this* life, his new life, would be about respectability and decorum and proper things. "I will write you a glowing recommendation. You can secure something better, something more exciting for yourself."

She continued to shake her head and reached for his hand. "Whatever I have done to offend, Your Grace—"

"Do not worry yourself on the matter. It is getting late, Miss Lockhart. You should retire. We can discuss this more at a later date. After the house party. There will be no changes made until then. Continue with your duties for now."

"After the house party," she echoed uncertainly, her eyes narrowing on him, studying him as though he were some unpredictable beast that might snap his teeth and take a chunk out of her flesh. "So you are not sacking me right now, then?"

"No. I am doing nothing right now." Her lips pursed, clearly not satisfied by his answer. "But I promise I will not leave you without prospects . . . or in dire circumstances. Not after your years of loyal service."

Hot color splashed her cheeks. "Heartening words, to be sure."

"I am merely giving you notice—"

"That you will *likely* soon *give me the sack*," she snapped.

Phrased that way, it did seem to be what he was saying. He stifled a grimace. Perhaps he should have thought ahead. Usually he was not one to mangle his words. On the contrary. He was usually very adept at conversation. Meg always said he had a silken tongue, in more ways than one. And yet Miss Lockhart confounded him and left him fumbling and inserting his foot into his mouth.

He took a breath and tried again. "I only wish for you to take the time to consider what your options are . . . and where you might go from here."

"Because clearly I *will* be going," she clarified. "Eventually." Her chin went up. "And yet I should not *worry* myself."

"I did not say that."

"Did you not?" she snapped, angling her head sharply and stretching her hand out for the paper. "If the menu meets with your approval . . ."

After a moment, he returned it to her. "It does."

"Excellent, Your Grace. You won't be disappointed." She nodded perfunctorily, lips pursed. With a quick curtsy that lacked her usual care and sincerity, she turned and departed the room.

# Chapter Nine ❧

*O*ver the following week, Susanna returned every evening to the duke's chambers, determined to perform the role of valet whilst Mr. Carter was recuperating, determined despite the duke's efforts to thwart her, despite his advice that she should start considering another situation elsewhere.

*Another situation . . .* meaning some place that wasn't *here.*

She vowed to change his mind with renewed vigor. He did not know her or what she could do. She would deliver unto him the most brilliant and successful of house parties. He would see what he had in her then, what she was capable of. He would see that he had to keep her here.

Each night was the same. She knocked, and he bade her enter.

She would then find him in various states. Either preparing for his bath, in his bath, or even once wrapped up in his dressing robe immediately following his bath. Never fully naked again. It seemed that he, too, wished to avoid that unfortunate happenstance. Thank the heavens.

There was no predicting what task he might be at when she entered the chamber. She could predict, however, his cool dismissal. He merely looked at her with a blank-eyed stare and proclaimed: "You may go, Miss Lockhart. I have no need of you."

Blast the man. He was determined to reject any offers of help from her and mark her ... unnecessary. Expendable. He would not make use of her.

*I have no need of you.*

Each time she heard those words, she felt them as a blow. An effectively delivered dig. She envisioned herself being sent on her way, dismissed, valise in hand, from Penning Hall. Like a beggar rejected and cast out who had dared to come ask for scraps.

It was an echo of the past. Of a time when she had been a girl of seventeen, a ragged valise in hand, forced out on her own, traveling over water and land by herself, not even sleeping lest she be accosted by the strange men eyeing a tremulous girl traveling alone. The world was not a kind place to a woman without fortune and family.

*I only wish for you to take the time to consider what your options are ... and where you might go from here.*

She could feel Penning's rejection keenly even though it had not happened. Not *yet* happened.

She imagined arriving on her aunt's doorstep, a

burden once again, as she had been all those years ago when she was scarcely a woman. Defeated. A failure. A blight. A sudden affliction her aunt must contend with. A young woman ruined in the tiny village of Kennaughly.

At least that was far from here. A blessing. Kennaughly was not London. It might as well be a different planet. The Isle of Man was far away and there was little of that life that bled into this one.

Her aunt, of course, could have refused her and cast her out into the great unknown as had her mother and stepfather. And yet she had not.

Aunt Ferelith had brought her inside the house, introduced her to all the staff and the *then* Duke of Penning. For good measure, to help her, to look after her, she had introduced her as Susanna Lockhart. A new name for a new start. Her aunt had possessed that foresight then, granting her a layer of protection from the forces that would devour and break a ruined woman.

Aunt Ferelith had saved her. It would be unfair to expect her to do it again. Susanna would not ask that of her. It was too mortifying a thought. She would not be that sad and desperate person again. No more. She had come too far. She *would* win over Penning.

This night he was standing before the mirror at his dressing table. "Miss Lockhart," he greeted flatly, not turning around as he stared at her reflection in the glass. "Still no Carter, I see."

She nodded perfunctorily. "He is still indisposed, although well on the mend. He will be ready to return to his duties soon."

He was shaving, she realized as she approached, observing him as he lathered his face thoroughly with shaving soap. She had somehow avoided witnessing him at this task in previous days. Any valet would do such a chore for the master of the house, but Penning was clearly managing it on his own. She felt a pinch of guilt. She would not prove herself to him by being unhelpful.

"Shall I assist you with that, Your Grace?" she offered, a tinge of hopefulness in her voice. Not that she wished to be near him, or put her hands on him, but she did wish to be of use.

Certainly she worked diligently all day, readying the house and staff for the forthcoming party, but that was behind the scenes. He likely did not realize the extent of her efforts, and usually that was the way of things. It was the way things were meant to be. The inner workings of a household *should* run smoothly without notice or mention. It was only when the inner workings failed that the employer ever noticed.

"Do you shave a great deal of gentlemen, Miss Lockhart?" The question, the way he emphasized

*Miss,* combined with the sardonic twist of his lips, told her he mightily doubted that.

He was mocking her.

He saw her as an old maid. A prim and starchy spinster housekeeper. Likely he did not think she had ever set hands on a man before, much less shaved one.

He would be wrong.

She inhaled. "I am perfectly capable."

He stroked the blade down his throat again in a sure motion. "I have made it abundantly clear to you that I have no need nor wish for your assistance and yet you insist on coming to my chamber multiple times a day." His voice rang with disdain. "Why is that?" he asked mildly. "Are you unable to take directions?"

Heat stung her cheeks. "I want to make certain of your comfort, Your Grace, and see that you are well served. That is my duty as your housekeeper." She was proud of her proper, deferential response.

He did not seem impressed. He continued to shave himself. The razor scratched against his cheek. He angled his face and his throat worked in the most distracting manner. She swallowed against the sudden lump beginning to form in her throat. It was altogether a mesmerizing sight. At least he wore a shirt of fine white lawn and she did not have the distraction of his bare chest again.

He did not look at her but at his own reflection as he echoed her own words, "Your duty . . ."

She gulped as those words faded, hanging there. Anxiously, she waited for him to finish whatever else he meant to say on the topic of *her duty*.

He continued, "Perhaps we should discuss the scope of your duties here at Penning Hall."

She lifted her chin. "Perhaps we should." Perhaps she should enlighten him of all she did and how he could not live without her. She felt a flush of awkward heat rush over her immediately following that thought—a thought which could be interpreted romantically. Fortunately for her he could not read her thoughts. "I realize you may not be familiar with what it is a housekeeper contributes, what it is *I* contribute—"

He tapped the razor in the basin before him, the clang of metal in the bowl loud and discordant . . . jarring. She suspected he meant it to be. His dark blue eyes met hers in the mirror again. "*You* want to school *me* on what it is you do in my house?"

He was twisting her words.

That did not sound right. Indeed not. Her stomach dropped to her feet. She should stop. She knew that. She told herself that. *Stop talking, Susanna.* And yet she could not seem to heed the advice.

"As I said, I have worked here for eleven years. The last five as housekeeper. There is no one better equipped for the role."

"I cannot fathom my late cousin's reasoning for placing one so young and . . ." He paused as though searching for the word to describe her. Through the mirror, his gaze swept over her and she tensed, dreading what awful thing he might say. In this case, *young* felt like an insult. What else might he apply to her?

When it appeared he would not expand on his thought, she said, "No one before you has ever voiced concerns over my abilities."

"Although, ultimately, no else's opinion matters now. Does it?" He stared down at the basin as he sloshed his razor clean in the water.

Her cheeks burned even hotter. "Indeed, Your Grace. Your decision is the only one that matters." Such an agreement cost her. It frustrated her to make such an admission.

He looked back at her and her chest tightened beneath his intense regard. She sensed he knew of her internal struggle.

"That pains you to say," he pronounced, shaving carefully close to his lips.

"N-no, Your Grace," she denied, wondering how he came to read her thoughts. Why was she so very transparent where he was concerned?

He hesitated and sent her a dubious look. "You are a terrible liar, Miss Lockhart. You don't like being told what to do, which, correct me if I am mistaken, is the very nature of a servant's existence."

"Rest assured, I have no difficulty putting myself under your charge, Your Grace. Shall I prove it? Ask anything of me." She squared her shoulders. "I will do it. Without complaint, I submit myself to you."

His gaze shot to her, his blue eyes so searing she felt singed to the spot, unable to move, scarcely able to breathe.

She held his gaze unblinkingly, conveying her earnestness and trying not to think of how very desperate . . . and perhaps provocative her words could be construed as.

His hand stroked downward and suddenly he jerked. His razor clattered loudly to the washbowl. Her heart plummeted to the pit of her stomach.

With a savage curse, he staggered back from the basin. His hand flew to his throat but not before she spotted the flash of blood.

# Chapter Ten ❧

*M*iss Ross!" Mr. Carter sat up a little straighter on the chaise longue where he reclined near the window, setting the newspaper he was reading aside. Mattie smiled. It amused her the way he always declared her name with that level of surprise. "What are you doing here?"

He always asked that of her, too—each and every time she managed to seize a moment alone with him like this.

*What are you doing here?*

It really was adorable he did not know the answer to that.

He cleared his throat and smoothed a hand over his thick brown hair, appearing charmingly uncomfortable.

He should be quite accustomed to her company by now. The dear man had not a clue. But he would. He would. She would make it so that he understood.

She had chosen him and he would come to understand that.

He'd moved from the bed to the chaise a few

days ago, insisting it made him feel less like an invalid. It also signified that her time with him had almost come to an end. He would soon be returning to his duties as valet to her brother, which meant she would have fewer moments alone with him like this.

Mattie had taken full advantage of his convalescence, visiting him multiple times a day. Talking to him. Reading to him. Bringing him food. Books. Newspapers. Puzzles. Sitting close and brushing his hand with her own, doing her best to make certain he was aware of her on a physical level—and taking satisfaction at the red creeping up his neck, knowing he was not unaffected by her.

"Well, good day to you, too, Mr. Carter," she replied pertly. "And I thought you were going to call me Mattie now."

She tsked and shook her head. She had insisted he call her Mattie too many times to count now. For some reason, he resisted. She supposed it was the fact that he was her brother's valet and he thought her forbidden, that they should maintain a stiffly formal relationship. Stuff and nonsense.

His features flushed, the red creeping all the way up from his neck to his cheeks.

It was charming that he had yet to figure it out. Sweet and perhaps a little naive, too. He had yet to understand that she was quite infatuated with him. That she was very much in pursuit of him. Dear beautiful unsuspecting man. He was eight years her senior, but in this way he seemed much younger.

He pushed himself a little higher into a sitting position. "Begging your pardon, Miss Ross. I mean no disrespect." He took a breath and then plunged ahead. "But you cannot continue spending time with me like this."

*Ah.* Here they went. He would attempt to chase her away. It would perhaps work on a less confident girl. On someone who did not know herself, who was given to embarrassment and self-doubt. And yet Mattie knew what she wanted. She was not capricious in nature.

"I can't? Why not?" She angled her head and settled herself into the chair beside his chaise, scooting close, the chair legs scraping over the floor.

He took a deep breath as though suddenly needing air. "B-because it is inappropriate."

"Hmm." She pretended to consider this. "No."

"No?" He blinked.

She nodded, smiling slowly. "No."

He gazed at her in consternation. "I don't understand."

"You are rather dense in this matter." She angled

her head coyly, climbing her fingers along his arm where he rested it on the chaise, moving up to his well-muscled shoulder.

He possessed a fine form. She had noticed it the moment she arrived at the hall. A fine form and a fine face and a fine manner. His kind eyes crinkled at the corners with good humor. He was a man given to smiles and frequent laughter. She loved that about him.

Lucian thought her too young to remember the sorrows and trials of their childhood, but she remembered. She remembered all.

She remembered the time after Papa died. The ghost of Mama floating through life, existing but not living, not being there for any of them—including herself. Those had been years without smiles and laughter. Then there had been Lucian. He thought Mattie didn't know, but she knew of the sacrifices he had made for them. She knew the worry and strain he had lived under taking care of them.

So much of her existence had been weighed down with an awareness that life was fraught and precarious, that unhappiness was an unavoidable condition for so many people, including herself, so that when the chance for happiness presented itself, one must seize it, claim it, embrace it fully.

Carter stared from her fingers on his shoulder to her face in growing consternation. "Miss Ross . . . you must not—"

She leaned forward then and pressed a hasty kiss to his lips.

He froze.

She pulled back, looking down at him, assessing, the hope in her chest withering. His brown eyes stared at her in horror.

Everything inside her sank. *Oh, dear.* Perhaps she was the naive one after all.

She had played out this scenario several different ways in her mind. In none of them had she considered he would not reciprocate her feelings. She had thought once he understood her attraction for him, he would get over his reticence.

Perhaps in this case, happiness could not be claimed. Not with Carter.

Now it was her turn to flush. Mortification burned her cheeks. "Oh," she breathed miserably.

"Miss Ross—"

"No," she snapped, tears of disappointment clogging her throat. She could not hear him say it. She could not endure it. "I—I am sorry." She slid away, pushing back, the chair legs scraping the floor, the chair falling back with a clang as she rose to her feet.

"Mattie," he rasped, seizing her fingers and tugging her forward, pulling her so that she fell atop his chest. And then he was kissing her, hands diving into her hair, lips devouring. *This*. This was what she craved.

Her heart soared.

He was kissing her and she was kissing him and she knew then that he understood. Finally. He understood that she had chosen him.

"Mattie," he groaned against her lips.

He understood.

And he chose her, too.

# Chapter Eleven ❧

Susanna rushed forward, overcome with panic that Penning had slit his throat—that the man would bleed to death right before her very eyes.

She reached his side as he steadied again on his feet, his hand covering his throat.

She grasped his arm as fear pumped through her veins. "Let me see, Your Grace."

Grimacing, he dodged her, stretching his neck to better examine his injury in the mirror for himself, lifting his hand away for inspection. That was when she saw the bright rivulet of crimson streaking down his handsome throat.

Alarm skittered through her. She hissed at the sight, seizing a linen from the dressing table even as blood dripped down from the fresh wound to mar the fine lawn of his shirt.

"Are you trying to sever your head from your body?" she reprimanded before she could remember to use a more deferential tone. She was too worried for him. She forgot herself.

His hot gaze collided with hers as she stopped

before him and shooed his hand away, pressing the fabric to his neck in place of his fingers.

"You distracted me," he accused, his deep voice rumbling beneath her hand that pressed to his neck.

"With mere conversation? Nonsense. We had been talking for several moments before this happened. Perhaps you need someone *else* to shave you instead of stubbornly insisting on doing everything yourself," she pointedly argued.

He rolled his eyes, and she shook her head. "This is not a simple scratch," she snapped, completely forgetting herself in that moment—herself and *him*. "You could have killed yourself, you know."

She readjusted the cloth against his neck, determined to stanch the flow. Hopefully the bleeding would soon stop. Worry pumped through her.

"Ouch."

"Oh, hush. The pressure needs to be firm."

He snorted. "Your distress warms my heart, Miss Lockhart."

She looked at him again and that was a mistake.

His face was too handsome and his eyes were too close, staring intently upon her, making her feel . . .

Well, making her *feel*.

When he looked at her like that she was reminded that she was a woman. With all the working parts that went along with being a woman. Just as he was in possession of all the working parts that went along with being a man.

Moments passed, thick and fraught with this awareness.

"Let me see again," he said as his fingers reached to circle her wrist, but she shook her head and held fast, not removing her hand from his throat.

"No. The wound needs pressure a while longer."

He slowly loosened his fingers from around her wrist, sliding down to grip her forearm, not severing the contact . . . still touching her, still keeping contact with that much bigger hand of his.

"Sorry," he murmured.

"For what?" Then she understood, spying their reflection in the mirror.

It was an alarming sight. They stood close. Her hand pressed to his throat in a way that felt highly personal. Intimate. Her pulse thrummed wildly at her neck. His hand lowered from her arm then and she saw what brought forth his apology. He'd bloodied the sleeve of her gown.

"Oh. 'Tis nothing. It's just a dress. The blood hardly shows." It was true. The blood was only slightly darker than the brown fabric of her dress.

"I'll buy you a new one," he said gruffly, and she found herself gazing at his lips, at the way they moved, hugging his words, and she wondered what they would feel like . . . taste like on her.

Heavens. She really was depraved. She had not known this about herself, but now she did. Disappointing, to be sure, to discover there had been some truth in what her stepfather said about her. She really was a wicked creature.

She had functioned for nearly a dozen years without the slightest interest in men. Not a flicker since Robbie. When the new vicar moved to Shropshire and every woman within a day's ride to the village mooned over the fact that a handsome eligible young man had landed in their midst and *he* would be pontificating from the pulpit every Sunday, she had shrugged and went about her life. She had assumed she was immune. That something broke inside her after Robbie. After all her family and friends turned from her. Apparently she had been wrong, and she was not happy with that discovery.

"That is not necessary."

"I *will* replace your gown," he insisted.

"Very well." No sense arguing with him.

She glanced down. "There is blood on your shirt, too."

"I have others."

"I can get it out," she said very reasonably if not with a touch of exasperation.

He lifted one impossibly big shoulder in a shrug to indicate that it mattered not at all to him. And of course it did not. He was a duke. He could wear a new shirt every day. With his endlessly deep pockets, those broad shoulders of his could have as many shirts as there were stars in the sky.

She swallowed against a suddenly thickening throat. What had he done in his past life to be rewarded with such a robust frame? And what had she done to be tormented by the sight of it? The nearness? The heady effect of it—*him*—on her senses? She inhaled sharply as though willing such thoughts, such *feelings* away.

She did not know any gentlemen who looked as he did, with his impressive shoulders that rivaled those of a seasoned pugilist. She suspected there was a good deal about the Duke of Penning's past the world did not know. At least not the world of Penning Hall and Shropshire and the *ton*. She was curious, though. *She* would like to know. She would like to unwrap the puzzle he presented. Her gaze skittered over him and the thought struck her, unbidden: she would like to unwrap *all* of him.

Her face burned. She did not know who she was anymore when it came to him. She had never been particularly . . . lusty, for want of a better word. Even in her liaisons with Robbie, she had hardly been an amorous creature.

They had been together three times. Their first time had been awkward and short-lived in a stable loft and then two other times occurred in a field of wildflowers on his family's lands.

As romantic as it sounded, as nice as it had been . . . it had not been particularly thrilling. She had felt physical stirrings, but nothing that manifested into passionate frenzy. Nothing that gave credence to the giggles and furtive whispers she heard among other women. Susanna had never quite reached the release Robbie had. Their couplings always left her vaguely dissatisfied.

She was no hedonist, determinedly seeking her own pleasures, contrary to the ugly things her stepfather had said about her. She had enjoyed the closeness and kissing and intimacy with Robbie . . . but had not longed for another man since then.

Until now.

In the company of the duke her entire body felt afire. Her breasts and womanhood roused and throbbed with awareness. It was quite singular . . . and unwanted.

Perhaps he was correct. Perhaps she should begin considering other situations. Although what else existed for her?

She was the housekeeper to a grand ducal estate. It was the *choicest* of positions when it came to domestic service. She could not hope for better.

"Permit me to look again now," she briskly murmured.

He nodded once and she placed her fingers beneath his chin, angling his face and forcing his head to the side as she pretended not to appreciate the texture of his recently shaved skin.

He did not take his gaze from her, even as she positioned his head at an angle that should have averted his eyes. He watched her as she peeled back the linen to inspect his injury and then tsked at the sight of the gash, still sluggishly bleeding.

She quickly covered it again, applying more pressure. "You really should be more careful."

"Perhaps you should not have been in here to distract me." His dark blue gaze moved over her face as he laid the blame at her feet. Speaking of distracting . . . they were beautiful eyes and this close she could see the striations of gray in their depths.

"So it is my fault?"

He looked at her in perplexity. "There is little about you that proclaims *housekeeper*, Miss Lockhart."

Heat burned her face, but she resisted demanding

what it was she *did* proclaim. "I am a good house-keeper, Your Grace. Perhaps if you gave me a little more deference you would see—"

"Deference?"

She winced at her poor word choice.

He continued, "Should I simply do as you say, then?"

Her face burned anew. "I did not mean—"

"But did you not just say you would submit to me?"

She had said that. She gave her head a small shake. He unnerved her.

He pressed on, "Which is it, Miss Lockhart? Shall I do as *you* say? Or will you submit to me?"

"Perhaps both can be achieved?" She was not certain what she was even saying anymore. He chuckled lightly and again she felt the enticing rumble beneath her hand.

"I do not think that possible."

"Then what do we do?" she whispered, achingly aware of their closeness, of the hint of whiskey on his breath, the hint of soap on his skin.

"You need to go, Miss Lockhart. That's what can be done." His deep voice, so husky and close to her face, rasped warmly against her forehead. "You. Leave," he said haltingly. "Before . . ." His voice faded.

*Before what?*

She moistened her lips.

He followed the motion of her tongue with his hot-eyed gaze and she thought she heard him . . . groan? It was soft. Perhaps he was in pain from slicing his neck?

Her gaze flicked back to his throat. She lifted the linen from his throat. "Let me see if the bleeding has stopped."

His fingers firmly circled her wrist again, halting her. "I don't care if I'm bleeding out. You need to go . . ." His voice faded and his eyes dropped to her mouth. "Before I do something we will both regret."

*Something like kiss me?*

Her heart lurched into her throat, and she did not know if it was alarm or thrill at the prospect. Of course that was not what he meant. The Duke of Penning was not even in the smallest bit interested in her lips.

Whatever the case, she did as he bade and stepped away from him, her hand unfurling from around the linen. Instantly her body dropped several degrees without his nearness.

"I will not leave you until I see your throat a final time."

A muscle feathered his jaw, but he obliged with the barest of nods. He presented her with a view of the column of his neck. "Satisfied?"

The bleeding had stopped. She nodded.

"Now go."

She moved backward, executing a less-than-dignified curtsy before taking her leave.

Once in the corridor, she shut the door behind her and leaned against its length, taking solace in the firmness at her back. It was becoming more and more difficult to keep her composure around him, to remember boundaries. That had never been a problem before with the previous Dukes of Penning. This man was—

And there, she realized, was the crux of the problem. She did not view him as the lofty and impenetrable Duke of Penning. To her, he was a man.

A whisper of sound attracted her notice, and she turned, observing the eldest Miss Ross emerging from the chamber that connected to the Duke of Penning's private dressing room. The duke's valet always slept in that room. Carter slept in that room.

And Mattie Ross was coming from his chamber.

Susanna would not have thought anything of it. The man was recovering, stuck in bed all day. Several people visited him, including Miss Ross. It was hardly noteworthy.

Except Mattie lingered there, standing outside

the door for a moment, caught up in her thoughts so much so that she did not notice Susanna several feet away.

It was then that she recalled that it had been a week.

A week since Mr. Carter had been confined to bed. He should be reaching the end of his recovery. It was hardly an infirm man Miss Ross was visiting.

Susanna held silent, thoughtfully studying the girl. A dreamy smile lifted the corners of her lips. Susanna opened her mouth to speak, to declare her presence, when Mattie suddenly lifted her hand and brushed her fingers over her mouth. A mouth that looked different. A little more pink, a little more plump.

Susanna held her tongue.

The gesture was probably innocuous. It did not signify anything. Why should it mean anything? Why should a girl emerging from a virile young man's bedchamber at night with a dreamy smile and swollen lips mean anything?

Susanna winced. She could almost believe that.

Susanna waited tensely, reminding herself that Carter was a gentleman and not the manner of man to dally with the sister of the duke he served. She wanted desperately to believe that and yet she was not entirely convinced as she stared at Mattie's rapturous expression.

Susanna remained where she was, holding herself as still as possible, watching as the girl skipped away . . . wondering just how much more complicated her life had become.

# Chapter Twelve ❧

Something was coming.

Susanna woke in the predawn darkness with a gasp, pressing her palms flat down on the mattress and pushing up in her bed.

She roused early every day. There was never a reprieve, discounting scheduled holidays and the time she took to visit her aunt, of course.

Susanna never slept late. Even on Sundays. The duke and his family had to eat—not to mention the staff. All the servants broke their fast, too, taking turns, rotating, every seat at the massive work-worn table that stretched the length of the great kitchen occupied.

She and Cook were usually the first awake, moving about the house, stirring the fires to life in preparation for the day. But even this was earlier than usual. Than *her* usual. Whatever compelled her out of her warm bed was decidedly *un*usual.

She flung back the coverlet and shivered in the chill of her chamber. Snatching her shawl from the foot of the bed, she wrapped it around her shoulders and moved to the grate, giving it a stir so that she might bring some warmth back into the chamber.

On bare feet, she trod across the threadbare rug to her window. She parted the curtains and gazed out into the gloom, seeing nothing save darkness set against only slightly less dark shapes: trees and branches and shrubbery. Nothing else.

Disquiet hummed over her skin. She did not know what she expected. The four horsemen of the apocalypse? Famine himself waving a sword in the air as he charged her?

Nothing.

There was nothing save the still of the coming dawn and yet something had roused her and ripped her from a dreamless sleep. Something turned her skin to gooseflesh on her arms and sent the tiny hairs vibrating.

Telling herself it was no more than nerves at the impending house party and the influx of two dozen guests about to descend on Penning Hall, she turned away from the window.

After all, it was not as though she were gifted with the sight—or even that she believed in such foolishness. Aunt Ferelith had always subscribed to such far-fetched notions. It was the islander in her. Like Susanna, she'd been brought up in the Manx ways. All the traditions, including a plethora of colorful lore, was spooned to her—to them both—alongside their mothers' milk.

Her aunt may have left the Isle of Man, but Man never left her. She was a true believer. A country fair never passed through the village without her aunt waiting in line for the fortune-teller. Not Susanna. Susanna did not believe in such things. She was not waiting for some horned and hairy *buggane* to materialize in the darkness and devour her.

No sense going back to bed. Sleep would not come.

She washed her face, dressed herself and then brushed and pinned her hair efficiently, as she had done countless times. Smoothing her hands down her serviceable brown dress, she emerged from her room, ready, if not eager, to face the day and the army of guests about to descend upon them like a swarm of locusts.

THE ENTIRE HOUSEHOLD had turned out and each and every staff member was in fine form as the first carriage rolled down the drive. Livery impeccable, pressed to a crisp. Females in their pristine white mobcaps and men with hair pomaded to a high shine.

Susanna's chest tightened with dread even though this was scarcely the first house party or even the first time illustrious guests ever graced

Penning Hall. It was, however, the first fete upon which her livelihood depended.

To be fair, the duke had not said those actual words, but he had not needed to. She knew.

The Duke of Penning and his sisters stood in front of the house, several paces away from the long line of servants. They were a dignified and proper trio—all three ridiculously handsome people. The duke tall and strong with his dark-as-sin hair and his lovely sisters, both fair as English roses. Looking at them, one would never assume they were not born to their roles.

They were portrait bait. Some artist, undoubtedly soon, would revel in capturing their images for perpetuity, the great portrait to hang in the gallery of Penning Hall. Perhaps, even generations from now, in a museum. They would all be long dead, buried in their coffins, but their faces would be immortalized. A humble reminder of where she fell in the hierarchy of things.

Ready smiles graced their lips as they waited for the first carriage to stop, buffeted in sudden wind. Susanna eyed the darkening skies. It looked as though a storm were imminent. Hopefully, the guests would arrive before the skies broke loose.

Susanna waited, too, not quite wearing a smile. More like a pleasant expression of deference. She knew her duty. She knew the attitude she was expected to project. Smiles were not required of her, or any of the staff, for that matter.

She eyed the duke. He smiled, but it did not seem quite genuine. Oh, he looked fine and handsome and congenial in the late afternoon light. And yet there was a flatness to his gaze, a stiffness in the line of his shoulders. For a man determined to make a success of this house party, he did not strike her as enthused.

A kick of wind ruffled the dark hair at the crown of his head and he looked suddenly young and vulnerable—two things he had *never* appeared before. The sight squeezed something within her chest.

Well, perhaps he was *young*. She suspected he was older than her. As stern and rigid as he appeared, he seemed closer to thirty. Or eighty. She stifled a snort.

He might be young, but vulnerability was not something she would have *ever* assigned to him. Dukes could be young, but not vulnerable. On the contrary. Dukes, by their very nature, were decidedly *in*vulnerable.

Like it or not, she would say she was the vulnerable one here, subject to his whims, to his moods and decisions. She and every other member of the staff were vulnerable. Such was life. *Her* life. The life of every servant.

His gaze shifted suddenly away from the road and the remaining carriages advancing on a cloud of burgeoning dust. His attention should be on that—*them*—his impending guests, but through the gathered crowd, over heads, his gaze found her.

Their stares locked and held and she could not fathom the thoughts behind the darkness of his eyes. She only knew that when he looked at her she could not breathe.

Thankfully, he turned away and looked to the road again. She inhaled. Exhaled. Filled her lungs. Fortified herself. She clasped her hands in front of her and gave a single rock on her heels before catching herself and holding motionless. Composure. That was what was needed here. That was the requirement for all the staff, but especially her. She squared her shoulders. She needed to lead by example. That was what Aunt Ferelith had taught her.

Mr. Bird stood to her left, at the head of the line. It was where the highest member of the staff took position, and as the butler he was that—even if he was *not*. As long as he bore the title, he would hold his position as the highest member of the Penning staff. She would never usurp him of that.

"Gor, have you ever seen the like?" Miss Barrow leaned in to whisper, her shoulder brushing Susanna's starched sleeve as she sent the barest of nods to the new carriage to pull up before the doors and the lady descending from it. The woman wore a white dress trimmed in peacock-blue feathers. A bold choice for a day of travel. As far as Susanna could see there was not a single stain or smudge to mar the perfection. Her bonnet was equally festooned, a sweeping blue feather dipping over her forehead.

She was by no means beautiful. Not in the traditional sense. Her nose was too thin and her chin rather too square for her face, but that did not stop one's gaze from traveling over her and absorbing the splendid form of her, from becoming lost in the cool blue of her eyes. She was stunning.

"No," Susanna finally responded to Miss Barrow, her voice similarly hushed. "I have not."

Susanna had the guest list committed to memory by now and she had a few theories on who the well-turned-out lady could be.

Miss Barrow resumed her deferential air, leaning away from Susanna, standing at attention, resolute, a consummate professional. The woman had ambitions. Susanna knew that. Ever since she'd joined the staff at Penning Hall a few years ago, she had worked hard, striving to move ahead, to move up, ready for when the opportunity should ever present itself. The Duke of Penning arriving with two young sisters, neither of whom were in possession of a lady's maid, had been that chance.

A pair of young gentlemen poured out of the carriage behind her, and she knew at least one of them, if not both, were here for the Miss Rosses. She also surmised, in that moment, who they were.

The Harthorne twins. The spotted-faced lads were identical. Even the spots on their faces seemed to match. Both bore identical angry-red blemishes on their chins. Lady Harthorne with her oh-so-eligible sons had sat at the top of Penning's list. Clearly the woman dressed in a stunning, feathered day dress delicately stepping down from the carriage was mother to the prospective candidates.

A gentleman disembarked behind her, groggy-eyed and perhaps a bit in his cups. Presumably he was the husband, but Susanna could not recall Lady Harthorne having a husband. He had not been included on Penning's list. Perhaps she had brought a friend? A brother?

Whatever his identity, he evidently spent the journey indulging in the spirits to be had on board. As Lady Harthorne and her lads greeted Penning and his sisters, he followed in an uneven gait toward his host.

Other carriages arrived. Evidently the guests had come in a caravan from London. Susanna supposed that was the safest course of action. High-waymen did not abound in these parts, but there was the rare incident. No one could be too safe.

Others began pouring out from conveyances. It was a flurry of activity, distracting Susanna from catching the name of the gentleman in the company of Lady Harthorne as he was presented to the duke and his sisters.

Susanna focused on the task at hand, nodding approvingly as footmen stepped forward and began assisting with the unloading of luggage. She motioned discreetly at young Tommy when he did not appear very motivated to move, merely gawking and watching the happenings like the green lad he was. Once he caught her gaze, he snapped to action and hastened forward.

She and Barrow greeted the ladies' maids accompanying the duke's lofty guests. Susanna directed the Penning maids to break off and escort each guest and their maid to their assigned room. Her staff was well trained. This was accomplished with nary a word from Susanna. Merely a head tilt and a directed swing of her gaze sufficed.

Mr. Bird watched, smiling and nodding rather blankly. Years ago this had been his purview and he'd seen it done admirably well.

Susanna held her position, waiting for instructions on how the remainder of her afternoon would be spent. This would be based on the wishes of the guests, of course. Would they all wish to retire to their rooms until dinner? Perhaps some or a few would wish for tea in the drawing room or in the garden. Cook waited below for directions, ready with refreshments.

Susanna watched and listened carefully, alert to the duke's conversation as he greeted the myriad guests and inquired on the comfort of their journey.

She overheard several of the guests expressing a desire to take a respite in their rooms until dinner. That meant trays of tea and biscuits would need to be sent up. And very likely baths. She motioned Nancy, one of the head housemaids, closer.

She leaned into her ear. "Inform Cook to start on"—she scanned the gathering crowd—"a half dozen trays. Oh, and the lemon iced biscuits. Those are Cook's best. And make certain water is warmed for baths."

"Yes, ma'am." With a quick nod, the girl melted away, well trained in her duty.

"Your Grace!" An elderly woman with shrill, cultivated tones arrived before the duke, puffing for breath as she clutched a small, quivering dog in one hand and leaned on a brass-headed cane with the other. "I cannot tell you how very glad we are to have arrived. It was a simply dreadful journey. Something must be done about those roads. We had scarcely left the city before poor Chauncey fell ill all over the squabs. I shall see that the proper person hears of it. The Queen's roads should be much better maintained. 'Tis a disgrace."

The quivering dog did not look too hearty, to be certain, but whether it was his general constitution or a result of the journey . . . only time would reveal. The staff would assuredly inform Susanna if they were constantly required to clean up after the little beast.

"I am sorry to hear that, my lady." Penning managed to sound sincerely contrite as he bowed over her bejeweled fingers. "I will endeavor to make it up to you and dearest Chauncey." He lifted his gaze and swept the line of servants, his dark eyes landing on her. "Miss Lockhart, can you see to it that Chauncey is given the choicest of bones from Cook?"

The man was serious. His blue eyes stared steadily at her, and she hoped she looked like her usual impassive self. The perfectly composed servant. "Er. Yes, Your Grace, of course."

"Very good." He looked back to the old lady. "I hope that sets his spirits to rights."

Susanna blinked. Who was this man?

He was not the same one she had observed

watching the carriages roll in with resignation resting along the line of his rigid shoulders. Now that air of grim resignation was gone from him. The earlier flatness had fled from his gaze, replaced by a sparkling liveliness.

He appeared truly *charmed* and riveted by this old dragon. Even she seemed a little taken aback at his charming manner. He presented himself as the most cordial of hosts.

Had he led a life treading the boards before he became the Duke of Penning? There was no glimpse of the surly duke she'd observed these last couple of months. The man was truly a skilled and convincing performer.

Lady Lippton's loose jowls shuddered as she searched for an appropriate response. Evidently Susanna was not the only one caught off guard at his charming verve.

He did not wait for her to recover her voice. "And what of your daughter, Lady Lippton? How fares she?"

As though summoned by the question, a young woman stepped forward and murmured in dulcet tones, "I fared better than poor Chauncey, Your Grace." She executed a low curtsy. "Thank you for your kind inquiry."

The young lady lacked her mother's . . . *everything*. She did not possess her vigor or volume or, very clearly, her advanced years. Lady Lippton must have produced her quite late in life. Or Lady Lippton was not as old as she appeared.

Lady Philomena was as delicate and willowy as a reed, and Susanna felt the urge to usher her inside and feed her a large bowl of Cook's heartiest soup and wrap her up in front of the fire before she came down with an ague.

The duke took her gloved hand and pressed his lips to the back of it. "Lady Philomena. How lovely to see you."

Somehow he had met her before, the delicate Lady Philomena. She knew he had not come straight away from London when he first inherited the title.

He had arrived with agents of the estate in tow, but clearly he had spent some time in Town, securing his sisters in the Penning's grand Mayfair residence before departing and descending upon Penning Hall himself.

He had even gone back twice once he was settled into the hall. Short trips for business and to fetch his sisters. Clearly he had managed to squeeze in some time to socialize if he knew Lady Philomena.

The demure girl's cheeks pinkened. Her skin and hair were almost the same shade, both pale as milk, and Susanna could not prevent the completely unkind thought. *Too much inbreeding.*

She knew noble families had done it. Cousins marrying cousins for decades. Noble families believed it kept their bloodlines pure. Aunt Ferelith had once whispered to her that it was how they ended up with one too many toes.

As Penning lingered over the back of her hand, he added, "I am so relieved you are here, Lady Philomena, and in hearty form. I know when I was last in London you were a bit under the weather."

"I am quite recovered, Your Grace, thank you." Even as she said this, she rubbed the back of her gloved hand against the tip of a nose that was suspiciously red . . . as though she had recently spent a great deal of time sneezing. The whites of her eyes were also less than white. They were tinged a concerning pink, as though she were ill or had spent a good amount of time weeping.

"My Mena is as hale and robust as the heather that grows on the moors. Fret not on that account, Your Grace."

Clearly young Lady Philomena was one of his bridal prospects. Susanna tried not to consider that. It was neither here nor there. Certainly not any of her affair if he chose this delicate creature to be his bride. She attempted to gaze straight ahead and not make a study of them.

It was a hopeless task.

Susanna looked her over from head to foot,

missing nothing. Not an inch of her fashionable dress on her slender frame. Of course he considered this lady. That was what this entire blasted house party was all about. She tried to envision this woman as the future Duchess of Penning. It was not difficult to imagine, and she best get accustomed to the notion. If not her . . . then someone else. It *would* be someone else. He *would* marry someone else.

Indeed, it was no concern to her if this was whom Penning chose. It was not her business that this wisp of a woman would likely be crushed beneath his more forceful personality. She knew firsthand how stern and humorless he could be.

*And alluring.*

No. NO. *No no no no.* He was not alluring. He was a duke. That was enough said. It was all. It was everything.

It mattered not in the least bit that a creature like this did not seem well suited to the marriage bed and rigors faced therein—to say nothing of the subsequent rigors of childbearing. Again. None of her affair.

It was no matter to her if Penning wished to focus on a woman so ill suited to him, to a female who would wilt in their first argument, who would break like a twig beneath the first stiff wind of marital discord.

What did she know of marriage or the ways of the *ton*?

Nothing. Nothing at all.

Certainly Susanna knew of strife, but she had never been married. She never even had interest in her before Robbie. Certainly no offers.

She had been so young, and her family wretchedly poor. They had nothing with which to tempt suitors. Everything she earned working as Ruth's companion went to her parents. Her stepfather did not wish to lose her wages. There was no advantage to her marrying. No expectation. No benefit.

That was for blue-blooded gents like him, living where the stretch of his progeny made a difference in the grand scheme of things. He might not have been brought up as the Duke of Penning, but that was what he was now.

Susanna would likely have better luck winning over this prim lady than the difficult Duke of Penning. Perhaps that was where she should focus her energies. As far as she could detect, there was not a glimmer of meanness to her. Nowhere in her pale gray gaze did Susanna read that. It was unlikely that *she* would turn Susanna away or dismiss her offers of help.

Lady Philomena blinked owlishly at the duke. Then she looked entranced by him as he flashed her a brilliant smile. Who on earth possessed such perfect teeth? It was obscene. The man was blessed with an absolute unfair bounty of riches.

The girl was clearly blinded—by his fine looks or charming words it could not be said. Quite probably both.

Lady Philomena's mother seemed equally under his spell. She gave her head a shake, her jowls flapping as she regained her voice and harrumphed. "But we are here at last, Your Grace," she declared, "and I am hopeful it will all be worth it."

The woman's gaze roamed over the vast stone edifice of Penning Hall looming against the purpling sky. Her rheumy eyes assessed it brick by glorious brick, not missing a single mullioned window or overhanging eave. Seemingly satisfied, she looked back to the duke. It was hard to say which—the duke or Penning Hall?—was treated to a more thorough assessment.

Penning looked back and forth between the two ladies, his eyes bright and direct as he bestowed that infernal smile on them again. "I am confident it will all be worth it."

He was mesmerizing—blast him! Susanna, too, felt the pull.

A shadow stepped in front of her, a looming figure, blotting out the duke and his admirers from her view and jolting her from her spellbound stupor.

Susanna startled back to the present. Not that she had been lost in the past, but she had been woolgathering somewhere else as she observed the duke with his prospective duchess and mother-in-law.

Now a man, a stranger, stood before her, demanding her attention as he gazed down at her in a way that made the skin at the back of her neck prickle in foreboding.

# Chapter Thirteen ✢

Susanna's gaze honed in on this mystery gentleman who accompanied Lady Harthorne and her sons. He appeared quite foxed, swaying unsteadily on his feet before her.

"You, there." He wagged a finger in her face, wearing a sloppy grin that made her feel fairly . . . tainted for some reason.

She focused on the task at hand and ordered herself to stop her daydreaming. She had a duty to perform and perform it well she would.

Susanna stammered, "Y-yes . . . sir?"

She was uncertain of his proper address. She had, unfortunately, missed those details when he was introduced to Penning. The housekeeper was generally not introduced to the guests upon arrival. Always Aunt Ferelith had known, though. By sight. By name. By reputation. She never failed *not* to know someone's proper title. It was rather galling that Susanna did not.

To be fair, by the time she came to Penning Hall the old duke was not in the best of health. He rarely entertained guests. She had little exposure to affluent and lofty individuals. His son, Mr. Butler, had spent most of his time in Town, so he had not brought members of the *ton* home with him. She had not been confronted with anything quite like this before. She had been spared.

Until now.

"What is your name again, lass?"

*Again?*

"I did not say, my lord."

"But we know each other." He nodded resolutely. "Aye. We do."

She opened her mouth to deny that assertion, and yet . . .

He was familiar. She frowned. He was correct. She had seen him before. Somewhere in the fogged memories of her mind he existed.

She narrowed her gaze on his slightly meaty features and sucked in a shuddery breath, peering at the face obscured through his well-trimmed beard. *No.* It could not be.

*No no no no no no no.*

His face was fuller now, more bloated than she remembered, the flesh thick and swollen beneath his eyes, doubtlessly from the passing of years and copious amounts of spirits, if his sour breath and yellow-tinged skin was any indication. He had done some *hard* living since she last saw him, but she remembered him. They'd met before.

She recalled him distinctly now, sourly, bitterly. The way he held himself; his air of total superiority and hauteur radiated from him the same way it had all those years ago that summer he had come to the Isle of Man. When he'd joined his friend from school. His friend. *Her* Robbie. One and the same.

She had been a simple girl then, humble, without a penny to her name. He had been on top of the social order. Nephew to an earl, she believed. He was far above and far removed from all of them. Even his friend Robbie. Robbie who didn't mind walking down the streets of a poor fishing village, mingling with the common Manx people, even learning their mother tongue, determined to do so, determined to be near Susanna, even spending more time than he should in the servants' quarters with her—or tagging along whilst she accompanied his young sister, stealing Susanna away behind trees for kisses, coaxing her into a bed of hay in the loft of a stable.

The man before her continued to wag that one finger at her. "Oh, yes, yes, yes. I know you . . ." He peered at her with squinting eyes.

Aye, indeed he knew her. He knew of Robbie's love for her. He had disapproved of it quite vocally. Even attempted to step in and stop him, dragging Robbie off to a house of ill repute in Castletown in the hopes that he would forget all about Susanna. He had not.

Robbie had rejected the companionship of those other women and returned to her instead—an offer of marriage on his lips.

"Ah, er. I don't believe so." Denial was the only option. She fought desperately for her composure—to conceal the panic she felt.

"No," he said emphatically. "What was your name?" His eyes drifted to the side, clearly searching his memory. She only hoped he never remembered. He had always been overly fond of spirits. Hopefully the influence of drink and the passage of years prevented him from ever remembering.

"Billings?" Penning's deep voice interrupted as he stepped up beside his guest. "This is Miss Lockhart, my housekeeper."

Billings. Ah. Yes. That was his name. Somehow she had forgotten it. That time in her life had been a blur of pain, and his face had just been one small piece of it, his name less than significant to her.

"Housekeeper? A little young for that, is she not?" he asked as though she were not present.

"Miss Lockhart is not as young as you think." Susanna blinked at that response, telling herself she ought not to feel a sting from it. Penning went on, "She has been housekeeper here at Penning Hall for a good many years."

"That so?" Billings looked her over again, continuing to speak about her and not to her. "She is . . . unexpected. My housekeeper is a stern-faced termagant, but she knows how to manage a home and set a fine table."

"Sounds like a quality housekeeper."

Billings continued to study her with a frown. "Lockhart," he mused. "No. That is not it. It was some dreadfully unfortunate surname. What was it again?" He looked at her expectantly, and she could only shake her head mutely.

He then frowned as though he just fully digested what had been said. Wagging a finger at her, he demanded, "You are Penning's housekeeper, you say? Truly? What are the odds of that?" He clucked his tongue, clearly still not accepting she was not the girl he remembered from the Isle of Man. "How did that come to pass? I would have guessed you to be some ham-fisted farmer's wife with a dozen babes at your apron by now." He sniffed and looked her over. "Stout peasant stock, and all that."

She shifted anxiously, miserably, on her feet, fighting off the instinct to run.

"You know each other?" Penning inquired.

She shook her head helplessly. "No." The carefully crafted fiction Aunt Ferelith had invented for her was under attack. She needed to tread carefully. She could not admit to it. She would not. That girl . . . Susanna Duggan did not exist anymore. It was another lifetime in another world.

She was Susanna Lockhart now. She could not admit otherwise. Too bad her aunt had not thought to give her a different Christian name to go along with her change in surname. It had simply been convenient for the two of them to share the same last name.

"Forgive me, but you are confused." She must stick to her denial, must protect her identity.

"Confused?" His lip curled. "About you? No, I am not."

"Oh, Penning!" Lady Lippton beckoned him to her side, waving her cane in the air as her luggage was being carried past her.

With a frown for each of them, the duke moved away to answer the summons, leaving Billings with her, and she breathed a little easier, her chest loosening with the duke gone, no longer able to witness this uncomfortable encounter.

A short-lived sense of relief, of course, because she was still with Billings.

"So," he said in an unsettling silky voice. Her chest tightened again. "Miss *Lockhart*." He leaned forward and said in a voice for her ears alone, "You think I would forget such a prime piece as you? I used to wank off that summer, thinking about how Robbie got to diddle you and I had to make do with the whores in Castletown."

Her face went hot and she retreated a step, feeling suddenly sick. Never in her life had she fought so hard to maintain her composure. Never in her life had she wished to inflict physical harm to another person.

So much for him not remembering. He remembered her distinctly. It was her worst nightmare come to life. She had always feared coming face-to-face with someone from home. Never had she imagined it could be someone as dreadful as this man.

"Sir," she said in a pathetically small voice. "You have mistaken me for someone else."

He looked her over with a leer. "Wouldn't you like me to believe that?"

She would. Desperately.

Penning returned then. "So. Have you two recalled where you know each other from?" He looked back and forth between them with those keen eyes of his.

She held her breath. This was it. The moment Billings would expose her.

The wretched man took a breath, held it, looking at her expectantly. Releasing it, he then said, "It seems I was mistaken. I thought she was someone else." He smiled at Penning. "This peasant lass from long ago." She flinched. *Peasant lass.* "A bit of tart I encountered years ago whilst I was on the Isle of Man . . ." He feigned a look of contrition, as though he suddenly realized he was speaking crassly in front of her and regretted it. "Begging your pardon, Miss Lockhart."

She nodded. And yet as his gaze met hers, understanding passed between them.

He knew her.

And he knew she knew him.

Just in time, it seemed, thunder cracked the air, shaking the very earth. It felt sadly apropos. The first few fat drops of rain fell. One landed on her cheek, then on her nose.

She gasped and looked up at the sky, lifting a hand to shield her face as though that would offer protection.

"Hurry this way, everyone," Penning called to the remaining guests, gesturing them indoors.

Lady Lippton squawked in dismay, and the duke stepped beside her, gallantly offering his arm to both her and her daughter.

With exclamations of alarm, the nobles and peers hastened inside in a throng. But not before she met Billings's gaze one more time. Not before reading the promise there. *We're not finished, you and I.*

Turning from her with a smirk, he disappeared inside the house.

She lingered, watching them all go as more rain fell, picking up speed as it struck her exposed flesh. She welcomed the cool wetness on her over-heated skin.

Hopefully, it would only be a light deluge. Anything more than that and all the guests would be stuck inside together. Trapped.

# Chapter Fourteen ❧

$\mathcal{I}$t was *not* a light deluge.

Unrelenting rain pounded the roof and it sounded as though the thunder itself might split the house open right down the middle. She could not sleep if she wished to do so—even if she *could*. Not when it felt like God Himself was visiting His wrath upon them.

Susanna carried a lamp and strolled the house, inspecting every corridor, every unoccupied room. Penning Hall was an old building. It had weathered many a storm over the centuries and still stood. She preferred for it to stand another century.

Determined to keep a vigilant eye and make certain no water found its way inside the house through a window left carelessly open or a leak in the ceiling, she walked the halls, a solitary figure in the sleeping house . . . a sentinel determined nothing untoward occur on her watch.

She had no way of checking the occupied guest chambers. Hopefully the guests would keep their windows closed and sound the alert if there was any need.

She needed her rest. Tomorrow would be eventful, but she doubted she would be able to sleep over the drumming rain. Or in her present state of anxiety. How could she? Knowing that despicable man slept beneath this roof plotting against her . . .

She was braced for it. Braced for the moment he would corner her. And yet she feared there was nothing she could do to prepare for that. He would come at her sooner or later. He knew who she was and he would not accept her denial. There was a reason he had not exposed her, and she knew it was not a magnanimous one. He was not finished with her and she dreaded his next move.

She had learned that he was, in fact, still unwed, but here with Lady Harthorne. And Billings's marital status seemed on the verge of changing. He was Lady Harthorne's betrothed. He had somehow wormed his way into that formidable woman's heart.

Susanna could not fathom why a widow with all her blessings—wealth, rank, title—would wish to marry him. She would be handing all that over to him the moment she said "I do."

Perhaps it was love. Blind love. That could be the only reason for her to sacrifice her autonomy. And that Billings was skilled at artifice.

She recalled that Robbie's mother and sister had

thought him the most charming, considerate of men. Ruth was quite enamored of him. He knew how to behave when it mattered. He was not a fool in that regard. The poor Lady Harthorne did not realize the mistake she was about to make binding herself to such a cad.

Shaking her head, Susanna continued her walk through the house. The library was on the second floor. Its exterior wall boasted floor-to-ceiling windows that overlooked verdant green lawns. Tonight the view consisted of water-sluiced glass and unremitting darkness, broken by the occasional flash of lightning.

She'd already checked the room at the start of her inspection, but decided to look in one final time before returning to her chamber, prepared to borrow a book since sleep eluded her anyway.

Susanna slipped through the double doors, frowning slightly as she realized the room was not shrouded in darkness as it had been when she looked in a short while ago.

Indeed not. Someone had entered the room since then. Not too shocking, she told herself. It was the library, after all. Members of the staff often availed themselves of books in the library, borrowing what they liked.

The original Duke of Penning had been very generous with his staff, permitting them to browse his library and read anything they chose from his vast collection. He had established the custom. She realized she should find out if the current duke agreed with keeping the tradition.

Susanna would have preferred the staff not visit the library on the first night of a large house party. Good sense should have stayed such an ill-advised impulse.

Light danced over the walls and over the countless spines of books lining the shelves. She scanned the space, hoping that someone had not left a lamp or candle burning. She was frequent in her reminders to the staff to be careful and not leave any lamps or candles behind in rooms lest they wanted the whole house to burn down. It happened. Fires were an all-too-common hazard. Not a week went by where she didn't read of some tragedy in the newspaper—a home or business up in flames, often with people trapped inside. She shuddered.

Such dire thoughts abandoned her as her gaze landed on the room's occupant. Her heart seized. She was indeed not alone. It was not a member of the staff. She gulped. There would be no reprimand forthcoming.

For a moment she thought she might slip away undetected from the room and avoid an encounter altogether, but then Penning spotted her.

He was reclining in a wingback chair by the wall of windows, his long legs stretched out before him in an indolent pose as he gazed out at the wet, inky night.

He held a glass half full of amber liquid, his fingers clutching the rim of the glass just by the tips, and it seemed a precarious grip. As though he might let go at any moment, shattering the glass into a thousand pieces.

His blue eyes appeared almost as black as the world outside the library windows. They locked on her and she was seized with her usual breathlessness.

"Why are you not abed?" he asked in a voice as deep and thick as gravel.

There was so very *much* gleaming in those penetrating eyes. Countless *gleaming* unspoken things . . . Emotions. Thoughts. Intangible all, but she felt each and every nameless one, senseless as that sounded. *How can one feel something you cannot name or identify?*

And yet she did.

She *did*.

She felt every single one. She felt . . . *everything* in his presence.

It only reinforced her need to run, to flee and put as much distance as possible between them. Cowardly, yes. Or perhaps it was simply prudent.

Whatever the case, it was impossible, of course, as they lived together in the same house and she had to see him daily whilst he was in residence.

It would be different when he took a wife. Not so . . . intense. Not so many of these bewildering feelings.

Perhaps she would not even see him every day then. That would be a good thing. Truly. It would be the Duchess of Penning with whom she interacted regarding the running of the household. Naturally. The duke would only be seen in passing and from a distance.

She felt a funny sensation in her stomach at the thought of that. A pang at the center of her chest. She did not know what that signified exactly, and she did not have the time to examine it even if she wished to. She was faced with him now and he was talking to her.

"Do not tell me your duties keep you awake this late."

*You know nothing of my duties.*

Instead of delivering that caustic reply, she said circumspectly, "Begging your pardon, Your Grace. I did not mean to disturb you. I was checking the house."

"Checking the house?" he queried, pausing to absorb that. "Is that something you customarily do?"

"Not every night, but when it storms, yes."

"Very conscientious," he murmured, and it did not feel like such a compliment.

She squared her shoulders, feeling the need to justify herself. "One year there was a storm and the entire ceiling of the conservatory collapsed. And we've had other minor leaks. It's best to take note and get ahead of any potential . . . calamities."

"Ah." He lifted his glass and took a deep drink. "You are a credit to your profession, Miss Lockhart."

Did he mean that? Did he now see all the good she did? That she was worth keeping around?

She studied him closely, trying to gauge. "I do try."

"I am beginning to see that."

Was he? Her pulse drummed wildly at her throat. Perhaps he was. Perhaps he was changing his mind about her. She could only hope. Only pray that her position here, her place in this world, was secure.

But then did it matter what Penning thought when her world was about to crash down around her because of one wretched man sleeping beneath this roof? Billings would not leave the matter alone. He would not leave *her* alone. She knew this with grim acceptance.

Soon Penning would have his reason to let her go. He would have no choice. His conscience need not be pricked. He would have just cause. His housekeeper, living under an assumed name, was not all she pretended to be. To the world, Susanna was a fallen woman. A scandalous, wicked creature. He could not keep such a person on his staff and around his sisters. That was not the way the world worked.

All those years ago, when a pair of women had discovered Susanna with Robbie trysting in a field of wildflowers—in the most shocking state of undress—Susanna had her first taste of how the world worked, of how life could turn and sour in a blink.

Susanna had lived with the hard edges of her stepfather's authority all her young life, but her reputation had never been called into question before. She had always been well liked in her community. She never faced the hard edges of life *outside* her home before, and that was another, a different kind of hurt.

Those women had wasted no time carrying the tale of what they had witnessed to all who would listen. The unsavory tale had reached the ears of everyone, from the lowest of villagers to Mrs. Davies herself.

It was mortifying, but the scorn had been muted at first, whilst Robbie lived. There was the chance, after all, that he would do right by her and take her to wife. Then she would be a proper lady, wife to an important and wealthy gentleman.

He had vowed as much to Susanna, and she had believed him. She had heard the sincerity in his voice and felt it in the tenderness of his touch. He loved her. She might have been young and too trusting, but she knew that.

He had gone with her to speak to her parents, vowing that he intended to speak with his father when he visited from the mainland. He promised them he would marry Susanna. His reassurances had mollified her parents. Somewhat. She had at least been spared a sound thrashing, which was what she fully expected to happen. Her stepfather was not a soft man. She often felt the palm of his hand cracking across her face for any real or perceived misdeed.

Once Robbie departed Mama had wept tears of joy, clapping her hands gleefully as she rocked before the hearth in their small cottage, the light of the fire gilding her lined and weathered features, making her appear far older than her thirty-five years. *Well, lass, looks as though you've done well for yourself. Landed yourself a fine gentleman!*

Her stepfather had not been quick to congratulate her. He was still skeptical. It was almost as though he resented her good fortune and did not wish her a happy future. His nostrils flared. *Could not keep those thighs shut, eh? Well, we shall see if the lad marries you. Don't see why he would since you've already whored yourself for him.*

He scowled at her as he pounded the mud from his boots, beating the heels onto the floor she had just swept that morning, hoping to make their humble home look less squalid for Robbie's visit. Not that her efforts had helped much.

She knew what his life looked like in that big house on the hill overlooking their tiny village. And she knew what her life looked like inside this dreary little cottage.

Robbie had not said a word, of course, but she had seen the distaste in his eyes, the quivering of his nose, when he stepped inside the only home she had ever known.

She fought against the hot tide of shame, telling herself that she had no reason to feel that way. She had been born to the conditions of her life just as he had been born into his. It was not something she could control. She had not chosen this world. A whim of birth brought her to this.

Her stepfather's skepticism proved warranted, however. Robbie would not marry her. That would be impossible. He drowned a few days later. An unlucky fate to befall Robbie, to be certain.

But also an unlucky fate for her.

The village's collective scorn was unleashed. She was grist for the gossip mill. The wolves were released and intent on devouring her. And devour her they did. Starting with her own mother and stepfather.

Especially her stepfather.

There was nothing to stave off the consequent beating. The man had been particularly vicious, and she sensed that he had been anticipating this, convinced that Robbie would never wed her.

He relished every slap, punch and kick. She had thought he intended to kill her. Like Robbie, she would soon be dead. Susanna dimly recalled her mother stepping between them before she lost consciousness.

Later, when she woke in the front yard, her entire body ached. Her things were beside her, packed in a valise, presumably by her mother. Mama, who might have stopped her husband from killing her, but she was nowhere in sight anymore. Nowhere around to pick Susanna up from the dirt and promise her that everything would be well.

She had died, she supposed.

She'd painstakingly gathered herself up and limped her way to the village, to the harbor. Eventually, she climbed aboard a boat headed for the mainland, leaving the only world she had ever known behind and coming to life again. Reinventing, becoming Susanna Lockhart.

# Chapter Fifteen ❧

$\mathcal{N}$ow I understand why the late duke promoted you to such an important position." The Duke of Penning's words brought her back to the present. She blinked as his face came into focus. "His faith in you was merited."

"Thank you, Your Grace," she murmured, dipping a quick departing curtsy, holding her chin at a dignified angle as she pushed those unpleasant memories aside. "I will leave you to your privacy." She turned away, but stopped at the sound of his voice.

"Sit. Stay a while."

Susanna turned slowly, caught off guard at the invitation. He used his booted foot and hooked it under the seat of a nearby chair, turning and dragging it closer to him where he sat beside the window.

The gruff Duke of Penning was inviting her to sit with him. After so many rejections and dismissals. Curiosity won out. She moved and settled herself down into the chair beside him.

He studied her for a moment before reaching

for the nearby liquor service and rolling it closer. His movements were easy and fluid as he plucked an empty glass and poured a few fingers' worth of whiskey for her.

"Here you go."

She accepted the proffered glass. Whiskey was not something ladies imbibed—or any female of good breeding. That included a housekeeper. For some reason, she did not think he would judge her for the social gaffe. He was not testing her to see if she would cling to propriety. He was inviting her to drink with him as an equal would.

She lifted the glass to her lips and took a sip of the fiery liquid.

He studied her closely and she attempted to hide her grimace. She must not have done a very good job for he chuckled and then motioned to the bottle. "I suppose you are not the one taking a nip from the bottle in here every night."

She looked askance at the bottle of whiskey. "Do you mean one of the staff has been sneaking your whiskey?"

"Oh, most assuredly. Unless it is one of my sisters, and I highly doubt that."

"Oh," she breathed, indignation rushing through her that someone among her own staff would be doing something so underhanded beneath her nose. Who could it be? The groom, Thomas, had shifty eyes and was always trying to lure a maid into a closet with him. And there was dear Mr. Bird. She'd glimpsed him before indulging in an infrequent claret, when the occasion called for it. Who knew what he would do now that his inhibitions were reduced and he was not quite himself anymore?

"I will get to the bottom of it, Your Grace. I promise—"

He waved a hand in dismissal. "When one of the staff shows up to work deep in his cups and disrupts the house . . . then I shall worry."

"That is very magnanimous of you, Your Grace."

He snorted. "You almost sound like you mean that, Miss Lockhart."

"I do."

"Come, now. You think me an insensitive bastard."

She gaped at him for a long moment. "I never said that." She would not have dared. She followed that insistence with a deep swallow of whiskey, needing the fortification if they were to speak so candidly. It burned a scalding path down her throat.

"You did not have to. You think I lack empathy, compassion. You think I don't see you or the others who serve in this house."

"Well . . ." Her voice faded. Was she bold enough . . . *stupid* enough to say it? "Servants are invisible, are they not? That is the mark of a good servant."

"Is it?" He looked her over in bemusement. "You must not be a very good servant, then, Miss Lockhart."

She flushed warmly, certain she should take offense and yet pleasure suffused her knowing he found her noticeable.

He continued, "You are a far cry from invisible."

She fidgeted and adjusted her fingers around her glass again, taking another sip as she wondered if he was waiting for an apology. Suddenly she did not feel so circumspect and that did not trouble her. Her desperate need to prove herself so that she might keep her position had abated. What did it matter, after all, if Billings was about to dismantle her world?

She felt as though time had slowed, the moments crawling as she watched a glass vase descending to the hard ground, where it would shatter to pieces, too many to count, too many to ever repair.

"How old are you?"

She looked up from her glass. A gentleman would not ask a lady such a thing, but then it was understood that she was no lady. "Twenty-eight."

"Quite young to hold such a position."

"I have my aunt to thank for that, and the former Duke of Penning."

"You mean the real one?"

"Yes." She nodded with a wince. "He was good to my aunt . . . and me."

"I wish I had met him. He was my relative, after all." He flicked his fingers, gesturing around them. "I suppose I have him to thank for this."

"Do you?" She angled her head. "Was he not merely a product of his birth? Just as you are? Perhaps you owe your gratitude to the fates and the laws of primogeniture that see you so well established in life."

His lips twitched. "Perhaps so."

He stared at her in that intense, probing way of his again until she had to look away, feeling too vulnerable under his inspection.

"He was a bit of a scholar, the late duke," she offered, hoping to tread into less charged conversation, "and he encouraged my love of his library. He would share it with anyone. Talk books with anyone." She motioned around her. "We would often discuss books together. He knew I was fond of the classics."

"The classics?"

"Yes. Greek mythology."

"Ah. What is your favorite?"

"Hmm." She considered for a moment. "It

changes. My answer could vary given the day."
*Given my mood.*

As a girl she had loved Persephone and Hades. The seeming romance of it had made her young heart sing. She'd pored over those books in Robbie's family's library alongside Ruth and her governess. Perhaps that was why she had been such an easy mark for Robbie and all his whispered promises of love. She had craved romance.

As she grew older, her heart changed and she could see only a childlike bully in Hades, determined to have his way over the desires of the woman he allegedly loved. And that was not love. It was obsession.

Given the present state of her life, she could relate to Sisyphus more. She admired his endless determination. "I'm fond of Sisyphus."

"Seems rather bleak, does it not? His endless toil, pushing that rock only for it to roll back down, setting him to the task of pushing it up the hill again and again. And again."

"'Tis not bleak at all. It speaks to the human spirit, to perseverance and courage. It signifies . . . hope."

"Fruitless hope?"

"Is hope ever fruitless?"

He studied her thoughtfully, nodding slowly as though in agreement. "You have an interesting way of looking at things, Miss Lockhart. You are quite the unwavering lass. Not soft."

*Soft?* No. She supposed she was not that.

She knew women *should* be soft, though. That was the expectation. What they were taught from the cradle on. Men preferred them that way.

Soft ladies did not challenge. They did not usurp the men in their lives. They bowed to the authority of their fathers and brothers and husbands and . . . well, men in general.

Mama had been soft, forever bending to the will of her husband like a willow in the rain, and her stepfather had expected the same from Susanna.

Mama's face may have been weathered from the salty sting of wind off the harbor, her hands tough and cut up from working the fishing lines alongside her husband, but she was soft. Malleable. Silent when Susanna's stepfather raised his voice and the back of his hand to her and Susanna. Silent when he called Susanna a whore.

Silent when he flung a battered Susanna into the dirt outside the door of their small cottage—the cottage her father, her *real* father, had built them.

No. Susanna was not soft. Indeed not. And she did not long to be. Not if it made her anything like her mother—a woman who held no loyalty to her child.

Susanna did not begrudge her mother for re-marrying. She begrudged her for choosing a man so callous, so miserable . . . so unlike Papa.

Susanna's memories of her father were fuzzy, but she remembered being tickled and tossed in the air. She remembered laughter. She remembered love.

"You are correct, Your Grace. I am not soft," she agreed, the challenge in her voice sharp, cutting, daring him to dislike her for that. For it was the one thing she did not regret about herself. Anything that marked her as different from her mother, stronger, more loyal, she would not regret.

# Chapter Sixteen ✦❧

There is nothing wrong with that." He shrugged. "You're strong. Nothing wrong with that at all."

Susanna eyed him suspiciously, but she sensed no veiled insult. Only sincerity. Perhaps even a smidge of admiration. His gaze felt different, too. A flicker of warmth alive there. A flicker of warmth . . . for her. *For. Her.*

It was a jarring moment, but far better than most of their previous moments. The moments of indifference or, even worse, coldness or dismissal.

She moistened her lips and steered the conversation in another direction. "Um. There is still the late duke's son. If you wished to meet his father, you should meet the son." Unless he was the type to hold one's illegitimacy against them, but for some reason she did not think that of him. He could not be so pretentious. Could he? He'd only just inherited the title, only just become a blue blood himself. "You are related," she reminded him. "Distantly."

"Butler, correct?"

"Yes. He and his family live outside Shropshire now. His wife is lovely."

"I am sure I will meet them." He nodded, sliding a bit lower in his chair, his boots nudging dangerously close to her own feet.

"You would like him."

"Would I?" He looked at her curiously.

"Indeed. You've much in common."

"Do we? Such as?"

He studied her as he sat there with such an air of indolence. What could she say? *He was the duke. You are the duke.* She cringed a bit. Perhaps they did not have as much in common as she thought.

She felt the interest in his gaze, his curiosity in her answer. "He is a nice man."

"Oh." He appeared contemplative at that. "You mean you think I'm a nice man, too?"

He was many things, but not *nice.*

Her lips twitched, and she couldn't help herself. Her fingers pressed to her lips, doing a poor job to stifle her giggle. "No."

A smile stretched his lips and that smile was devastating. Of course he was handsome . . . but when he smiled he was lethal to one's senses.

"Indeed," he agreed. "I am not."

A weighty silence fell. A burst of lightning lit the sky, illuminating his face, making the angles appear sharp and unrelenting.

"So." The single word fell alongside the steady

drum of rainfall and startled her, making her feel foolish. "What do you think of our house party?"

*Ours?*

It was kind—or foolish—of him to think she had any ownership in this. There was no *ours*. It was not *her* party. It would not be her success. It would only be her failure if things did not go well.

"It will be a lively gathering," she offered, ignoring the sudden constriction in her chest.

He and his sisters should have no difficulty emerging from this house party betrothed. If they wanted a betrothal, it would be theirs for the taking. Everyone was doting on them. The young ladies were all aflutter over the duke, and the young gentlemen's eyes devoured Mattie and Evie like they were the finest sweetmeats that they wished to gobble.

"What do you *think*?" he pressed, clearly not satisfied with her response.

"What do *I* think?"

"Yes. You. I see you watching, observing and taking note of everything."

"It is my duty to be observant. I am merely making certain everyone has what they need."

"You have been around long enough, seen many of these things through multiple dukes here."

"I have."

His lips twitched. "Ironic, considering your tender age."

"I have been here for a while," she agreed. It was strange for him to consider her young. For a housekeeper she was indeed young. And yet she was no blushing maid. Not in many years had she been that. She was firmly on the shelf and considered so by all. She was a woman who had died long ago and been reborn into this world, this life.

"What do you think? Do you see a future Duchess of Penning anywhere in the group?" He took another drink and she wondered if he was not a little inebriated. Surely he did not seek her opinion? What did her thoughts matter to him? She was his housekeeper. His was the only opinion, the only decision, that mattered.

"I could not say, Your Grace."

"Ah. You mean you will not." He snorted and refilled his glass. "You have an opinion. All women do, but I know *you* especially have thoughts. You have already revealed yourself to be most clever, Miss Lockhart."

"This is a personal matter. *Your* private matter, Your Grace. You should not seek anyone's counsel on the matter save your own."

"Ugh." He looked skyward. "Miss Lockhart . . . you are disappointing me."

"I am not trying to." Valiantly she was trying only to impress him and prove her worth.

"I did not mark you as reticent. Do not start with that now."

She swallowed another sip of whiskey. "Why don't you share with me your inclinations? Certainly *you* have formed opinions. Perhaps then I can give you my thoughts."

"Ah." He waved a hand through the air rather searchingly, giving a small groan. "I do not know." He leaned forward and propped his elbows on his knees as though confiding something intimate. "They all seem nice enough, but who is to say which will make me a proper duchess?"

"You certainly seemed to be enjoying yourself with them this evening."

He flashed a smile. "Watching me, then, eh?"

Then, forgetting herself, she volunteered, "Lady Miranda does have a braying laugh. At first I thought a donkey had joined us in the house."

He winced, seemingly not offended at all. "Indeed. She does. A fact the scandal rags made no mention of when extolling her virtues. That would not be a pleasant thing to hear every day."

"And yet a wife full of laughter is a blessing."

"You would think so, but that laugh?" He shuddered and shook his head.

"It seems trivial to rule a woman out based on such a small matter."

"P'rap it is not that small. You did bring it up, after all."

She grinned. Touché. "Well, what of Lady Philomena?" she asked.

"Now that one, I fear, shall never once laugh at all. The sound may well frighten her."

"I fear you are right. She is rather . . ." Timid. Bland. Boring. Dull. "Demure," she finished. "Perhaps you should work toward that goal tomorrow, Your Grace. See if you can become better acquainted with her and bring her out of her shell."

"I should try," he agreed. "It is too soon to dismiss either one of them. They are both highly eligible and are very favored this season."

"Well, then. There you have it. You know what must be done. You must spend more time with each of them, but perhaps take a little extra effort with Lady Philomena."

Her advice was sound, so why did she feel a little pang in the center of her chest at the notion of him spending time with the very ladies he had brought here to court?

To be fair, his own expression was twisted into a cringe, and she marveled at that. From the moment of their arrival, he had played the part of besotted suitor exceedingly well, as though he were enamored with each of them. She had been convinced, but now she suspected this was his authentic self. Not that charming, flirty, ingratiating swell from earlier. Thank God.

"Should not be such a chore. You appeared quite enchanted with them today."

"All in a day's work, they say."

*Do they? Do they say that?*

She marveled at his casual air and his expression—which now seemed so very unaffected. There was something beneath it. Something real and *affected*. The skin near one eye fluttered. It was a subtle thing. Hardly noticeable. And yet she noticed it. She saw it and thought it marked a level of restraint in him. Restraint from . . . what? What was he hiding? What was he suppressing? What did he bury deep?

A man of his rank, in his position . . . there should be nothing unattainable for him. He had his good name. Title. Property. Money. If he did not wish to take a wife—*any of these ladies to wife*—then he should not. It appeared a very straightforward matter to her.

"It cannot be . . ."

"Cannot be what?"

"It cannot be wrong to find someone you are attracted to. You needn't marry if you don't wish it."

"Lady Miranda is beautiful," he countered.

*And possesses a braying laugh you cannot abide.*

"I do not speak of superficial attraction, Your

Grace. What of twenty years from now? When she is not so beautiful? What then?"

Was she actually offering marital advice? He had asked for her opinion, but she could not believe she had obliged to give it. Aunt Ferelith would have never dared. This man had a way of making her forget herself and all her training.

"And what of you, Miss Lockhart? Have you no wish for marriage? Children?"

She tensed. "I'm a housekeeper."

"Is that all you've ever wanted to be? To the exclusion of wifehood? Motherhood?"

She had a blurry flash of Robbie's face. She could not recollect him very clearly anymore. Just a vague sense of him. Pale skin. Brown hair that stubbornly fell over his brow. She thought his eyes were brown, too, but she was not so certain anymore. She was not certain what he had looked like at all and that made her sad.

She had wanted to marry that lad. She would have married him, too, had fate not intervened and taken him from her mere days after he proposed to her in a field of wildflowers.

And yet she could not recall his features anymore.

"I am content in my role."

"Not precisely an answer to the question. You are good at evasion, Miss Lockhart."

They gazed at each other in the golden light of the fire, unspeaking for some time.

Finally, after several more moments, she elaborated, "I have found contentment here." For the time being. *Until the vase drops. Shatters.* "Is that not answer enough?"

Again with his silent scrutiny. She resisted fidgeting where she sat, but the struggle was too much. She shifted her weight in the chair.

Her heart was galloping hard in her chest. She took another sip if only to give herself something to do, but then she was only made much too aware of the sensation of her lips against the smooth edge of the glass, the fiery whiskey in her mouth, rolling past her teeth and sliding down her throat. She was aware of everything. Every part of her, every hair, every fiber, every pore . . . the rush and pump of blood in her veins. She felt it all. Heightened and acute.

A slow smile spread across his handsome features. "I suppose it is. We are not so very different, then. That is all I seek, too. Contentment."

"Well." She gave him a wobbly smile. "We don't aspire for things so far out of reach, do we?"

His smile lingered. "No. It seems we do not. Contentment should not be so very elusive."

She finished the last bit of her whiskey. It no

longer burned quite so much as it went down. A pleasant mellow warmth spread throughout her, relaxing her muscles and melting her bones. She could now understand why the drink was so favored.

He lifted the bottle, ready to pour her more.

Without thinking, she covered his hand where it clutched the bottle. They both froze, gazes fixed on where their hands connected.

She kept her hand there for too long, appreciating the contact, the size of his hand, so much bigger beneath her own. The ropy veins on his forearms stretching to the back of his wide hand.

Her stomach tightened, twisting.

"Thank you, no." One drink was more than enough. Her head already felt a bit wrapped in wool as it was. Perhaps that was Penning, though. This cozy moment sitting here with him, talking to him, exchanging words as though they were equals.

She started to lift her hand from him, but he snatched hold of her wrist, stalling her from full retreat. His long fingers wove between hers, lacing their hands together, pushing their palms flush. Kissing palms. Her breath caught. His palm swallowed hers. She could feel his pulse, the thump of his own heart into her open hand, into her, penetrating and merging until it worked in cadence with her own.

He glanced from their hands to her face, his expression thoughtful, intense.

She could not breathe. Could not move.

"We fit nicely," he murmured, his fingers tightening, squeezing around hers slightly.

Her heart skipped. *We fit nicely.* Her stomach dipped and twisted.

Oh, dear. *No. No. No.* She could not let that thrilling thought go to her head.

She slipped her hand free, almost surprised at how easy it was to do so. He did not hold fast. He let her go. Her hand fell to her lap, almost as though it belonged to someone else. She looked at it lying there for a moment, limp, empty.

With a blink, she curled her fingers inward, squeezing her hand into a fist and willing away the sensation of his touch, the deep pulse of his heartbeat.

Composed again, she inhaled a ragged breath. Rising to her feet, she murmured, "Thank you for the drink. I'm going to retire now."

"Good night, Miss Lockhart. Sleep well."

"You, too, Your Grace," she murmured. With a turn, she walked out of the room, confident she would not.

She would not sleep well at all.

HE WAS AN idiot.

What was Lucian doing touching her? Flirting with her? More than that. *We fit nicely.* Those words . . .

That went beyond flirtation. They were stupidity.

He didn't know how his resolve had vanished. When he had first met her there had not been this temptation. He had felt in control of himself. Angry but in control. The distance between them had not been a struggle to maintain. Now it was. Now that distance was closing.

However, the longer he was here, beneath the same roof with her, around her, near her . . .

His resolve was faltering and developing into . . . *something*. Into *this*. This unidentifiable *thing* that was now between them. This pulsing thing that led him to share a whiskey with her in a darkened room, staring out at the rain-soaked night.

He had vowed not to take advantage of her. He had resisted her night after night, day after day when she put herself before him and said things like: *Ask anything of me. I submit myself to you.*

*Bloody hell.* Were there words any more excruciating than that? He did not know if he could resist anymore. There was a hollowness in his chest. It had been there for as long as he could recall. Since his father died and left them lost and alone, scavenging to survive. Since he lost his mother—and not to death. Since he had lost her to her despair.

The hollowness had not improved with an influx of lovers into his life. Those women did not want him. They were only after a night's pleasure. They sought him for their own release. They did not care for him. Theirs was merely a physical exchange.

The aching hollowness within him had only grown more acute since he became Penning. Since he moved here. His body might not be his only commodity now, but neither was his essence—his thoughts, his feelings.

And yet when he was around Miss Lockhart he did not feel quite so hollow inside. Indeed, from the moment he had first crossed swords with her atop that hill, soaked to the bone and furious, he'd not felt the least bit hollow in her presence. The conversation they'd just shared was perhaps the longest he had talked to anyone since claiming the title.

It was a good thing Carter would soon resume his duties and he did not have to worry about being alone with her quite so much anymore.

He looked over his shoulder at the door she'd passed through, stifling this mad impulse to follow her. He envisioned that. Moving through the house, tracking her and finding her in her room, in her bed, soft and yielding in some virginal cotton nightgown. He imagined joining her there.

He swallowed tightly. He was not that man.

He was not a hunter. She was not prey.

He charmed and seduced, but only women who *wanted* to be charmed and seduced. In the past, the women had always been in control, the ones who possessed the money, who wielded the power.

Susanna Lockhart was different. She was not someone with money or power.

He was.

He was and she worked for him and he would never take her to bed. He would never know if it was her choice. Or if she was compelled because of who he was—all that he was.

He was tired. Focusing his energies and charms on Lady Philomena and Lady Miranda had depleted him, which was unlike him.

He was accustomed to winning over the fairer sex. He'd done it for years. His skill never fell short, his energies never waned. Until now. Now he found the whole practice distasteful, which was some irony. For years, to live, to survive, he had charmed and seduced and not minded it at all.

Now, yet again, to survive, he must charm and seduce. His change in status had not changed that. And this time . . . he did mind.

As long as he was the Duke of Penning, he held power over her. It was a power he did not want. He did not want to be above her unless it was in bed, her body arching sweetly beneath him. Not unless she was free to choose him.

A wife. That was what he needed.

He needed to hurry up and get himself a wife. It would be another much-needed barrier between them because he would not ever shame a wife by taking a member of their staff to his bed. Not under her nose. Not in their home. He had a code, rules he lived by, lines he would not cross. That was one of them.

The only problem was that the young ladies he had invited to Penning Hall were not the least bit tempting. He did not want them in his bed. He wanted her. He wanted the housekeeper he could not touch.

It was a hell of a thing, but he wanted Susanna Lockhart.

# Chapter Seventeen ❧

As Susanna expected, she was cornered the next day.

First thing in the morning, actually, and that was more than a little surprising as she did not expect Billings to be an early riser.

The Billings she remembered had been a sloth. He drank, ate and slept to excess. He'd come home that summer with Robbie, but Robbie had been left to his own devices during the day because Billings slept well past noon.

He dared to enter the servants' quarters, specifically the women's wing, strolling down the corridor as though he had every right to be there. Thankfully she was the first one up and moving about and no one else spotted him strutting the corridor with such purpose.

She slowed, dread eating up her throat at the sight of him.

"Mr. Billings," she greeted as though she was meeting a gentleman on the village Main.

"There you are." He clapped his hands once and rubbed them together.

She winced at the sound. The last thing she wanted was to prematurely wake the staff and rouse them from their beds so that they could wonder why one of the houseguests was talking to her in the women's wing.

She had managed to sleep a little following her time with Penning in the library, but mostly she had tossed and turned, wondering if she had imagined the entire encounter.

But she knew. It was him. Her eyes had not deceived her, unfortunately. It was not some manner of trick or her memory failing her.

He recognized her. There was no hiding.

And now, as he faced her, there was no escape. The past had come to call after all this time.

He wagged a finger at her. "I knew it was you yesterday." His gaze flicked over her. "You have held up well . . . although I have seen you better attired. You are dressed like an old woman in this." His hand fluttered between them. "The last time I saw you, you wore your hair loose." He licked his lips. "Such a sweet young piece you were."

In those days, she had worn the top half of her hair in thin plaits looped around the crown of her head, leaving the rest of her hair tumbling down her back. She had been young. So young and innocent and swept off her feet by the attention bestowed upon her by a handsome boy with breeding who thought her accent—the accent she had worked so hard to lose—quaint and charming.

Billings shook his head as he looked at her. "You bewitched him, you know."

"I loved him," she whispered. As only a young heart could love. Blindly. Recklessly.

He snorted. "Stupid girl. Do you think he would have married you? You were a housemaid—"

"I was his sister's companion."

He shrugged. "A hired companion. Same thing." His lip curled. "A servant." He uttered that like it was a dirty thing.

She lifted her chin. "He proposed."

Billings sneered. "Well. A convenient allegation as he is dead."

Her throat thickened and she felt an echo of the old ache. Not since Robbie died and her mother and stepfather cast her out had she felt it.

She was still reeling from the news of Robbie's death when she picked herself up from the dirt where her stepfather had tossed her. Her mother had slipped just enough coin into Susanna's valise to pay for her travel across the sea to the mainland, and then on to Shropshire. Silent tears rolled down her cheeks as she watched the Isle of Man fade and disappear into the horizon. The tears had never been far from the surface as she traveled, thinking of her mother and how she had never spoken up for her daughter. She chose a man over Susanna.

Susanna had not digested the pain of losing Robbie before the blow of *that* occurred. The blow of losing her home, her mother. There was no distinguishing between the two. One pain bled into the next.

Billings continued drolly, "I suppose we will never really know if he would have married you."

"I suppose not," she admitted, beyond arguing the point.

She had been compromised. Ruined and everyone back home knew it. That was the truth of it. All that mattered anymore. What did Robbie's intentions matter now?

The only thing that had saved her—aside from her aunt, of course—was that no one here knew of her ruined status.

Except this wretch standing before her knew, and likely everyone here at Penning Hall would know soon, too. He would see to that. She was a fallen woman living among them. All this time, they had been taking orders from a fallen woman. She shuddered at the thought of that. Some would not care—those that truly liked and cared about her—but many would.

She lifted her chin and asked, "What are you going to do?"

Obviously he would tell the duke and then she would be on her way out—without references.

"What will I do?" he mused as he moved closer, his steps thudding as he advanced. "An interesting question. I could tell Penning, but that seems a quick end to the fun. Disappointing, that."

She studied him closely, and saw in his features what she had realized back then when she first met him. He was a horrible man.

"I don't want the fun to end," he finished. He was *more* than a horrible man. He was a beast who took delight in the discomfort of others.

"What do you want?" she shot back.

His smile deepened. "You."

*You.*

Her very skin reacted, contracting over her muscles and bones in physical revolt.

He continued, "I wanted you then, but Robbie had his hold on you and got beneath your skirts before I had a chance."

She scoffed. "There was no chance of you *ever* getting beneath my skirts. Not then. Not now."

"Bold words." His hand moved down to grope his manhood as he leered at her. "I used to imagine tupping you. I knew Robbie was . . . and I wanted a taste, too."

"You are disgusting."

How could Robbie have called this man friend?

The two were nothing alike. And how was it one was cursed with an early death whilst the other still lived and prospered?

"I can keep your secret," he whispered, reaching a hand to touch her that she narrowly dodged. "As long as you're nice to me, Penning need never know precisely what kind of woman you are."

*Nice to me.* She understood his meaning.

"Go ahead. Tell him." It felt good to say the words. And frightening. Penning was looking for a reason to sack her. This was it. Billings would give him that reason. He could not have a ruined woman in his household.

He chuckled. "So bold. So defiant. Such fire. I like it. I like it very much." His smile faded. "But you don't mean it."

Perhaps not, but she knew she would not give him what he wanted. She could not give herself to him. She would accept her fate, whatever it may be—but not him. She would never accept him.

Sounds stirred from one of the rooms nearby. Someone was awake. Her gaze darted to the side nervously, hoping someone did not emerge from one of those doors to catch them talking.

"I'll give you some time. Let you think on it. I'll be here a week, after all." He turned, moving down the corridor toward the door leading out of the servants' wing. Pausing, he looked back.

"I won't wait forever, however. My patience *will* come to an end."

She knew he meant what he said. It was no bluff. He would go to Penning. Eventually.

Her choices were few. Wait for Billings to tell Penning. Tell Penning herself. Or resign from her position and leave before either happened.

Altogether, it seemed Penning would have his way. Her time was coming to an end here, and that made her feel a host of awful things—too many and too complicated to distinguish.

This place was her home. Her friends were here. *And Penning.*

She felt a little pang at the center of her chest knowing they would have no more of their exchanges. She would miss that look that came over his face when she entered the room. The dukes before him . . . they had not looked any particular way at all when she arrived in their midst. Only Penning reacted. Only his expression changed.

She would miss the way his chest lifted on a deep breath when their eyes met. She supposed it likely marked his distaste for her. Except last night he had talked to her as a person. It had almost felt friendly, companionable, as they sipped their whiskey. She would miss that.

She watched Billings slink away like the snake he was. The man had been bold enough to enter the servants' quarters in the predawn hours. She knew he would not stay away. There was nothing to keep him from finding her again—even if it was in the middle of the night. She would not be safe as long as they slept beneath the same roof.

For the next week she would sleep with her desk pushed against her door and a knife under her pillow.

# Chapter Eighteen ❧

*T*he last thing Susanna ever thought she would be doing was acting the role of chaperone to the Duke of Penning and his prospective bride.

*This must be what hell is like.*

She could not have known the task of chaperoning would befall her even when Lady Philomena's maid fell ill. She had assumed the other maid in Lady Lippton's retinue would step forward to accompany them on their stroll through the parkland and for a picnic by the scenic lake.

Only Lady Lippton could not part with her maid for some reason—not even for her own daughter. Her rheumy-eyed gaze had landed on Susanna and she had declared *her* fit for the role.

*Take your housekeeper, Penning. She will see that you behave yourself with my darling gel.* The old dragon chortled, greatly amused with herself.

It had been a moment of wrong place at the wrong time for Susanna. If she had not been standing nearby at that moment . . . it could well have been a scullery maid Lady Lippton chose.

"M-me?" Susanna had stammered.

"Yes, you, gel." She assessed Susanna then as though seeing her for the first time. "Frightfully young to be a housekeeper, are you not?"

She opened her mouth, but before she had the chance to reply, the duke smoothly cut in. "Miss Lockhart is quite the doyen of housekeepers. And older than she looks."

Susanna ignored her ripple of pique over that.

"Och. Indeed?" Lady Lippton lifted her quizzing glass to look Susanna over again.

"There is naught she does not know about managing a household."

Heat stung her cheeks. Was the man actually praising her skills as a housekeeper?

Susanna attempted to spare herself. "I am certain I can find one of the maids to accompany Your Grace on his picnic—"

"No. You are here now and they are ready. Off with you now."

The older woman was clearly determined that Susanna not delay this picnic in order to leave and search for another maid to take her place.

Lady Miranda scowled from where she sat nearby, her needlepoint forgotten in her lap, clearly unhappy to be excluded. "I shall be happy to join—"

"Go on, now," Lady Lippton said loudly, almost shrilly, her shifty gaze shooting a quelling glance to the other young woman who was here as a rival to her daughter.

So here Susanna found herself, sitting several yards away whilst the Duke of Penning sat on a blanket with Lady Philomena.

The girl twirled a parasol, shielding her pale face from the feeble rays of sunlight.

It had been two days since the guests arrived. The day following the storm had dawned bright and cloudless, but it had still been too wet to go outdoors. The house party had remained inside. Guests toured the gallery—oohing and ahhing over an impressive collection featuring generations of artwork collected by a long line of Dukes of Penning.

They also ate. Breakfast. Tea. Luncheon. Dinner. Tea. Supper. She had long ago learned that the rich ate and drank copiously. This group was no different.

They entertained each other in various rooms: the drawing room, the conservatory and the salon. Servants wore the soles out on their shoes hastening back and forth, waiting on the duke's lofty guests. Various ladies sang and played the pianoforte and harpsichord. After dinner, they had engaged in a rather robust game of charades that even the servants, standing in the corners of the room, found entertaining. Not that they dared reveal their enjoyment. Their carefully trained stoic expressions did not crack.

Even Susanna had been amused. The Duke of Penning especially had a flair for the dramatic and she found him mesmerizing.

Her chest pinched at the sight of him with his easy smiles and ready laughs. He was a truly charming man. Handsome *and* amusing. He was going to have his pick of brides.

Susanna sat on a blanket of her own apart from them, squinting against the sunlight and watching them dine on tiny, perfect canapés prepared with great care by Cook and Emily and Rose. Cook's assistants had been trained well. Nothing less than superb emerged from the duke's kitchen. Susanna knew the repast was delicious because she had sampled it all earlier in the day.

She watched them covertly from her spot. It appeared that the duke had taken her *stupid* advice for he wielded his silken tongue to coax the lady from her shell with seeming ease.

The ground was *still* far too wet after the recent rain. Moisture penetrated her blanket. The chill seeped into her. Not that it appeared to be a problem for either the duke or his lady. The grooms had spread out two blankets for them at her direction, so she could fault no one save herself for her damp skirts.

Thankfully the picnic came to an end. Truthfully, she wished it had ended long ago. She had reached the limits of her tolerance the moment the duke fed the lady a plump strawberry. It was ghastly to sit there and observe the doting couple nibble food from each other's fingers. Lady Philomena had clearly emerged from her shell. In fact, Susanna would not mind if she crawled back inside it.

The grooms packed up the remnants of their picnic and the three of them ascended into the waiting landau. Susanna sat across from them, trying to enjoy the breeze on her face as she did her best to ignore their interactions and feign invisibility . . . as a proper chaperone would do. It was a miserable five minutes.

Lady Philomena sent the duke long, dewy-eyed glances reminiscent of a lovesick puppy dog. Susanna wanted to retch. She could not escape the carriage or their company soon enough.

Everyone was taking tea in the garden upon their return, as she expected they would be.

"Would you care to join the others in the garden?" Susanna asked the two of them, knowing the quicker she got rid of them, the sooner she would be able to steal a moment alone for herself.

Lady Philomena motioned to her frilly day dress, a confection of powder-blue ruffles that overwhelmed her slight frame. "I should like to freshen up in my chamber and change."

"But of course." Susanna motioned to a nearby maid. "Jill here will accompany you."

Lady Philomena's maid was still likely indisposed. Apparently travel did not agree with her and it took her some time to recover when they journeyed anywhere. Susanna had marveled why they would keep her on staff until she spotted Lady Philomena's elegantly turned-out hair this morning. Then she understood.

Apparently the girl excelled at that task. She was a marvel. Styling hair was where her talents centered. She would not shirk that duty. She clearly knew what made her indispensable.

As Lady Philomena was escorted away, Penning's eyes found Susanna. There they stayed. She offered him a wobbly smile. They had not seen as much of each other in the past two days. Carter was up and about again, and she had returned to her usual duties, free to do so at last.

"Thank you for joining us," the duke said, as though she had any choice in the matter, as though to serve him was *not* her role in life.

She snorted. She would hardly characterize

what she did today as *joining*. Joining sounded so . . . lovely. So optional.

"I chaperoned you and Lady Philomena." She let that simple statement of fact hang between them.

A smile twitched his lips. "Yes. You did and you showed admirable effort not looking bored."

She opened her mouth to deny that she was bored—that they had not been boring. No words emerged.

"Go on, now," he prompted, smiling. "Admit it."

"Very well." She blew out a breath. "The afternoon was . . . a *little* boring, but she is perfectly enamored of you. Congratulations. You must be very happy." Her smile was becoming harder and harder to maintain. "You will have no trouble persuading her to your suit." Obviously. They were already courting. That's what today was all about, after all.

Suddenly that hint of merriment was gone from him. She, too, could not summon a cheerful mien. She could only see him on that blanket with Lady Philomena and know that was his future.

It should not have affected her at all. She should not feel anything for the Duke of Penning or the prospect of his imminent marriage.

At any rate, she was not remaining here. She couldn't. Not with the threat of Billings hanging over her head. Now she was simply formulating her next move . . . her eventual departure from Penning Hall.

She dipped her head in deference. "If you will excuse me, I need to check on preparations for the evening."

She did not wait to hear his reply, if he even did.

She hastened away, her steps a flurry to reach a place she could compose herself, away from his eyes or the eyes of anyone else.

She did not flee to the kitchens, where she knew her attention was needed. Not yet. She would assuredly put in an appearance there. She simply needed a respite first.

Without looking back, she fled down the corridor toward the back stairs leading to the servants' wing.

She was almost there. The door loomed like a beacon ahead.

"Miss Lockhart," a voice called, stopping her retreat. She froze, dread filling her at the sound of that familiar voice. That *dreaded* familiar voice. She already knew it so well. She had thought—no, hoped—he would give her more time.

She turned slowly. "Mr. Billings."

"Miss Lockhart." He said her name with heavy emphasis. "You have been rather elusive of late. Where have you been all day?"

"I chaperoned the Lady Philomena on her picnic with the duke."

"Ah." He grinned then. Stroking his beard, he stepped forward and disclosed with a conspiratorial air, "That is rich, is it not? You, soiled dove that you are, serving as a chaperone." He clicked his tongue. "What would her mama say? Think you that old witch would forgive such an insult?"

Her stomach sank to her feet.

He continued amid her silence, "That would be quite the humiliation for the duke and his lovely sisters." A sudden look of exaggerated astonishment came over his face. "Oh, my dear Lady Lippton might disapprove of that, too. She is such a stickler for all that is correct and proper. Maintaining appearances is very important to her."

The threat was implicit. She felt the weight of it wholly, deeply, keenly. She sucked in a breath as it settled over her. If she stayed here, if she refused him, if he revealed the truth of her past . . . she would not be the only one to pay the price.

Up until now, she had only thought of herself— *her* pain, *her* shame, *her* loss.

Now she saw how others would be affected— the duke and his kind sisters. *The duke.*

Somehow he had come to matter. Her skin tightened with uncomfortable prickles. She could not do that to them. They did not deserve that. The matter of what she deserved was of no consequence.

"I see," she murmured, calculating her options: surrender to Billings's vile demands or simply pack her things and go. Disappear.

"Do you, now?" He stepped nearer, lifting his hand to her face. She flinched, but he kept coming at her. Instead of touching her face, he grasped a lock of hair that refused to be tamed, that refused to be captured with the rest of her hair at the nape of her neck. He rubbed the strands between his fingertips.

"You enjoy this," she stated flatly, all of her cold. So cold.

His pleasure was her torment. That, she realized, was the thing that motivated him. He was a man of position and wealth, betrothed to a very influential lady. He could have all the affairs he liked. Beautiful women. Willing women. He pursued her because it was a game to him. A wicked, perverse game in which he hunted, and she ran.

His hand released her hair then, his fingers dropping to brush along her jaw. "You must have a magic cunny."

She gasped and jerked back. "You pig."

"I'd like to find out for myself. I can make it worth your time."

"I am not for sale."

"Of course you are. You're in service. You know what it's like to earn a wage. What difference if you do it on your back?"

"I am no whore."

He snorted then. "I know exactly what you are. Everyone in Kennaughly knows."

He was not wrong about that.

"I am the Duke of Penning's housekeeper."

"Are you?" He sneered. "And how long do you think he will keep you on once he learns the truth of your past?"

Cold washed through her followed by a wave of hot mortification. She always knew it could happen. It finally had. Discovery was here.

"Please," she whispered.

"You have a good thing here." He nodded thoughtfully. "Such a shame to lose it."

"W-what do you want from me?" she asked desperately.

She hoped fervently, perhaps vainly, that he could look at her, see her, hear the appeal in her voice, and find his conscience.

"A night in your bed."

She swallowed against a bitter wash of misery. "I won't do that."

He lifted that tendril of hair again and replied casually, "Pity. Then I will ruin you."

She sucked in a breath and blinked eyes that suddenly stung.

His breath brushed her cheek as he continued, "Are you certain? You are no untried maid. No stranger to cock. What's the harm? You might even like it, eh?"

She closed her eyes in a pained blink. "You're an animal."

"No. I am not," he said mildly. "I am a guest of Penning, betrothed to be married to the very important and very grand Lady Harthorne—"

"And what would *she* think if she knew of your unseemly behavior?" she challenged, anger lighting a fire in her. "What would *she* think of your proposition?"

He looked down at her with disdain, his nostrils flaring. Clearly he did not care for her show of bravado. "She would think you not only a whore, but a *lying* whore."

She inhaled a ragged breath, her fire diminishing. Indeed, why would such a lady believe a word she said?

"Come, now," he coaxed in a seductive rasp. The remaining space between them vanished. He closed it, backing her into the wall of the corridor, invading her space with his body, and still she only felt cold. "What is one tumble in the sheets between old friends?"

He thought them *friends*?

"Begging your pardon? Am I interrupting?"

Susanna gasped and looked over Billings's shoulder.

Shameful heat burned her cheeks as her gaze landed on Penning, standing there with a tight expression on his face as he studied her with Billings. His blue eyes narrowed as he took them in. Clearly he was drawing his own erroneous conclusions regarding what he was witnessing.

Billings was slow to step back from her. His movements were almost languorous as he moved away, a faint, amused smile on his face.

"Not at all," he murmured easily. "I was just having a chat with your Miss Lockhart here. I wanted her advice on how to get out a soup stain off my jacket." He made a ridiculous show of brushing at an area on his jacket.

It was an absurd explanation. An obvious lie. They all three knew it, but from the glint in Billings's eyes he did not care about that.

The duke's gaze shifted to her, and the anger there felt like a blow. It was palpable. A crackling energy on the air.

"Indeed," Penning murmured, and the single word was strained, vibrating with tension.

"I am certain you can leave your jacket with Miss Lockhart and she will have it laundered and ready for you on the morrow."

"That would be brilliant." Billings then cheerfully removed his jacket with exaggerated movements. He handed it to her with a smile on his face. "There you go, my dear Miss Lockhart. Thank you."

She accepted the jacket with a stiff nod, folding it neatly over her arm. "I will see that it is returned to your chamber, Mr. Billings."

"Very good." With a cheerful smile, he turned and left them with a jaunt to his step, as though he were not a monster. A monster intent on destroying her.

# Chapter Nineteen ❧

$\mathcal{T}$he duke did not move. He remained where he was, staring down at Susanna with those probing blue eyes, searching her expression as though he could see into her soul.

She stared back, waiting, hoping he could not, in fact, see to the core of her and everything she hid there.

He looked away, granting her an unfettered view of his too-handsome profile as he took a bracing breath. Looking back at her, he demanded, "What are you doing?"

*I don't know. I don't . . . know.*

She didn't know what she was doing, and even worse: she did not know what she was *going* to do. It was a terrible feeling. This helplessness. This certainty that whatever she did, whatever move she made, would hurt. There would be pain. There would be loss.

She patted the jacket hanging over her arm. "Simply attending to my duties, Your Grace."

"Is that all?" He glanced down the corridor

to where Billings had disappeared, as though he could still see him there.

A maid appeared then, emerging around the corner and walking toward them carrying a stack of linens. She gave them both a polite nod. "Your Grace. Miss Lockhart. Good day," she greeted as she passed them and vanished through the door to the servants' wing.

"Good day, Alice," Susanna called after her.

The door clicked shut behind the girl, and they stared at one another once again.

"It felt like you were doing more than that," he accused.

*Doing more than that.*

She turned those words over in her mind.

He added, "Unless seeing to your duties means being especially accommodating to our male guests."

Hot indignation burned through her and she lifted her chin. "I've done nothing wrong."

*Except for loving and losing someone eleven years ago.*

That was her indefensible crime. How was it that a person like Billings thrived whilst her actions were so very unforgivable? Polite Society would condemn her and cast her out and yet he stood at the pinnacle.

The duke looked down at her, clearly unconvinced

of her assertion. Before she knew what was happening, he took hold of her arm and pulled her along.

Her smaller strides worked to keep up with his longer ones. "Where are we going?"

"Away from prying eyes."

He led her from the servants' wing to another corridor and then down a set of stairs. They passed a few doors before he opened one and ushered her inside.

She knew this house better than she knew the sparse spattering of freckles on her arm, but even this room was not often utilized. She could not recall the last time she had stepped inside. The late duchess had considered herself an aspiring artist and used it as a painting studio.

A long-neglected easel stood near the French doors, ready to take advantage of the available daylight. A worktable that had long since been cleaned and organized for the next fledgling artist sat next to it.

He uncurled his fingers from around her elbow, freeing her. She strode toward the French doors, her steps biting hard and angry into the floor.

She shot a quick glance down into the garden and the view of one of the fountains tucked rather furtively into an alcove of lemon trees.

Exhaling, she spun to face him and motioned around her. "This feels a little dramatic, Your Grace."

"I did not think you would wish for anyone to overhear what I have to say to you."

Her jaw clenched. That meant only one thing. He was about to say something she didn't like. *Very well.* Something *else* she did not like.

Her hands curled into fists on either side of her, bracing for the dressing-down that was to come. It could not be worse than what she had already endured today. He was no Billings.

"Very well. Say what you will, Your Grace."

"I'm aware that you are a young woman with certain qualities . . ."

"Qualities?" she demanded, certain he did not mean that to be a compliment. The cad!

"You are young and attractive with a lively wit, Miss Lockhart, but I expect you to conduct yourself with more restraint while you are employed here."

He thought her attractive? She knew that should not be the one thing she heard, but her thoughts stalled there for a moment before she gave herself a nudge.

"Restraint?" she said slowly, shaking her head, attempting to understand . . . and then suddenly she did. And she was horrified. "You think I was . . . that he and I . . ." She waved a finger between herself and an imaginary Billings. A bitter laugh bubbled in her throat at the absolute absurdity of her willingly entangled with that vile man.

The duke arched a dark eyebrow, his face impassive, supercilious. His anger was gone. Back was the cold nobleman who had questioned her—when he was not eschewing her presence. He was once again the arrogant jackanapes who thought she should begin looking for another *situation*. "You looked quite cozy—"

"Things are not what they always look like, though, are they?" she retorted.

"Are they not?"

"I do not owe you . . ." She stopped abruptly. She was on the verge of telling him that she did not owe him an explanation, but she did. He was the Duke of Penning . . . *and* her employer. She owed him . . . everything, *all*. By the very nature of his position and hers, he had a right to question her and receive answers.

She wanted to vent her spleen on him then, but she knew she could not do that. Instead, she crossed her arms, hugging herself tightly. "I can assure you that I was not being *cozy* with Mr. Billings."

He did not appear convinced. "I have had my misgivings that you are suited to this role—"

"As you have expressed," she snapped. "Time and time again. Perhaps your guests should be treated to more discernment."

He blinked at that. "My guests?"

She knew it was a ridiculous suggestion but she could not help herself. She was furious. Furious at being bullied by Billings and furious at now being harassed by Penning and treated as though she were the one who had blundered.

"Yes, rather than treating *me* to this *indictment*—"

"Are you saying Billings overstepped?" A muscle feathered in his jaw.

She compressed her lips in mute frustration. *No.* She was not saying that because she could not. The duke taking issue with Billings was the last thing she needed. It would only make a greater mess of things. Penning was many things but not a man to tolerate the abuse of a woman under his care. Even if that woman was his housekeeper. Even if that man was a gentleman guest. He'd go after Billings and where would that get her except exposed and ruined?

"Make yourself clear, Miss Lockhart. Was Billings subjecting you to unwelcome advances?" His blue eyes burned into her. "It is a simple question."

There was nothing simple about it. About any of this.

With a tormented whimper, she spun around to gaze down at the garden. Susanna had to. She could not look at his face one more moment lest she say or do something she should not—something she could not take back.

"Miss Lockhart?" He spoke to her back.

She inhaled, striving for her composure. She could not remain standing here with her back to him, ignoring him as she gazed down at the empty garden—

Only no longer empty.

A couple glided into the little alcove, strolling past the lemon trees and taking a seat at the bench beside the burbling fountain.

Miss Mattie. *Mattie.* In the company of Mr. Carter.

It was a curious sight, observing the two of them together in broad daylight. Out of doors. Almost as though they were a couple stepping out together . . . in a romantic fashion.

No one was around. Not a chaperone in sight. Oh, and there was the not-so-insignificant matter that Mr. Carter was in service whilst Mattie was sister to a duke.

The girl was turned out smartly, of course. Fair hair arranged in soft curls around her face. Her day dress of pale peach appeared soft, too. Altogether she was alluring: a sweet, tender-cheeked young woman. A very compelling package of femininity. Any of the suitors the Duke of Penning had assembled should be delighted to be in her favor, to court her, to walk the gardens with her.

So why was she sitting in the garden with Mr. Carter? Sitting rather closely beside him? They appeared quite cozy—to use that dreadful word the duke had laid at her feet.

Then they were moving, coming together so quickly she could scarcely believe her eyes.

One moment they were sitting comfortable as two peas in a pod, the next they were kissing. Kissing quite passionately.

Astonishment washed over her, followed quickly by consternation. Blasted fools. Yes, she had rather suspected something might be developing between them, but *witnessing* the evidence in this manner was quite another thing. Mattie's brother would not approve. Penning had big plans for Mattie. A dalliance with his valet was not one of them.

She had suspected she would be the one to get sacked. With good reason. The duke had intimated at it enough, if not stated directly. The irony was that Carter, however, was most valued, most appreciated. Even Susanna could not resent him for that. He was a good and honorable man. Indispensable. She could not imagine him taking advantage of Mattie.

Mattie appeared quite enthused as she kissed Carter. Susanna felt a bit of a voyeur spying on their private assignation.

Then Penning spoke. "Miss Lockhart? Are you ignoring me or is there something of interest outside?"

She jerked.

Gasping, she whirled around. He was drawing closer, his gaze lifting from her face to peer over her shoulder. A step closer and he would have the shock of his life.

That could not happen.

She had to stall . . . had to keep him from looking, from catching Carter with his sister.

Through whatever means necessary.

She reacted, lurching forward and flattening both palms on his chest—his impossibly broad, unyielding chest. She held him back from coming any closer. Perhaps she even gave a little push, keeping him from advancing and discovering his sister in the arms of his valet. It seemed the only choice.

His eyes flared, looking down at her hands on his chest and then back up to her.

"What are you . . ." He inhaled deeply as though he needed a swift intake of oxygen, as though her hands stung him.

He lifted his chin slightly, appearing to move

his gaze past her, and she panicked. No no no no. Before his gaze could stray and he looked beyond her to the garden and the pair of lovers locked in an embrace below, she reacted. She reacted *again*.

They could not kiss forever, could they? Eventually they would stop. Eventually they would need to come up for air. She need only distract the duke until they did. Just a small distraction. A few moments.

She would kiss him.

The thought landed in Susanna's mind as the only alternative. Standing on her tiptoes, she lifted her hands and seized his face. Forcefully holding him between her palms, she pressed her lips to his, a desperate little mewl escaping her.

*God, he tastes good.*

She gave herself an internal slap for that, vowing to deliver it in person to herself later. This was not about her pleasure.

He was immovable. A motionless slab. Her fingers pressed firmly into his face as she stretched higher on her toes. The man was so blasted tall. He could help out by kissing her back. By bending toward her even the slightest.

He did not. He was not helping her out in this endeavor. He was not responding. It was rather mortifying and yet she could not stop now. Not yet. Not so soon. She needed to give Mattie and Carter more time. She was not certain how much time, but she knew every moment was of value to them . . . every moment she kissed Penning a necessary sacrifice.

A sacrifice she was determined to make.

# Chapter Twenty ❧

*O*nce, as a lad, he had witnessed an explosion of fireworks over the Thames, the lights in the sky reflected in the inky water. He had stood beside his father in solemn awe, his mouth agape, never having seen the like.

This was like that.

A sudden explosion of light and color in the dark canvas of night that left him in equal awe. Susanna Lockhart kissing him felt as intense and astonishing as all that.

He felt it viscerally. Deep pleasure suffused his gut, spreading throughout him, creeping into the very marrow of his bones. The wonder of it overcame him, made it impossible to move.

She tasted of the tart lemonade they drank at lunch. She had not sat with them, but Lucian had watched her covertly, achingly aware of her every move as she sipped from a glass of lemonade one of the footmen discreetly provided for her.

He had never been so achingly aware of one woman, his physical being longing for her heightened whilst he devoted his attentions to another. It had been a true test of his will and focus.

He had been able to deny himself, to resist her . . . because she had never made a single advance, a single overture. She had only ever presented herself as a proper housekeeper.

Even when she barged into his room whilst he was at his bath, she had conducted herself as the consummate professional. She might have flushed scarlet at his nudity, but there had been no reaction beyond that. It was an easy matter to resist someone who held herself apart from him.

But now she was kissing him. What was he supposed to do with that?

Lucian battled against the urge to kiss her back. He forced his lips to hold still beneath her artless ministrations. Artless but no less affecting. Her soft mouth moved over his coaxingly and he thought he felt himself slipping, his grip on restraint loosening . . .

Never would he have expected for her to put her lips on his.

*He* had thought it, of course. Or rather he had *fought* thinking about it. But now it was happening.

Her smaller hands on his face, slim fingers pressing into his cheeks, felt almost more intimate than what her mouth was doing.

And he wanted more.

He was finished. Done. No more fighting.

His hands moved, slipping around her waist to palm her back, pulling her into him at the same time he bent down and dove into the kiss.

He came alive, his mouth opening to taste her.

"Your Grace," she gasped, and he used the opportunity. His tongue swept inside, stroking her slick tongue with his own.

"Lucian," he growled, needing to hear her say it. Needing to be Lucian to her and not Penning, not the duke, not her employer, not some blue blood even he did not like. And he needed her to like him. That in itself was an astonishing thing. He didn't just want her. He *liked* her and he wanted her to like him back.

"Lucian," she returned, and at the first throaty sound of his name on her lips his cock went hard.

She sighed into his mouth, her tongue tentative under his, but her body felt warm and soft and pliant and fully his.

Wrapping his hands around her waist, he lifted her. She released a little yelp into his mouth, her hands flying to his shoulders for balance as he plopped her on the nearby table. Several of the paint and brush jars rattled, but he didn't care. Didn't even spare them a glance. They could have crashed to the floor into a thousand shards and he would not have cared right then.

He continued kissing her, and she kissed him back.

He slid his hands along her cheeks, marveling at her soft skin. He'd touched many a woman, but he would wager no one had skin as soft and perfect as hers. He realized with a jolt that he'd never done this. Never held a lover so tenderly, so desperately by the face—and had never been held likewise in turn.

It was a strange thing to find there was something he had not done with a lover. It felt special. The kind of thing he had not expected to experience . . . especially not with his prickly housekeeper.

His fingers delved into the luxurious mass pinned so very neatly atop her head. He had longed to touch those burnished strands. He longed even more to tug the hair free of its pins and watch the mass fall unbound over her shoulders.

He knew he should not. He knew she could not be seen in the halls of the house with her hair all a-tumble, but he did not give a bloody damn. He had been about restraint for so long now. Especially when it came to her. She had quite undone him. It was as though an avalanche had begun and it could not be stopped.

No force on earth would stop it—or him.

He dragged his mouth away to look down at her, to appreciate the flush of her upturned face. She was panting, her eyes half-mast. So lovely. He was lost, but from the look of her, so was she. He rubbed his thumb over her kiss-bruised mouth, still wet from their tasting of each other.

She released a slow moan, leaning into him. A full-body lean. She wasn't as tall or as broad as he was, but he felt her everywhere. Every inch of him vibrated with the sensation of her sinking fully into him.

His gaze moved over her, imprinting the visage of her like this, in this moment, not realizing until now how badly he had wanted to see her this way. Unfettered and wild and real. Her authentic self. This was Susanna Lockhart stripped down to her core. The one just below the surface.

He'd been denying himself this—*her*—anyone, really . . . but no more.

His hands flexed in her hair, rubbing her scalp—earning another moan. He learned even that about her—the sensation and texture of her head in his hands.

"Your hands are magic," she murmured, looking at him with eyes that had suddenly fogged over with pleasure.

He lowered his head to take her mouth in a kiss again, but a flash of movement caught his attention—something to his left, just outside in the garden. He glanced sharply, quickly, out the window, not about to be distracted long from this most delightful task, but then he froze.

He didn't blink as he stared.

At first he thought it only two lovers locked in an embrace, likely two guests of his house party who had crept away for a tryst in the garden as they were wont to do. But they were not guests. Indeed not.

It felt as though time paused and held still as he took in his sister. Absorbed her attired in the familiar peach dress he had seen her wearing over breakfast. That was where the familiarity ended, however. The girl amorously attached to the man in the garden did not bear resemblance to the sister he knew. And yet it was.

It was Mattie. And the gentleman she was kissing . . . no. Correction. The *man*, for he was no gentleman at all, was Carter. His valet. His bloody valet had not only his lips on Lucian's little sister, but his hands, too. One hand clutched at the bodice of his sister's gown, boldly cupping her breast through the fabric.

Red filled his vision. He backed from the table and advanced on the window with a growl as though he would break through the glass, forgetting his own desires in that moment as he banged a fist against the window.

The couple jumped apart, looking up at him with twin expressions of horror.

"Lucian!" Susanna arrived swiftly at his side.

He did not spare her a glance. He was too busy glaring at Mattie and Carter. "Do you see this?" He motioned to them. "Do you see them?"

He did not await her reply.

He gestured for his sister and Carter to stay put and then swung around, stalking from the studio.

"Lucian! Your Grace!"

He heard Susanna call after him, but he did not stop. He took the servants' stairs. There would be no running into any guests that way. Susanna's steps sounded behind him. He did not mind that she was following. It was of some comfort, actually. She was a reasonable woman. Loyal and discreet. She would be a calming influence when calm was the last thing he felt right now.

He'd trusted Carter and he'd gone behind his back and defiled his sister. The hot sting of betrayal climbed up his throat. His hands opened and flexed at his sides.

"Your Grace, please . . . wait."

He could not wait. Not even for Susanna.

He burst out the back door into the gardens. His legs worked furiously, just short of a run as his boots pounded down the paved path, intent on stopping them and punishing the villain he had trusted.

# Chapter Twenty-One ❦

*H*e found them precisely where he had seen them, waiting for him, both looking somehow terrified and grim. Accepting of their fate.

In truth, his sister appeared terrified *and* shamefaced, wringing her hands in front of her. As she should. Carter, however, did not.

His soon-to-be-former valet stood straight as a soldier facing a firing squad, which Lucian decided was rather apt. But there was also a certain amount of dignity in his bearing. Pride. As though he were not entirely ashamed of his conduct, and that only stoked the flames of Lucian's temper. He closed the distance separating them.

"Your Grace, no!" Susanna cried breathlessly from behind him just as his fingers closed around Carter's perfectly arranged cravat. He was a valet. He always looked perfectly tidy, damn him.

Lucian's fist shot out, connecting with Carter's face with a satisfying *thunk*. The man went down like a heap of bricks.

Mattie screamed.

Susanna jerked to a stop beside him. "What have you done?"

Without awaiting his response, she dropped to the ground beside Mattie, helping his valet to his feet.

"You're a bully, Lucian!" Mattie cried, glaring at him. "Might you hear what we have to say first?"

"There is nothing you can say that will make me regret flattening him out." He stabbed a finger at Carter. "In fact, I would quite enjoy doing that again. The man deserves it." He moved forward to put his hands on Carter again and Susanna stepped in his path, gripping his arms to hold him back.

"You're a beast," Mattie pronounced, on the verge of tears—a circumstance he blamed entirely on Carter.

"Your Grace." Carter managed to look dignified, even with his bleeding lip. "I understand the way this looks, but I love your sister and I wish to marry her."

"Of course you do," Lucian snarled. "And her hefty dowry."

Carter had the gall to look indignant. "I don't want her money. I would love her without it."

Mattie made a little sound of delight as she offered Carter her handkerchief. She shot Lucian a smug look.

Lucian snorted and rolled his eyes.

Carter accepted the linen Mattie pressed on him. "Thank you, my love," he murmured, dabbing it at his lip.

At that familiar endearment, Lucian lunged forward another step. Susanna tightened her grip and held fast to him, thwarting him from reaching Carter again—unless he wished to pick her up and bodily remove her, but he would not do that. He would not turn his aggression on her. It would stay rightly where it deserved to be—fixed on Carter.

He nodded to the blackguard over Susanna's head. "You're finished. Leave. Go. Today."

"Lucian!" his sister cried, splotches of hot color breaking out over her face. "No! You cannot do this."

"Your Grace, please. Let's not be hasty." Susanna squeezed his arm.

"I'm not being hasty. He's lucky I don't call him out—"

"I'll go pack my things," Carter replied, nodding with grim acceptance.

"No!" Now the tears were springing from his sister's eyes. She flung herself into Carter's arms. "Please, don't go." The bastard stroked the back of her head like she was some manner of pet—as though he truly loved her.

"Mattie," Lucian chided.

She glared at Lucian. "I knew you wouldn't understand—"

"Understand how he's taken advantage of you? I very much understand that."

"No! I love Carter. And he loves me, but you would not understand that. You know nothing of love because you're heartless. You've never loved anyone! You wouldn't know how to."

Her accusation stung more than it should. She was upset, angry. Carter had twisted her heart and her head. "Mattie, you're so young. You don't mean—"

"Stop! Do you even hear yourself? I'm not so young you won't marry me off to one of the swells you invited here!"

He winced. There was truth enough in that.

She continued, "I'm old enough to know what I want. I don't want you deciding my life for me anymore . . . I want Carter. And he wants me."

*Decide her life?* Was that what he was doing? He supposed he was. Of course he was. But then he had always done that. Someone had to make decisions when their father died and it became clear their mother no longer could. Lucian had decided everything. That had been his burden.

A burden that led him into taking off his clothes and climbing into bed with a woman whose name he had just learned. And then a dozen more after her. Just so he could feed his mother and sisters. And move them into a nice home. And pay for a governess to educate Mattie and Evie. He never stole. He never hurt anyone. But he made the decisions for them. Was he supposed to simply stop doing that now?

"Mattie." Carter reached for her hand and brought it to his lips for a tender farewell kiss that clenched Lucian's heart. The heart his sister claimed he did not possess. "I will go."

"No!" She clung fast to Carter's hand. "Don't leave me."

Susanna was talking then. Lucian blinked, focusing on her face before him. "Perhaps we can all just take a day and talk about this tomorrow after emotions have cooled?"

Lucian shook his head. "No."

Carter disentangled himself from Mattie's hold. He gave her hand a final pat. "I love you. Remember that."

"Carter!" Mattie's face crumpled as he turned and quickly strode from the gardens. She watched him until he disappeared from sight and then she turned savagely on Lucian. "You've done this. This is your fault. You could not even consider me with Carter . . . not even for one moment." She shook her head. "Why is it so difficult to believe that I might feel something genuine for Carter . . .

and he for me?" She waved a hand at Susanna. "I see the way you look at *her*!"

He stiffened and opened his mouth to deny that, but he could not summon a denial. Not after he'd just thoroughly kissed Susanna.

Mattie continued in a wild barrage of words, "You might be content to limit yourself to looking at her and wanting her . . . but that is not me—"

"Miss Mattie," Susanna interjected, "it is not at all like—"

"I want Carter. He wants me. He's a good man. He makes me feel good . . . lighter inside. I will *have* him." Mattie ignored Susanna entirely. "Unlike you, I'll not marry some insipid blue-blooded prig for whom I feel nothing. I won't. I won't, Lucian!" With a choked sob, she turned and fled, leaving him alone in the garden with Susanna, her shrill words reverberating on the air.

After several moments, he dragged a hand through his hair. "Bloody hell. That didn't go . . . well."

Susanna blew out a heavy breath. "No. It did not, but it went as well as I expected."

He remained there, feeling trapped, stranded in the rubble. Standing shoulder to shoulder with Susanna, he stared after his retreating sister.

He'd never fought with either Mattie or Evie beyond the petty quarrel, but this . . . this had been painful.

*As well as I expected.*

He blinked, canting his head. "What do you mean?" He rotated on his heels to fully face her.

Her eyes went wide. "W-what? Nothing."

"You said that went as well as you expected." He shook his head. "Did you know about this? About them?"

He waited, watching her, expecting clarification because certainly he was mistaken. There was no way she would have kept something like this from him. No way she would have condoned Carter trifling with his sister.

"I did not *know* . . ." Her voice faded and she looked away from him.

"Susanna," he pressed.

"I . . . knew they liked each other. I had no idea they were anything more than friends." She shook her head.

"The relationship gave you pause, though," he finished tightly.

She winced. "Perhaps."

"Perhaps," he echoed grimly. "*Perhaps* you should have brought your concerns to me. She is my sister, after all."

She nodded. "I erred. When I saw them kissing—"

"Just now?" he cut in. "When *I* saw them? Or before?"

The color rode high in her cheeks and he knew there was more than what she was saying. She twisted her fingers together. "I saw them kissing from the window, too . . ."

He angled his head, listening to what she was saying—and not saying. Her wide eyes were so guileless. She had trouble holding his gaze. She could not lie to save her life. He supposed that was a good trait and made her a decent person. Except that meant she had something to lie about, to keep from him.

Then he understood. "You noticed them before I spotted them?" he demanded.

She nodded jerkily. "I noticed them before you did."

"Ah." He nodded slowly, drawing in a ragged breath that felt like a sharp rock going down. "And that is why you kissed me?"

The question hung in the air between them, swinging like a great pendulum, slicing its way toward him. He repeated the question. "*That* is why you kissed me?"

The kiss that had been so unexpected and un-provoked suddenly made more sense. He had thought she'd been overcome with desire for him.

He thought she wanted him, but he had been wrong. She had only wanted to distract him.

The look on her face confirmed it. The blood drained from her countenance. There, in the afternoon light, her skin turned white as milk. She wasn't denying it, and he felt a fool. The truth stung. He should have known better. He'd been with plenty of women for reasons that had nothing to do with love or desire. Distraction was as good a reason as any. It shouldn't sting, but it did.

That kiss had felt real to him. It had made him feel something. Something for *her.* Something more than desire.

The moment she had kissed him he had permitted himself to bend, to feel, to thaw . . .

Her betrayal cut deep. Deeper even than the betrayal he'd felt at seeing Carter with his sister. And yet Carter he had sacked.

With that thought taking hold, simmering alongside his many turbulent emotions, he said, "Perhaps, like Carter, you should pack your things, too."

# Chapter Twenty-Two ❧

$S$usanna sucked in a hissing breath. *Pack your things.* He had said those words. He had sacked her.

"Your Grace?" She let the question in her voice hover between them.

"You heard me."

Indeed, she had. She only wished she had not.

He was sacking her. There would be no waiting until the house party came to an end. It was happening now.

She nodded. "Indeed. I will go, then." All at once she felt as though she were moving underwater, her motions sluggish.

She'd already accepted her time here was at an end. Or rather she had been in the process of accepting it. It was not an easy thing. Eleven years was a long time to devote to any place. She had come here as a broken girl. She was no longer that. No longer heartsick over the loss of her mother and Robbie. No longer suffering from the final rejection of a stepfather who never wanted her and resented her existence.

Now she would be leaving . . . heartsick in an entirely different way.

Leaving this place was her fate. Billings had left her with little choice. She knew that. She had only been struggling with the details of it—the way in which it would happen. Now that had been handled for her. She had offended the duke beyond repair. More than offended. The austere, unflappable duke appeared almost . . . hurt.

Of course, that could not be right. She did not have the power to bring him down.

"Might I suggest Miss Barrow take over for me until you find a permanent replacement? I realize she is Miss Mattie's lady's maid, but someone else can step into that role. Barrow will know what to do and see that the remainder of your house party goes smoothly." The calm of her voice, the composure she conveyed, relieved her.

He stared at her with those intense eyes of his— the blue that appeared almost black, especially in this fraught moment.

"How far would you have gone, Miss Lockhart?" His eyes burned as they raked her scathingly and she simultaneously shriveled beneath his regard *and* went up in flames. "If I hadn't spotted Carter with my sister? Hmm? Would you have allowed me beneath your skirts? Would you have let me take you right there on the table?"

"No!" she hotly denied, but who was to say what would have happened. The kiss may have begun as a distraction but it had turned into something very real. Something that, even now, melted her insides.

It was vastly unfair how he could ignite her when his words were full of contempt. His fulminating glare should inject ice into her veins.

His nostrils flared and his chest lifted high on a breath, and the only thing she could focus upon right then was how he made her weak-kneed and feverish. She recalled the taste of him. It wasn't right and she was not certain what it said about her.

She opened her mouth and closed it, uncertain what more should be said—what *could* be said. He would not understand that she had only been trying to help. She would have gone to Mattie and persuaded her to confess all to her brother in a much less incendiary situation. In a perfect world, that would have happened.

Perhaps then the subsequent ugly scene could have been avoided. One look at his hard expression and she knew he was not interested in her excuses, though, and she better than anyone knew the world was far from perfect.

She could only say one thing. "I'm sorry."

His uncompromising gaze said how little he thought of her apology.

Turning, she fled through the garden, wondering if she appeared as wild and heartbroken as his sister had looked.

SUSANNA FOUND MATTIE in her chamber with her sister. The two of them were fiery-cheeked and deep in conversation when she knocked once and entered the room.

"Susanna," Mattie said evenly. "Thank you for earlier. I know you did your best to calm my brother and reason with him . . . for the little good it did."

"It was no trouble," she assured her, even though that was colossally untrue. It had resulted in a great deal of trouble for her if her imminent departure from Penning Hall was any indication. "But I've come to . . ." Her voice faded, a thick lump forming in her throat that was as surprising as it was unexpected. She had not thought bidding farewell would be such an emotional task. She pushed back the swell of emotion and took a deep breath. "I've come to say good-bye."

"Good-bye?" the girls echoed in unison, surging toward her. Evie reached her first, grabbing both of Susanna's hands in hers. "You're . . . leaving?"

"Yes." She nodded. "Don't distress yourself. I will be fine."

"You can't leave," Evie declared in clear distress.

Susanna gave a small smile and lifted one shoulder in a shrug. "I have to."

Mattie narrowed her eyes. "Why?"

Susanna opened her mouth, but hesitated.

"Is it because of Lucian?" Mattie pressed.

Susanna sighed and admitted, "He would like me to leave, yes."

Mattie laughed once at that—a hard, rough sound. "No. No, he doesn't." She shook her head with conviction. "I promise you . . . if you do that he will be a real bear. More than he already is." Mattie and Evie frowned and looked at each other grimly. Then, to Susanna: "You can't go. You can't do that to us."

Susanna frowned. "He really does want me gone, and I really must go."

Mattie blew out a breath. "Is this because of me and Carter? Does he blame you for that?" She shook her head as though that was the most absurd thing she had ever heard.

Susanna was not about to get into the particulars of what happened between them. It was personal, and that might be the entire crux of the matter. Things between Susanna and the duke were personal. They were personal and they should not be.

"He's such an ogre," Mattie continued. "You can't let him bully you in this." She pointed to her chest. "I'm not letting him bully me. When this is all done, I *will* be with Carter, and Lucian will realize he was being difficult for naught."

Susanna hoped she was right. She hoped Mattie and Carter found a way to be together that did not destroy their relationship with Penning.

"Your brother aside, it is for the best that I go," she said. Whether she felt that way or not, it was the thing she ought to say. She didn't want to make things worse between Mattie and Penning. They were already at odds. She didn't want Mattie angry at Penning because of her. She didn't want to be the reason for their differences. And there was Billings. Unfortunately, he was not going away.

"That is not fair. You cannot leave. We need you." Evie squeezed Susanna's hand and bounced them on the air. "Penning Hall needs you."

"The staff is well trained. I won't even be missed."

"You will be *sorely* missed," Mattie disagreed.

"This is not happening. You cannot go. *Where* would you even go?" Evie shook her head.

"I have someplace to go."

"Lucian does not want you to go."

Susanna winced. "There is no mistake. He did not mince words. Do not fret yourself, though. I will be well."

Evie waved a hand "Pfft. He doesn't know what he wants."

Susanna smiled. "But you two do?"

They nodded, sharing a look again. "Yes. We do."

Susanna had a flash of Billings's face then. *As long as you're nice to me, Penning need never know precisely what kind of woman you are.*

Susanna took a fortifying breath. "I think it is time for me to start fresh someplace else."

"Rubbish." The sisters looked at each other again. "You do not want to go. And neither does our brother want you to go. He wants . . . *you.* He just doesn't know it yet." Mattie crossed her arms in quite a determined manner. "Just as he does not realize that Carter and I belong together. But he will."

Susanna needed a moment to digest that. Was it really so obvious to the onlooker that she and Penning were something . . . *beyond* employer and servant? That was problematic and concerning. She was a housekeeper. Not a mistress or a female on staff to be the lord of the manor's plaything.

Once she had been seduced. When she was young and did not know any better. Now she knew better.

Mattie continued, "He thinks I will relent and do as he says and marry one of Lady Harthorne's sons. I will not. I will marry Carter or no one. Carter will wait for me." She nodded resolutely. "We can both be patient." She wagged a finger at Susanna. "And you must be patient, too. Lucian will come around."

She blinked. *Come around?* Did the girl not know her brother?

"I am afraid you're seeing what is not there. The duke and I . . . we are not like you and Carter."

"Perhaps not yet," Evie piped in. "But we've watched you together ever since we arrived at Penning Hall and it is obvious to—"

"I just went on a picnic with your brother and Lady Philomena," Susanna cut in. "I was their chaperone—"

Evie giggled. "Chaperone? You?"

Mattie rolled her eyes. "That must have been a misery."

"It was fine," she lied, "and I am certain there will be an announcement forthcoming."

Evie shook her head, her lips pursed mulishly.

"He won't marry her. Mark my words," Mattie insisted.

"You girls"—Susanna shook her head in disbelief—"are woefully mistaken."

"No, we're not. He feels something for you and

the quicker you get him to admit his feelings for you the better. Then he will understand how I feel about Carter and he won't stand in our way."

"*This* is your plan?" Susanna didn't know whether to laugh or cry.

Mattie nodded.

Evie gave Susanna's hands another encouraging squeeze. "It's not a bad plan."

"It's a terrible plan," she countered. "It won't work." She looked down at their clasped hands before disengaging. Stepping back, she smiled regretfully to both of them. "I hope things work out for you and Carter, Mattie. And Evie . . . I wish only happiness for you, too. You girls both deserve that. Now . . . I have to go pack." In a rare display of affection, she pressed a quick kiss to both their cheeks and left them.

# Chapter Twenty-Three ❦

*You should pack your things, too.*

The moment the words had left him, Lucian wished he could take them back. He wished he could snatch them from the air with both hands and stuff them into his mouth.

He didn't mean it. He didn't want her to go. He felt no satisfaction.

He might have wanted to get rid of her in the beginning. But it was too late for that now. Now, after the kiss, he knew.

He was keeping her.

He'd been so furious . . . at Mattie, at Carter. Obviously at Susanna, too. She'd tricked him. Used her attractiveness, used his desire for her . . . and manipulated him. He realized now, however, she might have taken the brunt of his temper.

He was still angry, but not enough to cast her from his life.

He finished changing his clothes. Without Carter. His valet should be gone by now. Lucian tugged at the sleeves of his jacket as he assessed himself before his dressing mirror. His cravat was . . . fine. Not arranged to the perfection Carter would achieve, but he did not have time for anything else. He had guests—bloody hell—but first he needed to stop by Susanna's room and stop her from packing, as she was undoubtedly doing. The ever-efficient Miss Lockhart would not waste any time. He could not expect her to linger.

A knock that could only be described as anxious sounded at his door. He bade enter and Evie burst into his chamber.

"Lucian!"

He arched an eyebrow.

Her anxious expression might have given him alarm if he did not well know that his youngest sister was given to histrionics that were rarely ever significant.

"Evie," he returned.

She clamped her hand on his arm in a surprisingly viselike grip. "You must come!" She tugged him toward the door.

"Come . . . where?"

"It's Mattie."

He felt the first prickle of misgiving. "What about her?"

"She's with Carter—"

His misgiving erupted. "Bloody hell! Where?"

"They're in the wine cellar."

*The wine cellar?* That was spectacularly worse

than the garden. Or *better*, depending on one's perspective. It was much more private. He could well imagine the kinds of trouble Mattie was getting into at that very private location. His mind shied away from the thoughts and images of his sister engaged in intimacies with his valet. *Former* valet. There were certain things a brother should never consider.

The general staff were not permitted into the wine cellar. Only a few of the upper servants even had the keys. Carter or Mattie must have filched a key. He would get to the bottom of it. After he thrashed Carter to within an inch of his life.

He stormed past Evie and out of his room. He passed Lady Harthorne's twins on the stairs, grunting in response to their greetings. He should thrash those lads, too. They were supposed to be here to woo his sisters, a task they were failing at abysmally considering Mattie was even now—potentially—trysting with his valet.

He winced and broke into a run.

"Lucian!" Evie called distantly after him, but he did not slow. He did not wait. He did not stop until he passed through the kitchen and descended the steps that led to the cellar. The moment he arrived at its door, he realized he did not possess the key, but that did not matter. He tried the latch and it swung open easily.

He stepped inside the murky space. A small, narrow window positioned high on one of the walls allowed a feeble amount of early evening light into the room, filtering among the racks and barrels.

"Mattie?" He stalked deeper into the cellar, peering into the shadows, his shoes biting hard on the floor.

Silence met him.

"Mathilda?" he demanded, whirling around. Was she hiding from him? With a growl, he called out, "Carter? Bloody hell, show yourself!"

Suddenly the door released a long creak and then thudded shut.

Spinning around, he glared at it a moment before advancing on it. He closed his hand around the latch and—nothing. It would not turn. He rattled it again with no luck.

He slapped the flat of his palm against the door several times. "Hello? Mattie?" Then he recalled that Evie had just been behind him. "Evie!"

He thought he heard whispers. "Who is out there? Girls? Open the door!" He leaned his ear against the cool length, trying to make out the hushed words. The indecipherable distinctly female whispers continued only a moment more, much too faintly, and then they stopped.

He pounded on the door several more times.

"Who is out there? Mattie? Evie? Unlock the door and let me out! Someone! Let me out!"

Silence answered him.

He tried the door latch one more time, turning and shaking it almost savagely to no avail. *Fuck.* He was locked in the wine cellar. *Someone* had locked him in the cellar.

He pounded the door one more time and then leaned back against it with a curse. He had a house full of guests and a housekeeper intent on leaving that he needed to stop and he was locked in the bloody wine cellar. By his very own sisters, it seemed. They had been with him one moment and then gone. Who else could have locked him in here? Those little hoydens.

What were they up to?

IN THE RELATIVE comfort and safety of her chamber, Susanna pulled her valise from where she stored it beneath her bed.

Then she sat down, smoothing a hand over the well-worn coverlet. She stared straight ahead, struggling to put herself into motion. Into doing the things to prepare herself for her journey. She knew there would be a coach picking up in Shropshire midmorning tomorrow. She needed to be on it.

But at the moment she could only sit and stare. Gaze blindly ahead.

She knew she would leave early so that she would not have to see anyone. She contemplated that. She should say her good-byes to everyone. These were her friends. Cook, Bird, Barrow.

But she did not think she could bear it. Saying good-bye to Mattie and Evie had been harder than she expected and she had not even known them for very long. Saying good-bye to the others . . .

Her eyes began to burn and she shook her head. She rubbed the base of her palms roughly into her eye sockets. It would be a misery. She did not have to have experienced it to know what it would be like. Cowardly or not, she would spare herself that.

A rapid knocking on her door lifted her up from her comfortable spot on the bed. She opened the door to find Mattie standing there. Mattie, wearing a most panicked expression.

"Mattie?"

"Susi! He's gone mad! Come! Come at once! He's attacked him!"

"What? Who?"

Mattie seized her hand and yanked her from her room. "Lucian! He and Carter are in the wine cellar."

"Wine cellar?" She frowned and almost tripped. Mattie's hand wrapped around hers, saving her from falling.

"Yes!"

"Why are they in the—"

"I don't know," Mattie snapped as she pulled her along. "But they're going to kill each other if we don't stop them!"

At that, Susanna actually rushed ahead, over-taking Maddie. She didn't need to know why the two of them were in the wine cellar. She could learn those details later. Right now, she simply needed to stop Lucian and Carter from killing each other.

She reached the wine cellar out of breath to find Evie already there, one hand on the latch of the door. Susanna scarcely digested the sight of her.

She hastened ahead, pushing past Evie to yank open the door, expecting to walk in on the sight of carnage. Blood and mayhem. Penning and Carter battling to the death.

She burst into the space, her gaze adjusting to the thin lighting. Casks and racks of wine met her scouring survey, but nowhere did she see two bodies locked in mortal struggle.

"Mattie? Where are they . . ." She rotated, search-ing, and that was when she saw him sitting on the floor. Long legs kicked out from him, stretched out on the floor.

She stopped hard. Blinked. "Penning?"

"Lucian," he automatically returned.

"Lucian," she obliged, bewilderment sweeping over her. "What are—"

He suddenly lunged forward, awkwardly shoving to his feet. "The door!"

Too late. It thudded shut. There was a faint scratching of a key in the lock. She watched Lucian grasp the latch and attempt to turn it. Rattling it wildly, he struck the door. "Bloody hell! Open the door! You can't keep us locked in here!"

Susanna rubbed her head. "What is happening?"

He turned to fully face her. "We are locked in."

"What?" She stepped past him and tried to open the door herself. No luck. Locked. "No." She rattled the latch. "No!"

She spun around and fell back against the door as though she needed the support to hold up her suddenly unstable legs.

"No," she said again, this time quieter, a whisper.

Her gaze found his and read the grim resignation there. "This can't be happening."

"Yes," he affirmed. "It is happening."

# Chapter Twenty-Four ❧

$\mathcal{A}$t least she hadn't left yet. It was Lucian's single comforting thought. Although one look at her face and he could see there would be no comforting her. He had spent the last half hour resigning himself to this situation. His sisters were clearly up to something. Something that went beyond a mere prank.

"I don't understand what is happening."

"My sister . . . sisters, I suspect, have hatched some scheme."

Susanna looked back and forth between him and the door barring them from returning to the world. "Scheme?" she echoed, her voice full of the bewilderment he had initially felt.

He nodded. "Indeed."

"I don't understand."

"Which one led you here?" he asked.

"Uh. Mattie, but Evie had been here at the door . . . waiting . . ."

"Ah. Yes, then I imagine Evie was the one I heard unlocking the door the moment before you ran inside."

She nodded slowly.

He went on, "And what reason did Mattie give to lead you to charge in here full of furious indignation?"

She'd reminded him of an avenging angel bursting through the door. For a moment he had thought she was there to rescue him, but then he recalled their last encounter and doubted she would have that impulse.

"She said you and Carter were fighting . . . She made it sound very dire, as though you two were murdering each other."

And she thought to save them from each other. In truth, she more than likely thought to save Carter.

He chuckled. "You must admit Mattie is creative."

"She's a devil!" Susanna turned and pounded on the door with renewed vigor. "Mattie! Evie! Open this door at once."

Mattie's voice carried through the door. "Calm yourself, Susanna. We're doing this for your own good."

"My own good?"

"Yours and Lucian's."

Lucian came to stand beside her. She looked up at him. "She's unhinged."

"Mattie," he said in his sternest voice, trying

to recall why being trapped with Susanna was such a terrible thing. "Be reasonable. What do you hope to achieve? We have a houseful of guests. I will be missed—"

"We will make your excuses, explain you had a megrim and took to your bed early tonight."

"Thought of everything," he muttered.

His sister continued, "I think some time together will make you both see things clearly. Susanna, you don't want to leave this place, and Lucian . . . you don't want her to go."

Her disembodied voice settled on the air of the cellar that suddenly felt thick, the space tight.

Susanna darted him a look and then stared back at the door. "Mattie," she began in a cajoling voice, as though trying to convince a recalcitrant child to take one more bite of her dinner. "Why don't you open this door and we can discuss—"

"No," came the quick rebuttal. "This strife has to end between the two of you—"

"Strife?" Susanna shook her head with a scowl, her kind tone disappearing in the face of her frustration. "You act as though we're squabbling children."

"You're behaving as such."

"We are?" She released a humorless laugh. "We are mere employer and employee—"

Mattie made a sound of disagreement through

the door. "If that was the case, there would be none of this friction between the two of you."

"Friction?" she echoed. "I don't know what you're talking about."

"Lucian sacked you! You remind me of two feral cats circling each other . . . when clearly you only want to breed."

Susanna gasped.

Lucian tipped his head back and laughed. He could not help himself.

Susanna glared at him. "This is not funny!"

"No, it is madness, but what else can you do except laugh?"

She looked at him like she did not know what to think of him. Her lips twitched.

Then Evie's disembodied voice carried through the door. "You both need to admit that you fancy each other, kiss, marry and have a dozen babies."

Susanna's mouth worked, struggling for speech.

Lucian couldn't laugh anymore. For some reason images of *that*—of those things—took hold of him. And they weren't terrible. He already knew what kissing her was like. He would relish more of that . . . and he would especially relish exploring the deed that went into making those babies.

Susanna flattened her hand against the door. "Mattie, you are mistaken. You have the wrong idea here—"

"I think not. I think I have the right of it, and it is you who are mistaken."

Shaking her head, Susanna snapped, "Let us out of this cellar!" She turned to glare at him. "How can you remain so calm?"

Because remaining locked away with her did not trouble him. Not as it should. Also, because escaping his houseful of guests felt like a gift.

And yet he couldn't simply embrace this absurdity. He could not permit his sister to be right about this. Her mad scheme could not succeed.

"Mattie," he said, "you needn't pretend altruism is your single motivation here. Do not think me so naive as to believe that. This is also about Carter."

Silence met the allegation.

He pressed on, "Whatever happens, this won't change my mind about you and Carter."

*Whatever happens.* The vagueness of that unsettled him. He heard the implication. It hinted at acceptance. Acceptance of remaining locked in this cellar with Susanna. Acceptance that there might be something between them, and that he might be willing to embrace their forced isolation to explore that—which would be definitely wrong.

She was his housekeeper and he could not take advantage of that fact.

Mattie finally responded. "I won't deny it." She

sounded dogged, and he could envision the resolute tilt to her head. She had been doing that ever since the age of three when she was determined to have her way. "If you and Susanna could find your own happiness, then you would see that Carter and I should be together."

"Should?" he demanded, stepping up to the door. "That feels awfully absolute."

"It is absolute," she called through the door. "Love *is* absolute, Lucian."

He closed his eyes in a long blink. "Bloody hell. Save me from lovesick fools."

Susanna laughed lightly beside him.

"There is a basket of food in there," Evie called. "We assume the wine will suffice for drink."

He turned, searching until he spotted the basket stuffed to the brim with bread, fruit, cheese and other wrapped items.

"Oh, and we've left you a bucket and, er . . . other essentials, should the need arise."

They left them food *and* a bucket in which to piss? They had really thought of everything, it seemed. *Brats.* When he got out of here . . .

"How long do they plan to leave us in here?" he muttered more to himself, not expecting an answer.

"Until you change your mind about your sister and Carter, I imagine," Susanna supplied.

He looked down at her, trying to gauge whether she was jesting. "That's going to be a long time," he said wryly.

"And until we fall in love, I suppose," she added.

She was definitely jesting now. He could hear the humor in her voice and he rather loved that she could find humor in this situation. Most women would be in a panic.

*Until we fall in love.*

A multitude of things rose up on his tongue to reply, to reject her jesting words and express just how thoroughly ridiculous a prospect that was.

The words never came, however.

It's not that Lucian didn't believe in love, but he believed in lust and desire and infatuation *more*. He knew the power of those things. He did not know the power of love.

# Chapter Twenty-Five &

$\mathcal{S}$usanna pounded on the thick door until her fists ached, eventually slowing down as she tired, but not yet stopping. She could not stop. She could not quit. She could not give up. She felt as though she was trapped in a cage with an unpredictable animal. At any moment he could decide to devour her. Or even worse. Before *she* turned into the animal and decided to devour *him*. That would definitely be worse. She needed to get out of here before that happened.

"No one can hear you."

Susanna whirled around, her arms still raised, fists poised to continue knocking. He had made himself comfortable. Or as comfortable as one could be sitting on the floor, leaning against a rack of wine with the flat butt of a barrel at his back.

He'd found a blanket from somewhere, so he wasn't sitting directly on the floor, but it couldn't provide much cushion. Beside him was the basket of food, which he had begun to examine.

She lowered her arms and flattened her palms to the door. Swallowing against an unreasonable bubble of hysteria, she dropped her head to the flat length of wood and murmured, "What are we going to do?"

In the fading light, his features were in shadow, but even so she could read the vagueness in his expression. "Wait."

"Wait?" she echoed and then gave her head a small shake, rolling it against the door. "For how long?"

"I imagine someone will find us in the morning."

She whirled around to face him. *In the morning.* The bubble of hysteria in her chest expanded.

"In the morning? We're to stay the night here together?" *Together.* Alone.

"There is little choice." He bent one of his legs. Propping his hand on his knee casually, he flicked his fingers toward the door. "Bang all you like, no one can hear us down here. The staff is undoubtedly busy in the loud kitchen preparing for dinner."

She swallowed thickly as the situation settled over her. She was stuck alone with this man overnight.

"You have this wrinkle forming right here." He pointed between his eyebrows. "Ease yourself."

She reached a hand there instinctively and rubbed at the skin. "How is it you are so calm?"

He shrugged. "No sense in fretting over what cannot be changed." Pushing back up to his feet, he gathered another packing blanket from where it sat on a nearby worktable and then offered it to her. "Here you go. It will get colder down here once it's dark."

"Thank you." She hugged the blanket close to her chest, still standing, uncertain where to settle her body.

He returned to his previous spot, lowering onto the floor, his long legs sliding out before him on the ground again.

"You look almost . . . comfortable." Her voice rang with a hint of accusation.

One corner of his mouth lifted. "Hardly. I would much prefer that big bed in my room upstairs than this for the night."

*That big bed in my room upstairs . . .*

For some reason the words struck her as provocative. She could only visualize him in that bed, the counterpane stripped down to his waist. She could see him perfectly, that body of his she knew so well from her intrusions on him whilst he was at his bath. She shivered.

"You cold?"

She nodded jerkily and shook loose the blanket so she could pull it around her shoulders.

Fully wrapped in her blanket, she moved to the rack he leaned against. Keeping several feet between them, she sank down on the ground, convinced she would not sleep a wink.

Soon they would be cocooned in darkness. Perfect.

She felt him studying her expression. He stretched out some bread and cheese to her. "Hungry?"

She took it, knowing she should eat something. "They did think of everything."

"Except what I'm going to do to them when I get out of here."

She couldn't help herself from smiling at that. "You dote on them."

"Which has evidently turned them into monsters." She detected an undertone of affection in his voice, and she could not help but wonder how different her life could have been if she had someone like him for a brother or father. If she had ever locked her stepfather in a cellar she would likely have ended up as bait for the fish in the harbor.

She was still smiling . . . and pondering as she asked, "Are you really going to force your sister to marry someone else when she's in love with Carter?"

"She's infatuated with him. Not *in love*. There is a difference."

"If you say so." She shrugged, unconvinced.

He sulked for a moment, tearing off a hunk of bread and chewing. He stood abruptly and stalked about the cellar in angry movements, selecting a bottle of wine.

At the worktable, he snatched a corkscrew and opened it with a *pop*. Returning to his spot, he took a deep swig from the bottle. "You think it love? Truly?" Another swig. "I never took you for a romantic."

He offered her the bottle and she accepted it, studying it for a moment before placing her lips to the opening, where his mouth had been, and taking a drink. It was delicious, rich with notes of berries and cinnamon.

She was born a romantic. That was what led her to the bed of a man so far above her station at seventeen . . . and what consequently ruined her and brought her to Penning Hall. She might not believe in romantic things for herself anymore, but that did not mean she thought such things dead for others.

"So you'll sentence Mattie to a loveless life, then?"

"A comfortable life," he snapped, reaching for the wine again. "A *safe* life." Another swig. "She will be protected from . . . come what may."

"Safe," she murmured, turning that over and thinking it an interesting word choice. And . . . *come what may*. What did he think *may* come?

"Yes. Safe," he affirmed, and then a long stretch of silence fell in which he swapped the bottle of wine back and forth with her. They ate amid their swallows of wine.

Then, lulled into a sense of comfort by the wine and the cloak of darkness, she had to ask, "What do you think may . . . come?"

Long moments passed. She stopped accepting the bottle of wine. She was already too comfortable. A drowsy languor enveloped her. She didn't think he was going to reply to her at all . . . when he did.

"I have things in my past . . . things I have done that may come to the surface and that could be bad. For me and my sisters."

Her head whipped in his direction. As someone in possession of ghosts of her own, she could not help feeling intrigued. He was a duke now. A deeply privileged man at the pinnacle of Society. What could he possibly have to fear?

"Don't tell me you killed someone?" Murder was veritably the only thing she could think of that might be problematic for a man like him.

He laughed once, a short bark. "No."

"Well . . . what else could you have done to create such worry?"

He sighed.

Clearly it was not a question he would feel

comfortable answering. Who was she to him but a servant? A servant he'd sacked. He would not confess anything so very personal and potentially damning to her.

"Before I became Duke of Penning I survived by taking women to my bed . . . for money."

It was not murder.

And yet it could not have shocked her more. She knew women made their livings selling their bodies. For a short time, she had considered that might be her only option—if Aunt Ferelith had not offered her a different future.

It had never even crossed her mind that men could perform such acts for money. But of course they could. And Lucian was an exceedingly attractive man. Young and handsome. With deep, compelling eyes and lovely teeth.

He spoke into the silence between them. "Can you imagine if it was ever learned that the newly minted Duke of Penning made his living as a whore?"

She winced. "That would indeed . . ."

"Shake the very bedrock of our patriarchy?"

She nodded, then realized he could not see her. "Yes . . . I see how that could happen." They would not like it. She thought of all the self-important toffs . . . the blue-blooded nobles would take it as an affront to their entire way of life.

Those swells could visit brothels and keep mistresses and trade coin for sex whenever they liked, but one of them could never have come from *that* side of things. They would view Lucian like a muddy mongrel that had somehow crept inside the house and took residence in front of the hearth. They would reject him in spectacular fashion, duke or no. His sisters included.

"I could bear it myself. Say, fuck the lot of them. But then I have my sisters. I cannot disregard their futures."

His language should perhaps offend her, but she grew up surrounded by fishermen and sailors, her stepfather included. Rather than offend, it had the opposite effect. It made her feel closer to him, drew her to him. She felt an affinity with him. A connection. As though he might understand her, too. As though he might be able to relate to her past and what she had done.

"No. I suppose you can't. The girls need your protection. They're lucky to have you looking out for them." She moistened her lips. "Do your sisters know? What you did for them?"

There was a slight rustling and she knew he was looking at her, for however much he could see her in the darkness. "No. They don't know how we survived. I think they assumed our father left us with enough to see us through . . ."

But his father had not.

He made a humming sound. "Huh." A contemplative pause fell. "The way you asked that . . ."

"What way did I ask?"

"You asked if they knew what I did for them." She nodded. "Yes?"

"I don't think most people would recognize that I did anything for them."

She considered that. "Probably not. Certainly not all your blue-blooded friends who never had to worry about a thing like survival or sacrifice before."

He snorted. "I haven't any blue-blooded friends. That is for certain."

"Whatever you want to call them, then . . . you have a houseful of them upstairs missing you right now." She had a flash of Lady Philomena's face then.

He hissed out a breath. "Well. *I* am not missing them."

She stretched out her legs before her, not caring that her ankles and a bit of her calves were exposed. He couldn't see them in the gloom.

He surprised her with his next comment. "You know I am not sacking you."

"You're . . . not?"

"I was angry earlier . . . I don't want you to

leave. I was coming to tell you that before we got locked down here. I wanted to apologize to you."

He would apologize to her? For something that he had every right to feel angry about? *Who even is this man?* Clearly everything she had thought about him needed reevaluating.

Although . . . *did it?*

The man had flung himself from his horse rather than run over her on their first encounter. He did not even know her then, but he had risked his own life rather than harm her, a stranger. Was he not a nobleman in the truest sense? A man who knew all about sacrifice, and not just when it came to members of his family.

"Most of my anger was at finding my sister with Carter . . . and I directed that at you. I am sorry for that. I don't want you to go."

Except nothing had changed. Not really. She had to go. Only now it was that much harder to leave this place . . . *leave him.* Warmth suffused her chest. She had not realized how much his dismissal stung her. "It was a . . . fraught situation." He was still her employer. The boundaries between them still existed even if now they were blurred and she felt all woolly-headed around him—and that had nothing to do with her wine consumption.

"It stung my pride to think you were only kissing me to distract me." Was it her imagination or was his voice deeper, gruffer?

She smiled widely, stupidly, and then bit her lip, trying to stop that impulse. It should not have stung his pride because no matter what her motivation had been at the start she had loved and reveled in every moment of it. Certainly he knew that. Certainly he had felt the fire between them then.

Certainly he felt it now.

# Chapter Twenty-Six ❦

$S$usanna didn't know what to do with her hands right then. Her fingers fidgeted in her lap, twisting to the point of discomfort.

The darkness was its own protection. It lulled her, shielding her, making her think she could say anything without being seen, without consequence. A dangerous thing, indeed.

"Well, that kiss . . . our kiss . . . might have started out as a decoy, but it did not feel that way as it unfolded."

Silence.

The rasp of his breath.

She thought she heard the pounding of his heart before realizing, no. That was *her* heart in *her* ears.

Her stomach dipped and twisted, the sensation descending between her thighs, to her core. She shifted slightly, determined to ease the dull throbbing.

Perhaps she truly was that wicked creature her stepfather had claimed. He'd called her a woman of loose morals, destined to corrupt men from their righteous paths, and said that she deserved whatever wretched fate befell her.

This, being trapped in the dark with this man, did not feel wretched, though.

She closed her eyes, finding only more darkness awaiting her there. There was nowhere to escape.

She waited, wondering if he would pursue this line of conversation . . . The kiss they had shared may have started out not *real* but became so much more.

He did not speak.

More silence stretched, and then she whispered, "I won't share your confidences."

She wanted him to know that.

She wanted him to feel secure knowing the secrets of his past were safe with her.

"I know," he replied. "You have far too much integrity to carry tales. When I first arrived here it was clear you were loyal. You attempted to defend that imposter duke—"

She flushed in mortification. At least he could not see her burning face. "I was wrong."

"You were mistaken," he agreed, "but loyal. Who was I to you, after all, save some madman who nearly ran you over on his horse? Why should you have initially believed me?"

That warmed her. It made her feel like they

were almost . . . friends. The housekeeper and the duke. *Friends.* Except a friend, she realized, would confess her own secrets in turn. And she definitely had her secrets, too.

She moistened lips that suddenly felt too dry, wondering if she could do that. With Billings upstairs, threatening to expose her, confiding in another person felt tempting. It had been a long time since she had Aunt Ferelith in her life with any regularity. It would be nice to talk to someone, to lift the solitary burden of it all from her shoulders.

"I've done things in my past that would hurt me, too, if they came to light."

"Indeed."

He said nothing more than that. No prying questions. No employer demanding to know what manner of woman he employed. He simply let her words sit there, hanging between them with no potential explanation. As though he were satisfied with leaving it at that. She had never felt safer with a person, excepting her aunt, of course.

"I . . . uh . . ." How did one announce they were ruined at seventeen?

"You don't have to tell me."

"I want to."

Perhaps then he would understand when she inevitably left Penning Hall. He'd been decent enough to renege upon dismissing her, but nothing had changed. Billings still sat beneath this roof with full knowledge of her past and every intention of razing her to the ground if she did not *oblige* him. That would not be good for Lucian or his sisters. She could not remain here. Penning would not want her around then. Every day she spent here she tempted fate. She'd been fortunate it took eleven years for the past to catch up with her. But it had.

"I am no maid."

Silence.

She peered into the darkness as though she could make out his features. "When I was seventeen I worked as companion to a young lady of good family. A genteel family on the Isle of Man. They were English. I fell in love with the son of this family. Robbie. He wanted to marry me. We were indiscreet. Our . . . affair came to light." She winced, recalling the horrified faces of those women who had happened upon them together. "And then he died before he could marry me."

It was a strangely abbreviated version, but after all these years, that was what it amounted to. She was ruined. Shamed.

She burrowed deeper into the blanket, waiting for him to speak—to say something. Anything.

"How did he die?"

That was his question? After everything she confessed?

"He . . . ah, drowned." It had been all the more tragic for its senselessness. He had done what every local knew not to do. He swam too far out from shore at night. He and his friends had been deep in their cups. He'd lost his sense of direction and became lost, a victim to the undercurrent and his stupidity.

"It seems," she added, "we have something in common when it comes to checkered pasts."

"I would not say you falling in love and then losing the man determined to marry you is anything akin to my history."

"In the eyes of the world, I am not an honorable woman."

"The world is a hard place with far too many mean and stupid people."

She blinked eyes that suddenly burned. "But you are not mean or stupid."

And he very well could be. He was a man of wealth and power and rank and he could be cruel and stupid like so many others in his position. He could be a man like Billings. Instead he was decent.

"Oh, I don't know about that. I oftentimes feel fairly stupid."

"Why?"

"Because I want you. I can't *stop* wanting you . . . and that is stupid."

She sucked in a breath. "That's not . . . good."

"No," he agreed. "It *is* stupid and it is decidedly not good."

"It cannot ever happen."

"No. It can't," he agreed yet again. "Good night, Miss Lockhart."

Her gaze jerked to him where he sat, a few feet to her left, and she frowned. It was Miss Lockhart again. She'd admitted enjoying his kiss—essentially—and he admitted to wanting her. And now she was the proper Miss Lockhart again.

Never had so few words conveyed so much.

She was Miss Lockhart. He was the duke. And there could be nothing more than that.

With the blanket wrapped around her, she tried to make herself comfortable as the room sank deeper into darkness.

"Good night, Your Grace," she returned, although she knew sleep would not come in this space where confessions were made and they spoke of kisses and want and the nature of stupidity.

# Chapter Twenty-Seven ✈

Sleep did come.

When she opened her eyes, it was to sheer panic at discovering she could not see.

Darkness swallowed her. She waved her hand in front of her face but saw nothing. It was a strange sensation. She brushed her nose to make certain her hand was even there, before her face.

She whimpered, blinking, straining her gaze until she recalled where she was—and with whom. She was locked in the cellar with the Duke of Penning and there was no light by which to see anything. By some miracle, she had fallen asleep on the cold floor, the single blanket beneath her not providing much cushion. Was it the cold discomfort that roused her?

She eased her breathing and held herself still, listening for a sound from the man mere feet away, doubtlessly sleeping. She strained to hear as the very air pulsed around her.

Then she heard it.

A scrabbling followed by a slight squeak.

She jerked as though prodded with a rod. Then

nothing. Breathing heavily, she waited. It happened again. In some far corner of the cellar there was a brief scurrying.

They were not alone in the cellar.

She lurched to her knees with a shriek.

"Easy there," a deep voice rumbled in the darkness.

His voice wrapped around her like a comforting mantle. She bolted to his side, glad for the proof of life—a life not of the rodent variety.

"Rats," she managed to croak.

"Mice," he corrected, his voice close to her ear.

"How do you know that?" His arm slid around her and she did not mind that.

"Rats would sound . . . bigger."

*They would sound . . . bigger?*

She did not know whether to laugh or cry. She turned her face as though she could see his features in the darkness. "That's ridiculous. You're just trying to make me feel better."

"Is it working?" He was close, his words directly against her cheek.

"No."

"They're more scared of you," he pointed out in a reasonable voice.

"That, I doubt." She snorted, burrowing even closer, forgetting all about her earlier determination to keep at arm's length from him when she first sank down. The rules had changed. They were sharing the darkness with vermin. She would sit on his lap if need be.

A long stretch of silence fell in which she cocked her head sharply, several times, for any perceived noise.

"I don't hear them," she whispered.

"Your shrieking probably sent them from the room."

She sniffed. "Would that we could depart as easily."

He didn't respond, simply sat relaxed and comfortable—as far as she could tell—still holding her with his arm wrapped around her middle.

"They're gone," he pronounced, and she chose to believe that because the alternative—not to believe that—was far too disturbing.

After a few minutes, she asked, "Do you think it's close to morning yet?"

The kitchen maids roused first, before dawn, starting all the fires and readying things. Cook joined them soon after. If they knocked and made a fuss, they would likely be heard. Someone would come. Cook would unlock the door.

She leaned back against the base of a barrel, her shoulder nestling into his side.

"It's warmer," she murmured, "next to you."

His body emitted heat like a stove. Despite

that, she shivered and it had nothing to do with the cold that she had just remarked was markedly less.

She swallowed thickly.

Suddenly he shifted, tucking her closer to his side. "You're like a block of ice," he said gruffly, chafing her arm up and down with his broad palm.

Not anymore. She was not an ice block anymore. But she did not voice objection to being pulled closer against him, either. Not as she should. Her sleep had not erased their earlier conversation. Nothing could ever do that. It was imprinted on her soul with a heated brand. Her admissions. His admissions. They wanted each other despite everything . . . perhaps *because* of everything. Who they had been. Who they were *now*.

She should move back to her old spot away from him, but the threat of rats or mice or whatever else shared the darkness with them kept her where she was. At least she told herself it was that fear.

Not some other *base* need driving her. Not some other memory of what it felt like to be a woman in the most fundamental way.

She knew he was merely trying to warm her, but it felt far too intimate . . . and that was saying something indeed, considering she had marched in on him whilst he was at his bath and ogled him like he was the first naked man her eyes ever beheld.

The memory of that only added to her awareness of him—of *them* pressed so intimately together. Suddenly she wasn't just warm. She was hot. Hot and itchy and aching.

Emboldened with the knowledge that he wanted her, she turned slightly against him. Her nose found him first, bumping into his throat. She inhaled, well acquainted with the scent of his soap.

"Miss Lockhart." He said her name hesitantly.

"What happened to Susanna?" She tilted her face into his delicious-smelling neck and pressed her lips to his skin.

His breathing changed and it was gratifying to have affirmation that she was affecting him.

"Susanna." He breathed her name and she continued, opening her mouth, tasting his skin with a slow glide of her tongue. She worked her way up the arch of his throat, reaching his jaw, kissing there, nipping there . . . all in a desperate, starved quest to get to his mouth. That mouth she had tasted already and knew to be . . .

Her lips landed on his. *Heaven.*

She kissed his bottom lip, sucking, nibbling, tasting with her tongue.

"Susanna," he moaned into her mouth, and

then she realized that she was doing most of the work, most of the kissing. His hands weren't even on her. And the sound of her name was rather pleading.

She came up for air, her hands bracing on his shoulders, looking down at him because even in the dark she knew she was hovering over him.

"You don't want to kiss me." She felt foolish. Like she was another Billings, forcing herself on him. Perhaps it was an extreme comparison, but she did not feel wonderful in this moment. Slipping her hands off his shoulders, she eased back, inching away.

He snatched hold of her, his hands finding her arms. "Susanna . . . I am in agony for you."

Then he was kissing her. Without a doubt. Lips fused. Mouths open. Tongues questing.

She leaned into him, seeking, hungry, ready to claim and *be* claimed.

"Forgive me," he rasped against her mouth.

His words did not penetrate her desire-fogged mind. At first. She slid one leg over his lap, straddling him so that she could get even closer.

Apparently it was the wrong thing to do, sending him from her as effectively as a fire-hot poker to his flesh.

He was gone from her. Instantly. His lips, his body. Gone.

His hands clamped down on her arms and he removed her from him. She sat distantly from him on the cold floor, very nearly dissolving into a puddle of unsatisfied desires.

She curled her fingers into fists, her nails digging into the tender skin of her palms to stay the impulse to touch him, to haul him back against her, to force him to mash his lips against hers again.

She felt as though she'd been given her first sip of water after being stranded at sea. She desperately wanted to drink her fill. She craved it . . . needed it to live.

She blinked, fuzzy-headed. "Wh . . . why?"

"I've overstepped. Grievously. Please forgive me."

She blinked again, hearing the grave remorse in his voice. She gave her head a small shake, trying to make sense of his words . . . his apology. *Apology.* He was apologizing for kissing her. For giving her the most shattering kiss of her life. And she did know a thing or two about kisses. Time had eroded many things. The details and nuances had been lost . . . but she knew about kisses and how they had the power to corrupt and seduce. This had been one such kiss. He could have kept going. He could have continued to kiss her. She *wished* he had continued.

She wished he had finished shattering her with

his lips and his touch and the intimacy she had not felt in . . . well . . . ever.

Not even when she had someone who loved her enough to go against his whole way of life and marry her. At least Robbie had claimed to want her as his proper wife. He would have wed her. She believed that.

Lucian continued, "That was unconscionable of me."

"Why?" she asked again, this time without the stammer.

"You're in my employ. It was not my intention to take advantage of you or make you feel unsafe."

She could only sit there in the dark, soaking up his words, picking them out of the silence, trying to understand.

As though he sensed her confusion, as though clarification was needed, he added, "You are my housekeeper . . ."

"So?"

She thought they were beyond that. She thought they were . . .

She frowned. Well, she was not certain what they were. But they were not *nothing*. They were intimates. Friends? She shook her head in the dark. No, that did not feel right, either.

But they were definitely something.

Something more than merely housekeeper and employer.

"So that means I will not . . . cannot do this. I will not do this to you."

A roaring filled her ears. She heard nothing else. This was some cruel joke. She moistened her lips. It was all too much. The disappointment felt like the prick of a knife at her skin.

She gave her head a small shake and some of the roaring subsided. She focused on his voice again. "It was unforgivable of me to take advantage of my position and do this to you . . ."

*Do this to her?* What did he think he would be doing that was so wrong? Giving her pleasure? Giving her joy? Making her feel what no one had ever made her feel?

*Do this to her . . . to her.* As though she was an unwilling participant. As though he had subjected her to his unwelcome person.

"Lucian." She scarcely recognized her own voice. Not the throaty, needy dip of it, but she was fairly certain it was just the two of them in this cellar, so it must be her. Just as it must be her crawling toward him like some manner of siren, a confident Aphrodite or perhaps Peitho coming to him on her knees, a greedy supplicant, her hands stretching out until she found him.

She felt a knee, groped a strong thigh, taut and flexing beneath her touch . . . then she found *him*.

She molded her hand over him, her fingers feeling, caressing the perfect ridge. His shaft was thick and hard, rising up and tenting his breeches.

He made a sound—part groan, part sob. Gratified, she exerted a little more pressure on his thickening cock. She wished she could see his face.

Biting her lip, she stifled her own harsh breathing as she traced the shape of him. Then she pressed her palm down on the length of him, rubbing him, fidgeting as her sex clenched with an ache that bordered on pain.

He snatched hold of her wrist, peeling her fingers off him. "Susanna," he said in a guttural voice full of warning.

But at least he was calling her by her name. That felt like progress.

Still on her knees, she brought her face close to the vicinity of his, seeking his mouth, finding it and taking it. Kissing him hard. He kissed her back, chasing her lips with a growl when she pulled back to rasp, "I'm glad you changed your mind."

He went hard under her, harder, stiffening, and she instantly regretted the words, fearing he would stop again, pull away and spout about why they *can't* do this.

"Very well. I will take nothing from you, though. I will only give." And he still did not sound satisfied. On the contrary, he sounded angry with himself . . . angry but resigned.

"What does that mean?" Bewildered, she shook her head. "I don't know what—" She stopped abruptly and released a small yelp when he seized her by the hips. It was almost as though he *could* see in the darkness. He maneuvered her skillfully, adroitly, lowering her onto her back on the blankets with the flat of his palm on her rioting stomach.

His hands moved to her ankles. She trembled as he skimmed his palms over her stocking-clad legs until he reached the bare flesh of her thighs. She gasped, shaking now.

She wiggled, desperate to find relief for the throbbing burn between her legs.

His hands circled, drifting to the insides of her thighs, where he eased her legs wide for him.

She knew what came next. She was no virgin, after all.

He shoved her skirts all the way to her hips. "Lift up," he directed thickly.

She obliged and he slid her drawers down her limp legs, casting them aside.

And then his head was under her skirts. That was unexpected. Certainly not anything she had been anticipating. His shoulders were there, too, huge, wedged between her ankles and working their way up.

Her hands flailed at her sides, groping, searching for purchase. She stilled, shocked at the first touch of his lips to the sensitive inner skin of her knee.

"Ohhh," she breathed as he continued his wicked assault, climbing up her thigh with his lips and tongue and gently grazing teeth.

Definitely new. Definitely different. Definitely the most titillating thing she had ever experienced.

She could scarcely hold still. She twisted and wiggled, a moan building up in her throat. "What. Is. Happening?" Her hand slapped at the ground beside her.

He spoke into her skin, the tender part right at the inside seam of her thigh. "You are unraveling. Go ahead, sweetheart, come apart."

She didn't even know what he meant. She had never heard of such a thing . . . and yet she understood. She knew. She knew because she felt herself starting to splinter.

When his lips touched her, when they landed unerringly on her sex, she arched and flew out of herself. He didn't stop with that first kiss, however. He continued kissing and licking and doing dangerous, nefarious things to her with his tongue.

He found that secret part of her nestled at the top of her sex and sucked it deeply between his lips, his tongue flaying it until she was panting and gasping and making all kinds of embarrassing sounds. But she did not care. Because she could not stop if she wanted to. She shook, convulsions racking her as he continued to devour her. Clearly that secret little button was not a secret to him and she was heartily glad of it. Glad for his expertise. Glad for his hands and his mouth and his tongue and his teeth.

She felt what was now a familiar wave swelling up on her again. "Too much, too, too, oh oh oh oh . . ."

"That's it, sweetheart. Let go." Then he added his hand to the mix. His fingers in particular. A finger. He traced her opening and then slowly slid a thick finger inside her, plunging deep and curling inward, rubbing at some invisible patch of nerves that produced a rush of moisture between her legs, coupled with an exultant explosion of sensation. She couldn't even cry out. A ragged, noiseless gasp wrenched from her throat.

She gradually stilled.

He slipped his hand from her. The rest of him

soon followed. He pulled her skirts back down. He was gone for a moment, and then returned with her drawers. She lifted up and pulled them back on, fighting against the languor pulling at her limbs.

Properly attired again, she settled onto the blanket. "That's what you meant by taking nothing from me . . . only giving."

"I won't deny that it gave me pleasure, as well." He reached for her, dragging her down beside him. His bigger body curled around hers. She rested her head on his extended arm.

"But don't you want to . . ." Her voice faded with senseless modesty, especially considering everything that had transpired.

"Oh, I want to." He flattened his hand against her middle. "But I won't."

"Because I'm your housekeeper."

"Because you're my housekeeper," he agreed.

She exhaled with resignation, accepting that. She was his housekeeper. For now.

# Chapter Twenty-Eight ❧

$\mathcal{M}$attie arrived to free them early in the morning before anyone else in the house was awake.

Thankfully she was fully attired with her drawers back in place. Never had she been so glad for anything in her life as that. She grinned a little, realizing "that" could apply to both being dressed and being loved so thoroughly by Penning.

Both of them were respectable and fully attired. Even if they were wrapped up in each other like two sleeping cats.

Lucian was flat on the floor and she had curled herself atop him, using him as her own personal pillow. The creak of the door roused her from perhaps the deepest sleep of her life. She lifted her head groggily, wiping the drool from her chin.

As light flooded the cellar, Susanna's and Lucian's gazes met. Light was not the only thing to suffuse the room. Awkwardness swelled around them.

Embarrassed heat crept into her face, and she clambered to her feet, using the action to avert her eyes in what she hoped appeared to be a natural manner.

"Mattie," Lucian greeted. "Kind of you to free us from our gaol."

Mattie smiled cheekily. "Happy to oblige. Hope you each had a pleasant night." Her eyes definitely possessed a devilishly knowing twinkle.

They did not linger. Few words were exchanged as the three of them left the cellar, cutting through the still and silent kitchen.

At the point where they should go their separate ways—Lucian and Mattie to their separate chambers and she to hers in the servants' quarters—he seized her hand.

"I will speak to you later," he vowed in a rough voice that abraded her skin.

That felt rather ominous . . . but also thrilling.

Thrilling in a way it should not feel. She looked back at him.

His sister had not left his side. "When will you talk to *me*? What about me and Carter?" Mattie propped her fists on her hips in an aggressive stance.

He sighed. "There is no you and Carter."

"Yes, there is," she snapped. "Don't tell me you haven't changed your mind."

"Did you think locking me away for a night in a cellar would achieve that? Was that your goal?"

"I thought you might come to your senses and

decide not to be a tyrant." Her gaze darted to Susanna. "And I thought some time with Susanna might . . . soften you."

Another sigh. "We will talk about the matter later, Mattie."

Not an outright refusal. Susanna smiled. That was something. That was hopeful. Perhaps he would permit Mattie her love match after all. Eventually. At least someone could find happiness. Not her. Not Susanna. Not with him. But young Mattie could have that.

Lucian turned his gaze back to Susanna and it was full of such longing that she thought she was looking into her own gaze and reading all her own longing reflected there. "I will find you later and we will talk." He spoke with such determination that she could only blink and nod, a pained smile tightening her lips that she hoped he could not discern. She *hoped* she looked sincere and not sad. Not as sad as she felt.

They parted ways.

She found her valise where she left it on the bed and finished packing. Once she was finished, she rotated, surveying the room, marveling it would be her last time here. She moved to her desk and pulled out a sheet of parchment from the drawer.

Seizing a quill, she addressed it to the Duke of

Penning. Nothing too personal or revealing. Anyone could find the note.

She kept it straightforward and proper. She rendered her resignation very properly and requested that Lucian forward a letter of reference to her at her aunt's address.

There. She folded the note with satisfaction. Nothing to raise eyebrows.

She had no choice and he would realize that. He had too much to lose keeping her here, underfoot, a constant threat of scandal. She wanted him. Perhaps even loved him. God knew she felt deeper feelings for him than she ever had for Robbie. She had never even talked to Robbie the way she talked to Lucian. She knew him. Perhaps more than anyone. She alone knew his past—no one else did, excepting his lady clients, of course.

She knew because he had wanted her to know, and that meant more to her than she could have imagined. It brought flutters to her belly. A warmth to her chest.

And more than that. *He* knew *her*.

She shoved aside thoughts of how she might love him and marched from the room that wasn't her room anymore. From the house that wasn't her home any longer, either. From the man . . .

The man that had never been hers no matter

how she might have been confused, momentarily, into thinking that he was.

She had a coach in Shropshire to catch.

SUSANNA'S AUNT'S COTTAGE appeared as she rounded the lane, like some sort of mirage magically appearing amid the dunes of a desert.

She had visited several times over the last five years since her aunt had stepped down from Penning Hall. Considering she was only a short journey by carriage . . . it was really rather sad. *Wrong.* Especially as she had made all kinds of promises to visit when they left. To *frequently* visit.

She could have visited more, she realized. More than the two times a year she managed to get away for a mere night or two. There was no excuse for it other than her own lapse.

The truth of the matter was she always felt an intruder upon Aunt Ferelith and Agatha. They were the closest of friends and clearly preferred each other's company above all others—even hers.

Perhaps that was not fair. Most definitely that was not fair. And yet she always had a sense that they were holding back, pausing amid their lives during her visits. She could not quite understand it and yet the sense that they were eager for her to be gone was a very real experience for her.

They had waited a lifetime to retire, saving so that they could have their perfect home, their lives to lead without being subject to an employer. Freedom. She envied them that, which only made her feel rotten and disappointed in herself. Who was she to feel sore and neglected after all her aunt had done for her?

So she stayed away, for the most part, giving them their deserved space in their sweet little cottage together.

She panted as she neared their door, passing through the front gate with a light heart. Her valise had grown heavy in her grip. It had been quite the walk from the village square, where the coach had deposited her.

In moments, she would see her aunt. Soon she would be in her arms. Things always felt better—*right*—when Aunt Ferelith held her.

Wrong or right, grown woman or not, she looked forward to that. She *needed* that. Needed the comfort. Needed to feel she would be well. That *all* would be well. That somehow this pain in her heart would ease and pass.

Like a fool, she had fallen in love with him. Lucian. A duke. As before, she lost her heart to a man beyond her reach. What a terrible thing. Evidently, the years had not made her any smarter.

And yet *unlike* before, he had not fallen in love

with her. He did not love her back. What was more . . . this time felt different in other ways.

One would think at seventeen she would have felt more consumed, more attached, a deeper longing.

All that first-blush-of-love rot—except there was truth in it. She knew that. She *had* known that. She saw the evidence of it even now, in Mattie and Carter. Mattie was besotted. Her eyes starry-bright when she looked at Carter. Her voice full of wonder.

And yet Susanna could not recall such a whirlwind, such a tumult of emotions for herself with Robbie. Indeed not. Her feelings had been tame in comparison to what she felt now.

Her heart beat for him. *For Lucian.* She ached when she was with him and ached when she was not, which was now. If this was how love felt why did anyone ever wish for it? She wished to be rid of it. To be cured of it like any other ailment. She wished it gone from her life for good. Forever. And once she was cured, she would never be so foolish to let that happen again.

After several knocks upon the front door, it became clear that no one was home.

She blew out an exasperated breath and circled around the house to sit in the arbor swing.

She could not say how long she sat there, alone

with her thoughts, enjoying the view of their beautiful flower garden.

She was so deeply lost in her thoughts she released a startled scream when a voice spoke.

"Miss Lockhart?"

It was Andy, a boy from the village whom Ferelith and Agatha paid to help do things occasionally about the place.

He advanced with a bucket full of seed.

She rose hastily to her feet. "Hello, Andy."

The boy removed his cap from his shock of red hair and gave her a polite nod. "I did not know you were coming for a visit. Your aunts did not mention it."

Susanna did not bother correcting him that Agatha was not also her aunt. "I thought I would surprise them."

He shook his head with a frown. "Sorry. They are not here."

It was her turn to frown. "Oh. Where are they?"

"They took a trip to the shore."

"Oh, dear. I suppose I should have written to them that I was coming." She looked around rather helplessly then.

"You should wait for them. They will be back tomorrow and I am sure they will be delighted to see you. Your aunt Ferelith is always talking about how much she misses you."

Susanna smiled, warmed to know that her aunt mentioned her. She nodded. "Yes. I will do that." What choice did she have? She had nowhere else to go. And it was only for a day.

She followed Andy to the back door of her aunt's cottage, watching as he fished a key out from his pocket. "They asked me to feed the bird. Now you are here, so—"

"Yes, I will do that for you." She looked down at the bucket of seed in his hand. "In fact, I am happy to feed the chickens, too, until they return."

"Oh. If you are certain. I don't mind—"

"I am certain. It will save you the trip from the village."

Standing in the threshold of the back door, he gave her another polite nod. "Good evening to you, then, Miss Lockhart." He slapped his cap back on his head.

"Thank you. See you soon, Andy." She imagined she would be seeing a good deal of the boy. At least until she figured out what to do with the rest of her life. For certainly it would not be to live out her days here, leeching off her aunt and Agatha.

She closed the door and glanced around the tidy kitchen with its sweetly painted dishes and sprigged curtains that reminded her of sunshine, matching, coincidentally, the little yellow canary chirping in greeting from its cage beside the window.

"Hello there, Daffodil. How have you been, hmm? Are you missing your friends? Ferelith and Agatha will be home tomorrow and so glad to see you," she conversed, telling herself that talking to a bird was not the loneliest and most depressing thing in the world.

# Chapter Twenty-Nine ❧

Susanna lurched upright in her bed in the small guest chamber she always occupied when she visited her aunt. Her heart banged against her rib cage in time with the banging reverberating on the air, drifting up from the first floor of the cottage. She fumbled to light the lamp on her nightstand as the knocking continued.

Alarmed, and very aware of the fact that she was alone in the house, she vaulted from the bed to investigate, wondering if brigands roamed these parts and whether they knocked on the doors of the homes they invaded. Surely they simply broke inside, crashing a window or breaking through the back door. The bad people never knocked on your door.

Wrapping herself up in this comfort, she snatched up the lamp and hastened down the stairs to the tiny foyer.

Her bare feet sank into the soft rug, her toes flexing as she inched toward the door, holding the lamp aloft, prepared to use it as a weapon should someone crash through the door.

It certainly sounded as though that was a possibility. The individual on the other side of that door knocked with relentless tenacity. They clearly wanted *in* this house, and that terrified her. If they wanted inside, they would find a way. Determined people always found a way.

"Who is it?" she demanded, trying to make her voice sound formidable.

"Open the door, Susanna."

Relief gusted past her lips. Not a brigand.

She lowered the lamp and then something other than relief trembled its way through her.

"Lucian?" What was he doing here? He was supposed to be at Penning Hall with all his many important guests. What was he thinking to abandon his house party and follow her here?

He repeated himself, and the deep rumble of his voice felt like a caress, reaching her through the door. "Open the door, Susanna."

She hesitated, wondering if she could pretend she hadn't heard him—or didn't recognize his voice. Or pretend that she wasn't Susanna. Pretend that he had found the wrong house, and that she had not just spoken his name out loud.

"Susanna," he growled with a touch of desperation—as though he were privy to all her inner thoughts, wild and unreasonable as they were.

"Open. The. Door." Then, after a long moment: "Please."

It was the *please* that undid her.

Stepping forward, she mumbled hastily, "Yes. Of course."

Unbolting the door, she faced the Duke of Penning standing on her aunt's front porch and tried to reconcile the sight of him here, away from the opulent trappings of Penning Hall, in this reality of her life.

When he was so clearly *not* the reality of her life.

He was the dream.

Susanna's gaze hungrily raked over him, devouring him, noting his unkempt attire. His cravat hung loose, not even tied at his throat. His vest was buttoned, but his shirt looked very rumpled beneath it. His jacket he had forgone altogether.

She had never seen him in such a state except for when she caught him at his bath. He was always so very dignified and controlled, impeccably attired. Impeccably . . . duke-like. As he ought to be. As he presently was not.

She sent a quick self-conscious glance down at herself in her nightgown. In. Her. Nightgown. They were a match, it seemed.

"Lucian," she breathed shakily. "What are you doing here?"

Given their previous intimacy, she should not feel such qualms over her lack of clothing. However, that intimacy had been in the dark. In the safety and comfort of darkness. She had not seen his face or body. He had not seen hers. This was entirely different.

His blue eyes, dark and wild, stared down at her. He nodded at the lamp she clutched in her hand. "Do you intend to maim me with that? You wield it like a weapon."

She glanced at it, remembering she even held it. "Oh." She took a step back and set it on the small hall table.

He stepped inside and closed the door after him, not waiting for an invitation.

She edged away, as though his presence was too much, his proximity a burning flame.

"How did you know where to find me?"

"Your note. You left your address."

She blinked long. "Ah, yes. Of course." Her skin tightened, every nerve ending tingling and prickling in a way that made her stomach twist. "Why did you follow me?"

"Did you think I would not?"

"I did not think . . ." No. She had not. She had not even considered it.

He quickly glanced around the small foyer. "Did I wake your aunt?" He smoothed a hand over his wind-mussed hair. Apparently he had also gone without a hat.

"They are not here at the moment. I . . . I am alone."

Something shifted in his expression. He looked her up and down, reminding her again how very little clothing she wore. "I see."

"You left your house party," she accused.

"I did," he agreed casually. As though it was of no matter.

But it *did* matter. It was no small thing.

His arrival here might imply that it was an inconsequential thing for him to abandon his party, his guests, but she knew better. It could be disastrous for him and his sisters and their future matrimonial prospects.

"You should not have done that, Your Grace."

"And you gave your notice," he countered.

His words rang on the air with something akin to . . . frustration. Was he hurt? They'd danced around the matter of her employment—or rather the inevitability of her *un*employment—since he arrived at Penning Hall, but they both knew it was unavoidable. Expected. Almost from the start. She had been fooling herself to think otherwise. She could not remain on as his housekeeper.

"I did," she admitted, her chin tilting with defiance.

There was a tightness to his jaw that indicated just how unhappy he appeared to be over that fact. She opened her mouth and then shut it with a snap. She didn't owe him an explanation. It should be evident why she had left. He should know. He should understand why she could not remain under the same roof with him.

His gaze never left her face. He moved, stalking her in the small space of the foyer. She backed up until she collided with the hall table, jostling the vase of drying flowers upon it. Her hands shot out to steady it.

Still, he followed, came after her like a great predatory cat.

"I hated finding you gone. Do you know what that did to me?"

Straightening, she positioned herself in front of the table and shook her head mutely. Words were quite beyond her.

His chest lifted on a ragged breath. "You belong under my roof. With me."

She retreated another step. The table bumped the backs of her thighs through her nightgown. She could withdraw no farther. "I served my notice."

His gaze sharpened, roaming her face, and his voice came out hoarsely. "Oh, I am aware of that.

You were quite clear in your letter. You are no longer my housekeeper."

It stung to hear the words even though it had been her decision. Even though she had done this. He stepped forward another pace until their bodies were flush.

Her senses reeled, overwhelmed at his nearness, the push of his chest against her breasts, the breadth of him surrounding her, towering over her. She was keenly aware that only the thin fabric of her nightgown separated them.

"You don't know, do you?"

Bewildered at the question, she shook her head. "Know . . . what?"

"What you've done," he explained, although it was not much of an explanation. She still did not understand his meaning.

"You have set yourself free. You no longer work for me. You are not subject to me, Susanna."

She digested that for a bit, swallowing against the impossibly thick lump in her throat.

"Oh," she breathed, acutely aware of him bending slightly and his hands reaching for the hem of her nightgown. His gaze held hers for a moment, but she could not find her voice. In one swift move, he pulled the nightgown over her head, leaving her naked, his taller body pressing her into the table, the hard edge digging into her hips.

The only sound was the rasp of their breaths. "You are my equal now, Susanna." She wondered at that. He was a duke. She . . . a no one. Could that be true? As though he could read her thoughts, he seized her shoulders, his strong fingers pressing into her tender skin. "You are a free woman," he added, gazing at her intently. "Free to choose."

She shivered but not from the cold. Not because of the air on her bare skin. On the contrary. She felt achy and hot, as though a fever coursed in her blood.

"Tell me to leave. Tell me to go or I shall continue," he went on, his voice hard, his blue eyes like obsidian flint. "My restraint ends now."

She could not refuse him. His tether had slipped and she was glad for it.

"I don't want you to go," she whispered.

A heartbeat passed and his mouth came down on hers as he simultaneously lifted her up on the table, coming between her thighs, the rough scratch of his trousers a delicious sensation on her tender skin.

He broke away for a fraction of a moment to tear off his vest and his shirt, not giving her nearly enough time to appreciate that sight in the glow of the lamplight. Then his mouth returned, kissing her so hard that her head fell back.

Her legs came around his hips and his big hands were under her, grasping her bottom, bringing her sex to grind against his hardness, still barred from her, unfortunately, by the fabric of his trousers.

Her hands clung to him, gliding over the bulge of his shoulders and the firmness of his back. He didn't stop kissing her. Not once. She did not know kissing could be like this. She did not remember it this way. Deep, desperate, endless kisses that squeezed the coil in her belly tighter and tighter and tighter.

He was a flurry of sinuous movement. Raw strength and power.

With a move she could scarcely digest, he tugged open his trousers and shoved them down his hips. His cock was freed, grinding into her weeping sex. She gasped, astonished at the sensation, at the wildness taking over her.

She wanted this. Wanted him.

He pulled back and she whimpered at the loss of him, biting her lip as he looked down between them.

She followed his gaze, watching as he gripped his swollen cock. Her core clenched in need, the hollowness aching to be filled as she watched him pump himself in one long stroke.

She watched, riveted, her mouth watering.

Some of her eagerness edged into panic as she assessed the burgeoning size of him, looking down between them at that plump head nudging against her opening.

He must have read something in her expression. "Do not fret," he growled, one of his hands landing on her hip, anchoring her. "We're made for each other." He hauled her to the edge of the table.

She gasped as he leaned forward and lightly bit down on her throat, the pleasure-pain searing through her. "I do not think you're going to fit."

"I shall," he assured her, his cock pushing inside her yielding heat bit by slow bit until he was lodged fully, to the hilt. "See, sweetheart? You're so wet for me."

She nodded sloppily. He was inside her. Incredibly. She felt full, bursting with him, physically and in every other way.

His hands held tight to her hips, anchoring her as he withdrew and drove back in to the hilt, rattling the table under them.

He made a groan of appreciation. "It's better than I dreamed."

She whimpered, the sensation of his pulsing cock overwhelming and unfamiliar. It had been so long and so few times. This . . . *him* . . . felt so new. Heady and exhilarating. She felt every inch of him, deep in her sex, in her body, heart and mind.

He moved slightly, carefully it seemed, stretching her. His shoulders and arms quivered beneath her and she knew he was holding himself back. It was maddening. The slow friction of him sliding out and in drove her wild. She writhed under him. Her inner muscles tightened, clinging to his shaft.

She moved her hips for a better angle, taking him deeper. He hit at some magical spot buried deep inside her and she cried out, a rush of moisture drenching his cock.

"Fuck," he ground out in her ear.

It snapped something loose inside her. Her hands reached down, grasping his buttocks, urging him on.

"Susanna," he choked. "I'm trying to . . . have a care for you . . ."

She made an inarticulate sound at that, and then ground out: "Don't."

His eyes burned fire and he drove into her then, harder, sliding her back on the table. He changed his grip on her, lifting her up, his strong fingers digging beneath her, into the swells of her bottom, locking her into position for the pounding of his hips against her.

His eyes blazed down at her. "Bloody hell, you're sweet . . . tight, milking my cock . . ."

His filthy words sent her careening over the edge. She tightened her grip on him, hanging on. His biceps flexed and bulged under her fingers.

She burst, erupting into a sizzling flash of flame.

Susanna shuddered with a choked cry. And yet he did not stop. Her breathing had barely evened before the coil tightened in her belly again. He continued to stroke inside of her. Her body bounced from his thrusts. The sound of flesh smacking together filled the air.

One of his hands drifted, left her backside to grip her shoulder. He held her tightly there, bettering his leverage as he raced toward his own end, thrusting harder, faster . . . and bringing her to another climax.

With his other hand, he reached between their bodies and found that little button of pleasure he had discovered before, rolling it once before pinching it firmly. And that did it.

She came apart, gasping and moaning.

He soon followed, slamming into her one last time with a ferocity that threatened to slide her off the table if not for his grip on her shoulder. His body draped over hers as he spilled himself inside her. He chuckled low and deep, the sound a purr that vibrated against the over-sensitized skin at her throat.

They were still joined. Her heart pounded like an incessant drum in her ears, matching the pulse of him within her.

Her fingers worked against his smooth skin,

fluttering over the tight warmth, uncertain where to go, what to do next. He lifted his head and looked down at her, his eyes fathomless, deep and unreadable.

His rough voice rumbled against her bare breasts. "I didn't know it was possible."

"What?" she whispered.

"For it to be like this. *Better* than what I dreamed."

Her heart gave a painful squeeze. He stroked the arch of her eyebrows and gazed down at her as though she were the most fascinating creature he had ever seen, which was really quite something since she knew herself to be the most ordinary of people.

He tenderly brushed the hair back from her face. Taking a fistful of the mass, he leaned in to inhale it as though it were the most fragrant thing.

"Now," he declared, scooping her up in his arms. She yelped in delight and clung to his broad shoulders. "Where is your bedchamber, sweetheart? We have the rest of the night ahead of us."

# Chapter Thirty ❧

Susanna woke to the delicious aroma of food. Propping herself up on her elbows, she peered around the cozy bedchamber, aware of the vague soreness of her body that was testament to a night spent in bed with Lucian.

No sight of Lucian, but clearly he was in the house, unless her aunt and Agatha had returned and decided to make breakfast, and that was an unlikely scenario.

What a shock that would have been. Certainly, the inevitable debacle of her aunt finding her in bed with a man would have woken Susanna.

Lucian strode into the room, bearing a tray. She could scarcely take note of what delicious-smelling items occupied the tray as she was so distracted by his chest—particularly the enticing twin indentations marking his hip bones and leading to what she knew to be the promised land.

Her mouth was watering and it had naught to do with the food he carried anymore.

She held the coverlet to her breasts as she scooted back against the headboard.

"You cooked?"

"I found food in the larder. Eggs in the hen house." His warm gaze traveled over her. "Impressed?"

"Yes. This is very . . . domestic of you. I did not know you knew your way around a kitchen."

"I know how to do a great many things." He gave her a lascivious wink that she felt directly down to her core.

"You did not have to go to such trouble."

"We need to eat. We must replenish the well." He settled down beside her, settling the tray between them on the bed. He picked up a slice of jam-slathered toast, took a hearty bite, and then offered it to her. He was like the sun. Bright and joyful. The sight of him warmed her. She obliged and took a bite.

"Hmm," she mumbled around the mouthful, attempting to not feel so awkward, but that seemed to be her existence. Especially with him. Awkwardness marked by moments of desire and pleasure and, occasionally, strife, but even then the strife only stimulated her, thrilled her and awakened her as though she had been lost inside a long, deep slumber these many years.

He leaned in and licked a bit of jam from the corner of her mouth. Her breath caught and she flushed with warm pleasure. All of this was dangerous and far too wonderful. It could be both things, she realized. Dangerous. Wonderful. She could grow accustomed to it and yet none of it could last.

She would stay here and he would go back to his life. As was proper.

And then she would try to make sense of what had happened between her and Lucian.

"Eat up." He offered her a sausage. She accepted it and chewed, marveling that food had never tasted so good. Everything was better. Sweeter. The food. The bed and the room that had always felt so comfortable and cozy. It was *more* now with him. It had never felt like this. Never so close to perfection. It was indeed frightening because she knew that perfection did not exist. "We need to get on the road soon."

She slowed chewing. Swallowing, she asked, "We?"

"Yes. As much as I would like to linger in this bed with you, I have a house party to return to." He cringed. "A house party full of guests that likely think I am dying of some plague."

She wiped delicately at her mouth. "You said *we*."

He looked at her very soberly. "Yes. I did."

"But . . . I am not your housekeeper anymore."

He nodded. "I know that."

"Then how is it . . . how can I accompany you?"

"That is the very reason why you can accompany me. Why you can return with me."

She shook her head. "You are not making any sense." Did he wish for ruin to befall his family? To befall her?

He might be a man and seemingly immune to such things as ruin, but his sisters were not *un*-besmirchable, and they, she knew, were his ultimate concern. As they ought to be. They were young and innocent. Susanna was many things, but not that.

"I am making complete sense." He fed her another bite of toast and then himself another bite. Chewing, he leaned in and gave her a resounding kiss. "Come, sweetheart. We must be on our way."

Folding a sausage into his mouth, he launched his big body from the bed and landed lightly on his feet.

With his sweet endearment ringing in her ears, she watched him with wide eyes as he began dressing himself, quite unsure what was happening. She did not understand. She did not know . . .

She did not know anything except that she wanted more of this. She wanted to prolong this and have more of this deliciousness, more of *him*.

And yet she knew her aunt and Agatha were scheduled to return later today.

She needed to reach a decision soon. Stay. Or go with him.

Whatever the case, Lucian had to leave. He could not remain in this cottage with her and scandalize Ferelith and Agatha. However would she explain his presence?

And yet the thought of him going back to Penning Hall without her, leaving her here whilst he rejoined his guests, those ladies hungry for him . . .

"Very well," she agreed, feeling a bit reckless. "Let us go."

He grinned and her stomach flipped. That must be it. *That* smile on *that* face on *this* man. That was the fantasy—the dream he had supplied to countless love-starved women.

It was her dream, too, apparently.

Why else would she agree to return with him? She could not resist him. Clearly she wanted the dream of him for a little bit longer.

He continued to grin. "Yes?"

"Yes." She smiled like a fool. A fool in love, and his smile widened impossibly further, his straight white teeth truly a marvel. "Lucian?"

"Hmm?"

"We need to feed the bird and chickens before we go. And leave a note for my aunt."

"Then let's get busy." He leaned down, coming over her on the bed to place a delicious open-mouthed, tongue-tangling kiss to her lips that quickly escalated.

He tugged down the bedding to expose her breasts. "I think we have time for this first, though."

"Do we?" She gasped as he lowered his head and drew her nipple into the warm cavern of his mouth, sucking deep until she was arching and moaning under him. She threaded her fingers through his hair.

"This is important business, too," he said in mock seriousness.

"Is it?" she choked out as he brought his fingers to her other breast, tweaking and pinching and playing with that nipple as he continued to love on her other one.

His lips spoke around the hardened tip of her breast. "With you . . . always."

FINISHED WITH THE chickens, they entered the house through the kitchen door, laughing, hands all over each other because they could not *not* touch each other. Lucian had to feel her. The slim slide of her fingers, the flutter of her pulse at her wrists, the soft skin of her face . . . her even softer lips.

He folded her into his arms. She fell easily against him, her mouth trembling with laughter as they kissed.

"Well, Susanna. Aren't you going to introduce us to your friend?"

Susanna lurched away from him with a small squeak. Hand pressed to her chest, she cried out, "Aunt Ferelith! Agatha! You gave me a fright."

Two women stood at the threshold of the kitchen, eyeing Lucian with suspicion. The one who spoke— Ferelith, presumably—was petite. The top of her gloriously silver-gray head would barely reach his shoulder.

For her diminutive stature, she was not insubstantial. She was hearty with ruddy cheeks and a formidable stare, which she now leveled on Lucian. Her eyebrows were ink-dark, unlike her hair, and the effect was altogether striking—especially as they were now drawn tight over her eyes.

He straightened, hoping to achieve a dignified air, counter to the man who had just been caught slavering over Susanna. This was not how he had imagined first meeting Susanna's beloved aunt. She had every right to be concerned, if not alarmed at his presence in her house, alone with his niece.

"Ladies." He executed a smart bow. He cast Susanna an uncertain look, wishing to proceed at her direction and not blunder—at least no more than he had already done.

Susanna waved a hand at him. "Aunt Ferelith, Agatha . . . this is . . ." Her eyes met his. "The Duke of Penning."

Aunt Ferelith's eyes widened and then closed in a pained blink. She hissed out a slow breath and he thought he detected the faintest muttered epithet. No doubt she was drawing the worst conclusions. No doubt she thought him the lowest scoundrel. Agatha patted her on the shoulder in seeming comfort.

"A pleasure," he said, filling the silence neither one of the older women seemed inclined to fill.

At Ferelith's silence, Agatha greeted, "Happy to make your acquaintance, Your Grace."

"We did not expect you back so early," Susanna volunteered.

"Clearly," Ferelith snapped.

Hot color splashed Susanna's cheeks, and he reached for her, wrapping his fingers around her cool hand, determined that she feel his full support. She was not alone in this. In anything ever again.

Her aunt followed the action, her eyes sparking with some unnamed emotion. Her lips worked, evidently at a loss for speech as he laced fingers with Susanna.

Agatha was not at such a loss, however. The woman was almost as tall as Lucian. She moved with grace, her long legs covering the space quickly as she set the kettle on the stove. "Shall I make us some tea? We can sit down and have a nice visit."

"Your Grace," Aunt Ferelith pressed as though her friend had not spoken. "What are you doing with my niece, your housekeeper, unchaperoned in our home?"

"Aunt!" Susanna cried, her mortification turning her cheeks scarlet.

Her aunt held up a hand to halt Susanna's objections.

Lucian met the woman's stare directly. "She is not my housekeeper any longer."

"Oh?" Ferelith lifted a supercilious eyebrow. "You've sacked her, then?"

Agatha busied herself arranging cups for tea, inquiring brightly, clearly hoping to inject some much needed lightness into the exchange, "Who is hungry? Shall I make us all some lunch?"

"Of course not. I love your niece," he announced.

Susanna sucked in a breath.

He felt her gaze on him, soft and tender, but also as fiery as a brand.

Agatha clapped her hands together. "Oh! How delightful. Did you hear that, Ferelith?" The woman stared beseechingly at Ferelith, and there was something else in that gaze. Silent words passed between them. "They are in love, Fer."

Ferelith was no longer intent on him. Her attention focused on her niece now. "Susanna?" she asked quietly.

Susanna only glanced at Ferelith for a fraction of a moment before fixing her gaze back on him—as though looking anywhere else was an impossibility.

His heart battered against his rib cage as he waited for her response.

"I love him, too, Aunt."

He grinned like a fool then, giving her hand a squeeze. She squeezed him back.

"Well," Agatha gushed. "That is splendid. We're so happy for you both. Aren't we, Fer?"

Finally, Ferelith nodded, a slight, grudging smile on her face. "Very well, then." Looking to Lucian, she demanded, "Love is all and well, Your Grace. But what are you going to do about it?"

"I am going to marry her. If she will have me." He only stared at Susanna as he uttered this.

She nodded jerkily, a beatific smile curving her lips, and his heart clenched in his too-tight chest.

No one spoke. It was just the sound of water sputtering in the kettle and chickens clucking outside.

Susanna stood frozen, unblinking, her hand still in his.

Then another sound surfaced. Agatha weeping happy tears.

"Oh, Aggie." Shaking her head, Ferelith went to her friend, embracing the woman that loomed over her by a considerable foot.

Aggie fluttered a hand in apology. "Forgive me. I'm sorry! Just so happy for you both." Her tear-flooded gaze landed on Lucian. "We always hoped our Susanna would find someone to love . . . and who loved her." She sniffed and wiped at her nose.

Ferelith looked up at her fondly. "Oh, you goose. You're such a fusspot."

Agatha gave a watery smile. "I know I am." She inhaled a ragged breath. "It is just everyone deserves love."

Ferelith looked a bit emotional then, too, blinking rapidly. "Yes. We all do."

And Lucian understood then that these women loved each other. A quick glance at Susanna revealed that she knew it, too.

Ferelith turned a rather pointed look on him. "We look forward to the wedding." There was an edge of challenge to her voice. As though she thought he might recoil at that.

He nodded readily. "The first pew shall be reserved for you both."

He knew he did not have Ferelith's full trust yet, and that was perfectly understandable.

Lucian was happy to spend the rest of his life proving himself—to Susanna and these women.

# Chapter Thirty-One ❧

*T*hey arrived at Penning Hall shortly before dinner.

Dusk was settling over the ground in shades of bruised purple and pink as they rode their mounts into the stables and handed them off to a pair of grooms.

Lucian had brought two horses, hopeful, if not confident, that he would return with Susanna.

He resisted the urge to take her hand and walk her directly inside the house . . . to his bed-chamber. He wanted to deposit her there, to keep her there where she belonged, in his bed for the rest of their days. Perhaps they could emerge for food. Or perhaps not. Perhaps they would just have everything brought to them. It was a delicious fantasy.

But he couldn't do that. Not yet. Not until he got rid of his house full of guests.

They entered through the servants' entrance. At the base of the stairs, he stopped her, backing her against the wall, staring down at her intently.

"You are not my housekeeper," he said with a steely determination he hoped she believed.

She nodded, looking away nervously, and he felt certain that she still struggled to believe him.

He said her name. "Susanna?" Her gaze shot back to him. "You are not my housekeeper," he repeated, hoping she did not think he brought her back to keep her on staff as his paramour.

"Very well," she conceded with a small smile. "But . . . what am I supposed to do, then?" She gestured around with a little lift of her hand.

It was understandably complicated. He had not thought through every detail yet, but he would. They would decide how to best move forward. Together.

"In two days, the guests will depart and then we can—"

"Lucian! Susanna!" Lucian looked up to the spot where his sister stood at the top of the stairs. "You are back," she said unnecessarily. "Thank goodness. I told everyone you would be joining us for dinner even though I had no idea where you were or if you would return anytime soon. I've been running out of excuses."

He nodded grimly. "No need for that. I will be at dinner." He turned back to face Susanna.

She motioned for him to go. "Hurry along. You must go change for the evening."

He nodded again and dipped his head, murmuring for her ears only, "I will come see you after dinner and we will discuss all."

Her smile turned tight. "Do not rush on my account."

He frowned, disliking that. Disliking that a great deal.

Seizing her hand, he pressed a kiss to it, not caring that his sister watched.

Susanna's amber-brown eyes softened, melting in a way he knew was coming. He didn't think there would ever come a time in his life when he would not want to see those eyes.

"I *will* rush," he vowed, and her smile returned in a more convincing manner.

She nodded. "I will be waiting then."

Turning, he reluctantly started up the stairs toward Mattie.

His sister watched him ascend with her hands propped on her hips. She was already attired for the evening in an elegant gown of green silk—the kind of gown he wanted to see Susanna outfitted in. She deserved silks and satins and jewels and all the finest things. He wanted to give her all that. All that and more.

"Come, brother. There has been much chatter over your absence." She looked him up and down, wrinkling her nose. "You need a great deal of sprucing up."

"Thank you," he said wryly.

"I have reinstated Carter." Her chin went up, daring him to object. "He is in your chamber waiting for you."

Lucian sighed. He hadn't the energy to battle his sister on this point right now. Nodding, he followed her to his bedchamber whilst it slowly dawned on him that he might lack not merely the energy to fight her on her determination to be with Carter. He might no longer possess the will.

He smiled to himself and shook his head at such a turnabout. *Susanna.* Without even trying, she had changed him. With her, he was happy. Stupidly, perhaps even blindly, happy. If his sister had a chance at that kind of happiness, how could he stand in her way?

SUSANNA KNEW SHE should have stayed in her room until Lucian came to see her. That was the plan. She was no longer the housekeeper and yet she was here. In the servants' quarters. In the chamber that, by rights, belonged to the housekeeper. It was a complicated business indeed. She should stay out of sight until all the guests took to their beds.

Except she was hungry.

Her room did not come equipped with a bell. No room in the servants' wing did. She was going to have to take care of her hunger herself.

The servants' wing was quiet when she emerged from her room and walked down the corridor, everyone busy attending to their assigned tasks above stairs. It felt strange not to be participating. *Participating? Overseeing* was more apt a description.

The kitchen, however, was a melee. Servants running to and fro. Pots banging. Dishes clanking.

"Miss Lockhart!" Cook called. "Splendid to see you up and about. Hope you're feeling better." Several others echoed similar sentiments.

She was unaware of what explanation had been given for her absence, but bandying about that she was unwell made sense.

"I am better, thank you. In fact, I'm feeling a bit peckish."

Cook waved to one of the maids. "Fetch Miss Lockhart some of that consommé, Marie!"

Soon, Susanna was sitting at the kitchen table, dining on a delicious consommé and crusty bread slathered in fresh butter. She felt cosseted and a little guilty. It was strange to be an observer and not partner in the staff's efforts as she usually was.

"There you are, Miss Lockhart. I've been looking for you."

She looked up, startled at the unexpected sight of Billings in the kitchen. Her stomach sank. In the tumult of the last couple days, he had slipped from her thoughts. Clearly she had not slipped from his if he had dared to enter this space to find her. This was decidedly not his realm.

She was not the only one startled at his presence. Attired in his evening finery, he could not hope to blend in down here. The buzz of the kitchen came to a sudden halt. Everyone gawked at him in their midst. The staff who were sitting vaulted to their feet in due deference.

"Mr. Billings," she murmured.

"A word, Miss Lockhart." He inclined his head, indicating she should follow him from the room.

Alone.

"No."

Initially, she thought the word was only in her head. *No.* She did not realize it had emerged from her lips until the sudden rush of whispers rippled through the staff.

He narrowed his gaze on her. "No?"

And then she did not regret it. She nodded and said with more conviction, "No." There was no way she was following this man anywhere.

He stroked his bearded face. "Very well. You wish to do this here, then?" He spread his arms wide.

Her stomach knotted and she glanced miserably

around her at the familiar faces. People she had known all her adult life. They all eyed Billings with distrust. In his short time here, he had not endeared himself to the staff. Understandable. He treated them like they were muck beneath his boot and put on this earth to serve him.

These people had been her friends and family for eleven years. If her choices were to enter a space alone with him *or* endure him here among them, in front of them . . .

She chose them. Unequivocally.

"I'm not going anywhere with you."

He dropped his hand from his beard. His nostrils flared. "Oh. Very well." He nodded once. Hard. "We will do this here, then. In front of all your little friends. You and I had an understanding—"

"No," she cut in, really warming up to the sound of that word.

"No?" He slid a step closer, a sharp glint of warning in his eyes.

"No," she repeated with a nod. "There was no understanding."

"Well it was clear to me . . . as you are such a tart—"

A collective gasp swept over the room.

One of the kitchen lads, brawny Theodore, lunged menacingly toward Billings, stopped only by Cook. No matter the infraction, there were rules. Billings was a gentleman and a guest of His Grace. Theodore may have lost his head, but Cook had not.

"As you are such a tart," he repeated, "I did not think my proposition would be so repellent."

She inhaled a ragged breath. He was really doing this. In front of everyone.

A dull roar filled her ears, blocking out the voices of the staff. She sensed their movements, the stirring of their outrage, the working of their lips, but she could not hear them.

She could see only Billings, could gradually focus only on his sneering mouth, and the words coming from him: "I wonder what Penning will say once he learns that his housekeeper is a bit of gutter rubbish."

"I imagine he will call you out for daring to malign his future wife."

*That* she heard.

All sound returned then, flooding her senses, arriving like the boom of cannon fire.

"Penning." Billings laughed, rocking back on his heels. "That's rich." The merriment slowly faded from his face as he realized Lucian was not jesting.

Lucian looked him over coldly.

"Future wife?" Billings demanded into the stunned silence of the kitchen.

"Of course. If she hasn't changed her mind

and will still have me after I've allowed a bit of filth like you offend her in her home. It is her choice."

"Choice?" Billings laughed harshly. "Penning! What are you talking about?" He waved at Susanna. "What is it about this woman? Does she have a magic cunny that makes highborn men forget—"

He did not finish getting the rest of the words out of his mouth.

Lucian charged across the kitchen and struck him in the mouth, knocking him down to the ground.

The staff murmured in approval. A few even clapped.

Billings cursed and spit blood into his hand. Staring down into his palm, he lifted wild eyes to Penning. "You knocked out my tooth." There, glistening in the blood, was one far-from-white tooth.

"Serves you right," Cook cried out.

Billings staggered to his feet, blood dripping down his chin. "Name your seconds."

Lucian nodded, and Susanna reacted, lunging herself at him, wrapping her arms around him. "No! I won't have you do that . . . You will not risk yourself for me." She would not endure it. Not again. Not him. This time she would never recover.

He framed her face with his big hands. "Shh. You deserve to be honored and protected—"

"No!" she snapped, shaking her head. "I *deserve* you. You in my life. *You* alive. *You* not dead." A sob choked her at the mere prospect of that notion, of losing him. That loss, that grief, it would be unbearable. He pressed a shushing kiss to her cheek. "Don't fret, Susanna. You will have me, I vow it."

Billings harrumphed in disgust. "Penning!" he shouted, clearly finished with being ignored. "I said name your seconds—"

A woman's voice intruded. "Oh, stuff it, Billings."

They all swung to stare at Lady Harthorne. She descended the stairs, resplendent in a gold silk gown the likes of which had never once graced this kitchen, to be certain.

Billings blinked at her. "Isadora? D-darling?" He held out his bloody tooth and pointed to his face with his other hand. "Look what he did to me."

"I'm sure you deserved it." The lady's gaze flicked back to Lucian and Susanna in regret. She sighed and shook her head. "My apologies for the disruption to your household. We will take our leave tomorrow."

"B-but, Isadora! He struck me!"

Her wily gaze cut back to him. "And do you care to tell me why, hmm? Why did he do that to you? I am *vastly* interested to know what could have provoked such an action."

At that, Billings fell silent, darting a quick, panicked glance to Susanna. Clearly, it occurred to him how badly this might go for him if the details of his little blackmail scheme were revealed.

Lady Harthorne made a gratified sound as though she had her answer. "Now. Go upstairs like a good lad. My maid will see to your tooth."

He held out his hand where his tooth languished in a puddle of blood, as though to reinforce that his tooth was in his *hand* and not in his mouth where it belonged.

Lady Harthorne waved a hand airily. "Perhaps she can glue or sew it back in." Shrugging as though it were no matter, she turned to Lucian and Susanna. "Again, my apologies. We will depart in the morning." With an elegant swish of her skirts, she gathered the sulking Billings and departed the kitchen.

Lucian turned to face her, his arms still looped around her in embrace.

It was then that she fully realized they had an audience.

The entire household staff watched them as though they were a circus troupe. Heat crawled up her face and she attempted to disengage herself, but Lucian's arms only tightened around her. "Where are you going?" he murmured.

"Lucian, they are watching," she muttered awkwardly.

"Good. Let it be known. As a matter of fact, you are due this . . ."

Her face was on fire now. "Lucian," she growled low, under her breath. "What are you doing?"

"Giving you what you deserve." He loosened his arms around her. Still hanging on to her hands, he dropped to his knee before her. "Susanna Lockhart."

She felt the stares of everyone on them—on *her*—but she could not look anywhere except at the beautiful man before her. "Yes?"

"Will you marry me?"

"Lucian," she breathed.

"Be my wife."

"Blimey," one of the nearby kitchen lads muttered. "He just proposed to our housekeeper."

She shook her head, fighting tears, fighting a smile, fighting laughter. "Oh, Lucian. You're starting a scandal."

"That is a foregone event." He shrugged. "So marry me. And we can enjoy scandalizing all of Society together. If we're lucky they won't invite us to anything."

She giggled and tugged on his hands so that he rose to his feet before her. She stepped into his embrace, dropping her neck back to look up at him. "Yes. I will marry you."

The staff applauded, but all that faded to a dull roar in her ears. His voice was the only thing she heard, the only thing that mattered. "I love you."

# Epilogue ❧

*Christmas morning*
*Eight months later . . .*

*L*ucian opened his eyes slowly, blinking awake.

Frost coated the mullioned glass of his bedchamber window. Even through the frost he could make out the falling snow drifting down in powdery flakes.

Out here, in the country, the snow stayed white and pristine. Flawless. It did not turn to gray, muddy sludge like in London. He smiled softly, contentedly. *More* than content. It was his first Christmas at Penning Hall. His first Christmas as the Duke of Penning.

The covers shifted beside him and a breathy sigh reached his ears.

His first Christmas as a married man. With Susanna. His wife.

He was looking forward to the day ahead. They would celebrate in fine style. There would be gifts and parlor games and feasting with his family. A family that had grown in a short amount of time and now included, in addition to his sisters: his wife, his brother-in-law, Carter, Aunt Ferelith and Agatha.

He had seen the goose Cook was preparing. It would feed an army. He could appreciate that only as someone who went to bed hungry once upon a time.

He rolled away from the window and faced his wife, pulling her warm, yielding body against him, burying his lips into the delicious arch of her throat.

She opened those beautiful amber eyes of hers. "Hmm. Good morning," she murmured, threading her fingers through his hair.

He kissed her then. "Merry Christmas, wife."

"Merry Christmas," she returned with a sleepy smile.

"We best get dressed and go downstairs before my sisters invade the chamber, eager for us to start the day. No doubt they are anxious for their gifts."

She chuckled. "You speak of them as though they are still little girls."

"Why should they behave any differently this Christmas than all the ones previously?"

"Um. Because Mattie is a married woman now, and Evie is being courted most earnestly by the Viscount Collier . . . who I suspect will put in an appearance today."

"Oh? So what you are saying, wife, is that you think we have time?" He rolled atop her. She welcomed him, parting her thighs to settle him more intimately against her

"For us?" she murmured, kissing his throat, his shoulder, his mouth. She smoothed a hand over his cheek tenderly. "There will always be time."

Don't miss Sophie Jordan's exciting new series,

 ## *The Scandalous Ladies of London,*

which chronicles the lives of affluent ladies reigning over glittering, Regency-era London, vying for position in the hierarchy of the *ton*. They are the young wives, widows, and daughters of London's wealthiest families. The drama is big, the money runs deep, and the shade is real.

The first book, *The Countess*, is available now!

# Explore more books by
# Sophie Jordan

### *The Duke Hunt Series*

### *The Ivy Chronicles*